what
happened
that
night

what happened that night

deanna cameron

wattpad books

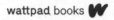

Copyright © 2019 Deanna Cameron. All rights reserved.

Published in Canada by Wattpad Books, a division of Wattpad Corp.
36 Wellington Street E., Toronto, ON M5E 1C7

www.wattpad.com

No portion of this publication may be reproduced or transmitted,
in any form or by any means, without the express written
permission of the copyright holders.

First Wattpad Books edition: September 2019

ISBN 978-0-99368-991-8 (Hardcover)
ISBN 978-0-99368-998-7 (eBook edition)

Names, characters, places, and incidents featured in this publication are
either the product of the author's imagination or are used fictitiously. Any
resemblance to actual persons (living or dead), events, institutions, or locales,
without satiric intent, is coincidental.

Wattpad, Wattpad Books, and associated logos are trademarks and/or
registered trademarks of Wattpad Corp. All rights reserved.

Library and Archives Canada Cataloguing in Publication
information is available upon request.

Printed and bound in Canada

1 3 5 7 9 10 8 6 4 2

Cover design by Sayre Street Books
Images © Wandering Introvert/Shutterstock

what
happened
that
night

author's note

There are a limitless number of topics and subjects someone can write about. A world of possibilities is waiting to be typed, and it can range from something as fantastical as warrior princesses storming the castle to something as real as young adults struggling with the aftermath of their sexual assaults. The latter is one of the topics of this book. It's about how wounds still throb even when they've closed over. It's about the reluctance some might feel to tell the truth because of the scary unknown of what happens next. It's something many, many people experience, and I truly believe that it's a story that needs to be told. Literature has such power to evoke feelings, responses, passions. It gives others the opportunity to see something from another perspective and to realize that this is important. It's important not to shame. It's important to know when to listen. It's important to know when to speak up.

But reading about this topic can be understandably triggering for those who have personally experienced it. When this book was still being posted weekly on Wattpad, I remember a few readers saying it was too hard to read, and I told them the same thing I'm about to say (type) now: that's okay. If you need to put this book down because of the feelings it stirs up, I want you to do that. I want you to find the story that brings you into a world you want to be a part of, and I hope you find it soon.

If any of you reading this have experienced something similar to what happens in this book, there are resources out there available to you. RAINN is an organization dedicated to 24/7 help for victims of sexual assault, with a hotline number you can reach through dialing 1-800-656-HOPE (4673) to speak with a trained staff member. You can also get help through visiting their website online at www.rainn.org. The Office on Women's Health is also available through calling their hotline at 1-800-994-9662 on Mondays through Fridays. RAINN, as mentioned above, has resources to help male victims of sexual assault as well.

chapter one

Bright yellow crime-scene tape blocked the Tomlins' property, looping around the telephone poles and their mailbox, on that Tuesday morning while my family prepared breakfast. Since there were only two police cars parked on the shoulder of the road, my father speculated maybe they were robbed in the middle of night or something. My mother grabbed the phone from the kitchen counter as she cooked, her other hand reaching to turn down the heat on the oven burner as bacon sizzled in a pan.

"I didn't hear their house alarm go off," she was saying to my dad, cradling the phone on her shoulder and flipping the bacon over with a fork. "I'll give them a call. Maybe—" Her face shifted as the sound of a frantic voice came on the other line. The noise (so loud even we could hear it) interrupted my father mid-sip of his coffee. "Hello, Lisa? It's Samantha."

He set down his mug, brow furrowing, as the piercing voice on the other end of the phone continued. "What's going on?"

My mother's hand was still on the burner dial when she let

out a breath, a word lost somewhere in the exhale. My father was mouthing something at her. I turned to my sister, Emily, sitting beside me as she stirred her cereal, barely looking up as my mother finally took her hand off the dial to cover her mouth, a gasp issuing through her teeth.

My chest tensed.

My mother was focused on something in front of her, like if she stared at the handle of her frying pan intently enough, she'd be able to understand whatever was being said. The bacon started to burn, so my father turned off the heat and moved the pan, still looking at my mother, raising his eyebrows whenever she met his gaze, her lips still agape.

Finally she tilted the phone away from her mouth as the voice on the other end quietened slightly, and she craned her neck to look at my father. I was annoyed with Emily because she was chewing so loudly on her cereal, I couldn't hear Mrs. Tomlin on the phone.

Mom's eyes were beginning to turn pink and water as she told us, "Griffin died last night."

"*What*?" my dad asked, eyes widening. The pan slid out of his hand and fell into the sink with a deafening crash. "What happened? How did he die?"

I was too shocked to say anything at all. *Griffin died last night.* But he couldn't have. I'd seen him last night, playing Marco Polo, eating hot dogs at our neighborhood's Labor Day party.

Dad leaned closer to Mom, like he thought he'd heard her wrong, he must have heard her wrong, before she started crying silently, her hand over her lips. Then he glanced over at us, as if just now realizing that we were still sitting there, watching. "Clara, Emily, head up to your rooms, okay?"

4

"What about school?" Emily asked. "We have to leave in, like, ten minutes."

My father shot her a look as he placed both his hands on Mom's shoulders, squeezing as she cried into the phone receiver.

I looked over my shoulder, through the window to the Tomlins' house across the street, almost expecting there to be visual proof of this impossible event—that Griffin was dead, that he was really gone. But all I saw were the same two police cars still parked alongside the curb, the crime-scene tape fluttering in the breeze.

A hollowness opened in my chest as I heard my mother tearfully ask what had happened to him . . . we'd just seen him the night before, and he'd been fine. Then a numbness settled into my fingers and extended to my arms and my legs and everywhere in between. I slumped against the back of the chair and listened to the faint sound of the hysterical voice through the phone, feeling as if nothing was sinking in. Everything felt blank and unreal.

Griffin Tomlin was dead.

chapter *two*

four months later

I heard my mother entering the house through the patio door downstairs from my bedroom, the *shwoop* of the door closing behind her, and the clomping of her boots against the floor as she maneuvered around the table and chairs in the dining room. I imagined her peeling off her dirt-caked gardening gloves as she walked into the kitchen, past a chair no one sat in anymore, and dropping them on the counter.

In the three months since Emily had been arrested, my mother had become more obsessed with gardening than ever before, spending hours outside as she tugged out weeds, planted autumn flowers, and filled her watering can with the hose. The head of her trowel was dented and white at the edges from scratching against pebbles in the dirt, and the elastic of her gardening gloves was worn and stretched. The back of her neck was sunburned from spending so many hours tending to the flower beds. They used to bloom with vibrant petals but now, in January, there was nothing for her to plant. Nothing for her to nurture.

I thought maybe she would've tried to convince my father to buy her a greenhouse so she could continue her intensified obsession with botany and not focus on the fact that her daughter was awaiting trial for the murder of her best friend's son. Instead she would go outside, brush the snow from her garden, and stab her trowel through it to crumble the frozen dirt. The only garden she hadn't touched was my father's vegetable garden. Most of the vegetables had been dug up by an animal last August, but the rest died in October when Emily was arrested and, unlike my mother, my father stopped caring about plant life.

A few of our neighbors—ones who used to be friends—peered out from the safety of their windows and watched her crouch in front of the flower beds, always a glimmer of anxiousness in their eyes. It was the first murder committed here in Shiloh in years, the first in decades committed by an actual resident. Everyone looked at my mother and thought, *This is your fault. You raised her. How could you not know?*

But no one had thought my sister, Emily Porterfield, was messed up. They'd thought she was perfectly normal too, with her cheerleading uniform and her pom-poms waving frantically in the air like fireworks at the games. She'd babysat their children. She'd sold Girl Scout cookies to them in the spring. She'd walked their dogs and even scooped up their poop instead of leaving it there. Emily Porterfield just wasn't messed up.

Downstairs, I heard our answering machine playing a message left half an hour ago, while she was outside and I was in my bedroom. The message was from my father, apologizing for working late again tonight, mumbling we should eat dinner

7

without him, don't wait up. A moment later, my mother pressed the Delete Message button.

Sometimes she asked me if I knew why Emily had killed Griffin Tomlin, if it was just an accident, if I knew why Emily had snuck out of the house and crept across the street into the Tomlins' backyard that night. Every time she asked me a question about her, about him, about them, I would tell her no, even when it wasn't true. No, I didn't know why she'd done it. No, I didn't know why she went there. No, no, no. Sometimes I imagined Emily in a white cinder-block room, dressed in a jailhouse uniform instead of her cheerleader one, and her lips mouthing the word *liar* at me.

Because I knew why she'd done it.

I knew that Emily hated Griffin Tomlin the moment I'd told her something I never should have.

My parents and I haven't talked about it, but every day I've driven Emily's car to school.

Before she was arrested, we drove to school together. We'd stop at the Starbucks across the street and order mocha lattes, listening to Carrie Underwood songs. After she was arrested, my parents seemed to have an unspoken agreement that no one touched her things. Her bedroom door remained closed at the end of the hall; her granola bars were still in the cupboard, pushed to the back, hidden behind soup cans; one of her socks was still on the floor in front of the washing machine.

But after Emily's defense attorney managed to convince the police to release her car after it had been impounded (on the grounds that no evidence was found related to the case), I started driving it to school every morning. The first morning I did it, a part of me hoped it would still sort of smell like her inside, like if she couldn't be there, then maybe the fruity notes of her perfume would be, clinging to the seats. Instead it smelled like cleaning products, the scent stinging my nose. Everything of hers had been taken out, even the trash in the glove compartment. It was like a totally new car, complete with a pine-scented air freshener, but with old memories lingering in the cracks between the seats, like crumbs.

When I pulled into the school parking lot, there were still a few kids sitting in the comfort of their heated cars. The heater in Emily's car was broken, just like everything else seemed to be. I turned the engine off and sat there drinking my latte, feeling its warmth against my fingertips. Through the windshield, I spotted Kolby Rutledge trudging through the slush.

He was wearing a black puffer vest with a collar and a pair of jeans that were a little worn in the knees. His beanie was pulled over the tops of his ears, his brown hair poking out from underneath, and his Timberlands were damp from walking through slush and snow. His cheeks were rosy from the cold.

I felt a pang of guilt watching him jog up to the school's front doors. Griffin Tomlin used to give him a ride every morning after Kolby had totaled his car last winter skidding on black ice. Kolby's parents couldn't buy him another car, and the insurance didn't amount to much, so Griffin had driven him to school—until last September, anyway.

I reached across the console and grabbed my backpack from the passenger seat. A few of the kids hanging out in their cars looked over when they heard me slam my door, then quickly glanced away. My classmates usually ignored me, just like they had when Emily was in the driver's seat and I was in the passenger's, where we'd both belonged.

I expected everyone to treat me differently after my sister's arrest, to shove me around, sneer, and mutter under their breath as I walked past them in the hallways, torturing me in lieu of my sister, but they didn't. They mostly just stared and whispered to each other whenever they saw me. A few asked if I knew why she'd done it or if she could get the death penalty, oblivious to the fact that New York State abolished it years ago. Somehow this felt worse than if they'd been bullying me for what Emily did, because maybe that would've been something I deserved. I would have been prepared for it. Instead they just stared, their eyes full of pity and morbid curiosity.

But they wouldn't just stare if they knew what I knew.

After I walked inside and started heading down the hall, I noticed a girl standing in front of Emily's old locker, her fingers twisting the dial of a hot-pink lock. Her skin was the color of deepened amber and her hair was ebony in a fishtail braid. She was dressed in a pale pink sweater with a rose-gold choker necklace, and had peach nail polish on her fingers. Her sneakers were pink too.

I stared at her for a moment, feeling thrown by all the pink she wore as she opened the locker, the hinges creaking in such a familiar way I felt an ache in my chest at the sound.

After Emily had been arrested, the police had cleaned out her locker for evidence, as if during Math and Biology classes she had been scribbling her homicidal plans for Griffin Tomlin or something. For a few months, it was left empty and vacant. Someone—I didn't know who—scribbled in black marker *YOU SHOULD BE*

DEAD on it a few months ago. It was gone now, scrubbed clean, but it still felt like the words were there, festering unseen.

The girl grabbed a pink notebook from inside her—Emily's—locker and a pen before closing the door, turning to head down the hallway.

At home, Emily was preserved, almost like petals pressed between book pages. Last month, when I'd grabbed the one mug Emily used to use for her tea, my mother's eyes brimmed with tears. She lied in a wobbling voice that it was okay for me to use it, but I put it back anyway.

It felt so surreal that here, out in the world, people were actually beginning to move on from Emily Porterfield.

After last period, as I walked out into the parking lot, I noticed a dark figure lingering around the hood of my sister's Mini Cooper. He was tall, with broad shoulders, and wearing a familiar black puffer vest.

Kolby Rutledge.

I felt a slight twinge of panic seeing him there. His hands were stuffed into his pockets and his nose was turning pink as he half-heartedly kicked his boot into a pile of slush. I hadn't really spoken to him since Griffin Tomlin's funeral.

He'd come a few minutes into the service and stood in the back of the church, since all the pews were full. He'd been supposed to sit with the Tomlins, because they said Kolby was like a brother to Griffin, but when he hadn't shown up, my mother took his place beside Mrs. Tomlin, squeezing her hand. A part of me wondered if he was late so he wouldn't have to sit with them, so close to the open casket, and listen to the overwhelming sound of Mrs. Tomlin trying to stifle her sobs or Mr. Tomlin constantly clearing his throat.

He'd left soon after the funeral too, lingering only for a couple of minutes to give Mrs. Tomlin a quick and awkward hug. He nearly bumped into me on his way out, and I mumbled a soft *sorry* I don't think he heard. If I had known then, I would've apologized for more than just getting in his way.

I barely knew Kolby. He was always with Griffin, like they were a package deal or something, and while he wasn't really *shy*, he didn't speak much either. I didn't really know that much about him, except that he and Griffin had become friends on the baseball team in middle school. They were on the high school team too, but after Griffin died, Kolby quit.

I never really spoke to Kolby unless Griffin was there between us, like some sort of bridge.

Except for the night of the Tomlins' Super Bowl party. And now, apparently.

Kolby had taken off the beanie I'd seen him wearing earlier, and a few snowflakes were caught in his hair. His eyes were a deep shade of brown, the kind that reminded you of coffee with cream and sugar. I had always thought his eyes fit with Griffin's, which were a remarkable ocean blue—and that if irises were elements, then Griffin's were water and Kolby's were earth.

"Hey," he said.

"Hey."

I unlocked the passenger door and tossed my backpack inside, glancing at him over the hood of the car as his eyes focused on the tires, and I felt the urge to say something. Like I should apologize because now he has to walk to school in the middle of January. Or that my sister killed his best friend. But instead I asked, "Admiring Black Beauty?"

"The car's red," he said, his voice flat.

I shrugged uncomfortably, feeling his gaze on me as I started to brush the snow off the windshield with my hand. Kolby paused before taking his hand from his pocket and brushing the snow from the driver's window, his fingers ashen as they glistened with snow. Every few seconds he would stop to shake his hand, as if to warm it up. I wanted to say he didn't have to clean the snow off with me, but whenever I tried, I'd look at him and lose my nerve.

"Emily named it that. Something about a horse—I don't know." I did know, though, but I wasn't sure if this was okay, talking about Emily, especially to him.

He nodded, the muscles in his jaw clenched as he shoved his pale, wet hand back into his pocket. The prickling feeling of disquiet intensified with every second as he stood only a few feet away from me.

"Did she . . . has she ever said—?"

"No," I interrupted, shaking my head and looking away, already knowing what he was about to ask. His eyes held a sense of vulnerability in them that made my chest ache out of guilt for lying to him. But if I couldn't even tell my mom, then I definitely couldn't tell him.

"No," he repeated, the word almost a sigh.

"No," I reaffirmed.

The clouds concealed the blue sky, turning it a shade of white that made me feel heavy and tired as I pulled into the driveway.

Shouldering my backpack, I caught a glimpse of something in the rearview mirror. Standing in front of his mailbox, in a pair of plaid pajama pants and snow boots, was Brandon Tomlin. His back was turned to me as he grabbed the mail; the same tousled curly black hair that Griffin had had reached his shoulders now.

Brandon was five years older than me and acted like he thought he was cooler sometimes, even though he was twenty-two and still living with his parents, working at the local movie theater. I'd seen him at the funeral, sitting beside his father, rubbing his eyes throughout the service. When our family was about to leave and we'd hugged the Tomlins good-bye, his breath stank of something sickly sweet as he wrapped his arms around me. He was wobbling, teetering on his toes, and I held on to him tighter when I caught Mrs. Tomlin looking over at us, not wanting her to know her now-only child was drunk at her youngest son's funeral.

Now, he shoved the mail under his arm and swatted his hand against the mailbox lid to close it before heading back up the driveway.

I almost wanted to tell him why she'd taken Griffin away from him and his parents. But I knew none of them would believe me about what happened between Griffin and me.

I never would've believed it either.

chapter *three*

Somewhere, somehow, at some point between six and sixteen, I'd fallen in love with Griffin Tomlin.

Love might be one of the stronger words to describe an attraction toward someone with ocean-blue eyes and a laugh as infectious as the common cold, but between the summer nights of gazing through my window at his house and the block parties, it began to feel like the right one.

My feelings seemed kind of ridiculous, especially since he never once showed any interest in me. There were a few moments that almost made me wonder if he cared—like one time, during one of my parents' parties, all the teenagers decided to play basketball and Griffin picked me for his team on his fourth turn—but eventually, after analyzing each of those rare instances, I realized these were just moments of niceness, which almost hurt more than him ignoring me. He kept inviting other girls over to his house and texting them on his phone during block parties, and then he invited Amy Gard to junior prom. Later I overheard him telling Kolby that they did it in the back seat of her dad's Toyota afterward.

Griffin Tomlin was not in love with me. He didn't even *like* me like me.

Or at least that was what I'd thought until the night of our school's production of *Into the Woods*, when I saw him in the audience, sitting with Kolby Rutledge on his right and his parents on his left, watching as I sang about pitch, and shoes, and decisions. Then, as the song concluded, he grinned at me and lifted his hand in a wave before the stage lights went dark.

After the play ended and the rest of the cast members, still in their costumes, gathered in the school lobby for fruit punch and themed cookies, I spotted my family near the entrance, the playbills in their hands. I realized after a moment, however, that it wasn't *just* my family, but that my sister had brought her boyfriend, Wilson Westbrooke, and I could already feel myself getting annoyed. They had only been going out for a few months, but she brought him *everywhere*, even to my birthday dinner the month before. He was also four years older than her, never washed his shoulder-length hair, and sometimes vaguely smelled like weed.

I was about to wave at them anyway when two strong arms—sun-kissed and muscular—wrapped around my waist and lifted me off the ground. It wasn't until I saw Kolby pouring a glass of fruit punch at the snack table, alone, that I realized the toned stomach pressed against my back was Griffin's. Suddenly I was self-conscious that I might be too heavy for him or that the stage makeup might make me look like a raccoon up close.

"Clara!" he said.

I'm in Griffin Tomlin's arms, I thought, and I hoped he would never, ever put me down.

"Who would have thought that our very own Clara could sing and dance, huh? Did you think so, Kolby?"

"You were really good, Clara," Kolby responded, grabbing a cookie shaped like a crown from one of the platters on the table.

"Good? Just *good*?" Griffin repeated. I felt his arms loosen as he let me drop onto the floor, the soles of my shoes making a smacking sound as I landed. I wanted him to put his arms back around me before they'd even left my sides.

"It's all right," I said, even though I wasn't quite sure what I was saying was *all right*. I glanced up at Griffin, feeling a jolt in my chest when he looked back down at me. "I'm really glad you came. You didn't have to. I mean, I'm really glad you did but it wasn't—it was just *really* nice of you," I said.

Griffin bent down and pressed his lips against my cheek. "Anything for you, Cinderella," he whispered against my ear.

I had to bite down on my lip to stop myself from reacting as he reached over and grabbed a sugar cookie in the shape of a glass slipper, winking at me as he bit off the heel before my parents finally spotted me.

chapter four

The girl with an apparent obsession with pink was back at Emily's locker, trying to attach a glitter-framed mirror to the inside of the door. Her hair was pulled into another braid and she wore a bright pink cardigan, neon pink socks, and a black corduroy skirt.

I watched her as I filled my water bottle at the fountain. She slowly retracted her fingers from the mirror, a hesitant expression on her face. When it stuck, she grinned triumphantly, like she'd accomplished something more than just adhering a decorative mirror to a locker. She was brushing the glitter off her hands when I heard my name being called from behind me.

"Clara!"

Water spilled over my fingertips as I jumped. Mrs. Foley, smiling through turquoise lips, was waving her hand in the air as she approached me, wearing an olive-green vest over an orange T-shirt. She wore khakis at school, but whenever I saw her in the grocery store or something, she had on drawstring pants messily hacked off into shorts.

Mrs. Foley was someone who simultaneously did and did not seem like a music teacher. She wore weird lipstick shades and wooden clogs that clacked against the floors when she walked. Not only did she direct the school musicals but she organized fundraisers almost monthly to keep the school glee club open. Her insistence that I audition for the musical was how I'd first got to know Mrs. Foley. She'd noticed I didn't have enough change at a vending machine and given me a dollar, saying the only way she wanted me to pay her back was by trying out for the school's spring production, *Mamma Mia*.

She'd said I could just be in the background if I wanted and stay out of everyone's way, including the audience's. Then when I auditioned, she gave me the role of Sophie Sheridan, the main role of the musical. I almost backed out when I found out, but Mrs. Foley convinced me not to, telling me to trust her on this one.

"Hey, Clara," she greeted me. "How are you? We miss you in practices."

"Hey, Mrs. Foley."

She watched me for a moment as I twisted the lid onto my tumbler, slowly so I could focus on something other than her standing there expectantly. "Bex misses you too. She says that you haven't talked in a few months." *Ten to be exact,* I wanted to say, but I didn't. Instead I hoped that she'd just leave on her own so I wouldn't have to respond.

Mrs. Foley sighed. I looked up for long enough to see the defeated look in her eyes that drowned out the sparkle I normally saw in them. "Listen, honey-pie, I know things suck for you right now. But we're here for you! Even if you don't want to be involved in the spring musical—which would break my heart because

19

we're doing *Shrek* and I think you'd be a perfect Fiona—we're still your friends." She smiled but when I looked away, she shrugged. "But it's all up to you, honey-pie."

I nodded, mumbling, "I really have to get to class."

The sky was bright blue that afternoon as I headed through the school doors. I was on the second to last step when my fingers brushed against something as I went to move my hair from my face—something soft, warm, and polyester. I turned to see Kolby Rutledge staring at me, going the opposite way up the stairs, as my hand touched his vest.

"Hey," I said dumbly, quickly retracting my hand and shoving it into my pocket. Somehow it still felt like I was touching his vest, the sleekness against my fingers. "Sorry. I wasn't looking."

He nodded as if he already knew this, and maybe he did.

"It's okay," he told me. Kolby had always had a deep voice. Not weird deep or James Earl Jones deep, but just *deep*, and I remembered how much Mrs. Foley loved it. She was always pestering him about auditioning for a musical, but he turned her down each time. He was quiet, and used the least amount of words possible in each sentence. I wondered if that was because he didn't like talking or if he just didn't like talking to me.

"Sorry . . . again," I said after a moment, sighing the last word as I went around him on the steps.

"Clara?" He shifted his weight as if he were uncomfortable. "When I asked you if you knew why she did it, were you lying?"

My muscles tensed at this, but I tried not to let it show in my face. "Why would I lie about that?"

"I don't know." He exhaled. "You're not answering my question, though."

He looked at me for a few seconds in a way that made me want to cringe and turn away, like he was searching for an answer I wasn't about to give but he seemed to know was there anyway. Then he nodded, like I'd confirmed something he expected. It wasn't until he started to walk down the steps that I realized that look, that nod, irritated me.

"I wasn't lying," I told him. "I don't know why she would . . ." I was beginning to get frustrated as I struggled to say something that made sense. Frustrated that I was always being asked this question and always lying in response. "Just because I'm her sister doesn't mean I know why. You knew Griffin, so wouldn't you know if he did anything to make her want to kill him?"

He inhaled deeply, glancing away from me for a moment. When he looked back, I couldn't tell if he was hurt or if he pitied me, or maybe both. So when he started to say, "Clara," I just nodded and walked away.

I was halfway across the parking lot when I heard someone calling my name again. A girl this time.

"Clare?" I stopped mid-stride, my blood turning to ice in my veins, as I heard the voice of the only person in the world who called me Clare.

Bex.

My best friend.

"Hey . . . Clare." She smiled hesitantly at me. "Hey, wow. I haven't seen you in, like, forever." She laughed awkwardly. I knew what she was doing. She was trying to pretend that the past ten months had never happened and that we hadn't spent them apart.

That we were still best friends.

But the thing was?

We really weren't, not anymore.

"Yeah," I mumbled. Her hair was dyed a bright shade of blond, but before—when we were really still *friends*—it had been darker, and longer. Now her hair was shoulder length, bouncing with beachy curls. My hair was longer then too, but I'd cut it a few months ago, up to my own shoulders. It reminded me of the first thing Bex ever said to me, when I'd walked up to her at the counter, an application tentatively curled in my hand.

Hey, your eyes are green, just like mine.

I got the job, working with Bex at the ice cream parlor, Scoops!, the summer before the school's production of *Into the Woods*. In between dunking the ice cream scoopers in cups of water and informing customers that we did *not* serve frozen yogurt, we became friends. We would sneak handfuls of sprinkles when the place was dead and swap magazines back and forth. We blasted music from her phone until one day she got so sick of her songs that she stole my phone and plugged it in while I was in the bathroom. I was washing my hands when I heard the unmistakable sound of a song from *Wicked*.

"What is this?" she asked when I came back out, staring at my phone in her dock. "Is this . . . *Broadway*?"

At first she thought it was pretty weird; the songs were either too long or too short, and too many of the notes were belted dramatically. But one day, as she was serving a chocolate twist, I heard her humming a song from *Rent*, and the next thing I knew, she was cast as the Baker's Wife in *Into the Woods*, trying to steal my gold slippers and kissing my husband. We cracked jokes about trading shoes and spouses.

Hey, your hair is short, just like mine, I could've said to her now.

"I've got to get home," I said instead, when I could tell she was bringing herself to say something, maybe ask why I'd ignored her calls or why I always kept my eyes forward whenever I passed her in the hallway. But like she always did, when I started to walk away from her, she just gave up and gave me the one thing I wanted now—to be left alone.

When I pulled into our driveway, something was sticking to the pane of one of the windows on the second floor of our house. I stepped out of the car, swinging my backpack over my shoulder before walking onto the snow-covered lawn.

I stood on the tips of my toes, pushing my glasses farther up my nose, and my heart dropped. I turned to look around the neighborhood, in case I saw someone lurking behind a telephone pole, watching as I realized someone had egged my window. Well, actually, *Emily's* window.

I heard a rumble on the pavement behind me and turned to see Brandon Tomlin pulling a garbage can up his driveway, staring back at me. His hair was tousled, again, and his patchy beard was thickening on his face. He wasn't wearing a jacket or coat, just a T-shirt and some sweatpants. He looked at me, lazily and resentfully at the same time, before he disappeared into the garage.

I blinked, my fingers cold and numb, as my mother's car pulled into the driveway behind me. I watched through the windshield as she gasped, staring up at the dripping egg yolk and shattered eggshell on Emily's window.

"Go inside, Clara," she told me, getting out of her car and glancing around her, but Brandon Tomlin—or anyone else who might have wanted to egg Emily's window—was out of sight. When she saw I was still standing there, she shot me a look. "*Now*."

When my father came home from work and saw the crusted egg yolk on the window, the few pieces of shell that had fallen on the driveway, he wanted to call the police. He was *angry*. He was cursing under his breath as he got a dishcloth and the ladder from the garage, and climbed up to clean up the mess.

He had shrugged off his jacket, and even though his breath was coming out in frosty puffs, he didn't seem to realize he might've been cold up there. "Did your mother call the police yet?" he said down to me, his voice snapping like a ruler against knuckles. It seemed pointless to me now, since he had already scrubbed off most of the egg.

"Calling the police isn't going to do anything, Eric." My mother stood on the front porch, wrapping her cardigan more tightly around herself, her eyes red, her cheeks flushed. We'd caught her in one of those rare moments where she had nothing to prove, nothing to ignore, and nothing to pretend. "It's not like they can fingerprint the eggshells or anything."

"At least we'd be doing something!" my dad retorted, his voice dripping with annoyance like the egg yolk dripping from the window pane.

My mother nodded bitterly as she moved to step inside, muttering, "Like bothering the police."

My father hesitated, his hand clutching the dishcloth, and his grip tightened around the side of the ladder. He peered over his shoulder, calling out, "Samantha!" But she closed the front door before he could say anything else.

chapter *five*

I was standing in front of my mirror later that night after the play, using a makeup wipe to scrub away the eyeliner and eye shadow dusted across my face to look like soot, when my phone dinged. I had tossed it onto my bed after checking a text Bex sent me, asking about that hug she'd seen Griffin giving me earlier. There was a winking emoji in lieu of a question mark. I rolled my eyes when I read it, but I also felt a tiny glimmer of hope because it wasn't just me noticing it, thinking about it, and about him and me, anymore. Other people saw it too.

I was aggressively cleaning off my left eye as I opened the message, my heart racing as I read it and realized it wasn't from Bex.

Meet me outside in five. Please?
Griffin

The wet grass prickled against my bare feet as I stood in the backyard, droplets of water falling from the roof and plinking onto our patio. It was dark outside but the moon and the streetlights kept everything dimly lit as I waited for Griffin. I had changed out of my pajamas and into a pair of shorts and a camisole, quickly swiping a tinted lip balm over my lips and ruffling my hair.

My mind raced as I remembered how he'd lifted me off the ground earlier that night and how close he'd stood to me even after placing me down, whispering *Cinderella* in my ear. A little secret just between us. Now he wanted to see me again, after midnight.

There was a rustling in the distance, footsteps, and then I was blinded by the glare of the motion-sensor light as Griffin Tomlin climbed over our fence, landing on the grass near my dad's vegetable garden. He squinted at me, bringing his forearm over his face to shield his eyes from the glare.

I darted to the other side of the yard. The odor of the rain and freshly cut grass was heavy in the charged air but still, I could've sworn I smelled the scent of his soap as he smiled at me, bringing his arm down as the motion light flicked off and it was just us, alone in the dark and the rain.

"Hey," I whispered.

As I looked at him, a raindrop fell on the curve of his cheekbone, rolling down his face until it landed on his shirt, but he didn't seem to notice. He was only looking at me, and that felt both wonderful and terrifying at the same time.

"So, um," I said, feeling the fragile wings of butterflies grazing my rib cage as my heart expanded, "did you need to talk to me or something?"

"No," he said, tilting his head to the side. "I didn't *need* to or anything. But I wanted to."

I wasn't sure what that was supposed to mean. Maybe it would've been obvious to either Emily or Bex that he was flirting, but it wasn't to me. Because he was Griffin Tomlin and I was Clara Porterfield, in the same galaxy but never in the same orbit. It just felt so impossible to think that someone I wanted could actually want me back.

"Okay," I breathed. "About what?"

Something filled his eyes, something that looked so sincere and inviting and kind. If his eyes were really the ocean, and if he had asked me to jump, I probably wouldn't have thought twice about squeezing my eyes shut and diving right in, right into him.

"You. How I kind of want to kiss you right now." Then, before I had a chance to react, I felt the warmth of his hands on either side of my face, fingertips in the strands of my hair, and his lips against my own.

I closed my eyes.

When he pulled away from me, his lips, the lips I had just kissed, curved into a smile. *You just did that,* I thought, and it was all I could think. Griffin Tomlin had really kissed me, and it wasn't a dream or a fantasy or anything, but real.

"I didn't think you were going to do that," I finally whispered after a moment.

"Well, I did want to do more than just talk," he told me. Then he glanced away from me, over to one of our neighbors' houses. "It sounds like someone's outside. I should probably go." He kissed me again, so quickly I only realized he'd done it when he pulled away. "I'll text you again, soon."

I was still so stunned—Griffin Tomlin kissed me—that all I

did was nod, barely even registering his words and swift movement as he ran across the lawn and over the fence, waving, just like he had earlier that night, until he was out of sight.

The next day, I thought he would call me or run through the backyard again in the middle of the night, like it was our thing, dark-backyard kissing. But he never called me or texted me. I even left the light on in my room until almost three in the morning so he wouldn't think I was asleep, but it was Saturday. Maybe he was really busy on Saturdays. Maybe he had baseball practice or was working, *or, or, or.* But then Sunday came and went, and there was nothing. I told Bex to call me to make sure that my phone was still working, but of course, it was. It was only Sunday, though. Maybe he had baseball practice or was working.

Or, or, or.

On Monday, I decided to find his locker between classes, hoping that he might be there. I was also hoping that when he saw me coming around the corner, he would hesitate a little, as if he were just as stunned as I was that he'd kissed me. Then maybe he would smile at me before giving me a totally believable reason for why he hadn't called me all weekend and then kiss me again, for the third time. Then we would go to class, and Bex would notice my smudged lipstick, and mouth something like, "Did you just make out?" and I would nod, because, yeah, I'd just made out with Griffin Tomlin.

When I turned the hall corner, he was standing at his locker, but he wasn't alone. He was standing in front of a girl with red hair that curled around her shoulders, her arms crossed tightly over her chest. Griffin looked almost—maybe—annoyed with her as she spoke, a crease forming between his eyebrows. He shrugged in response to whatever she said and tilted his head to the side, looking away from her.

He looked almost . . . defensive.

A second went by before she tightened her arms around her chest and shrugged too, appearing defeated in some way. He mumbled something I couldn't hear before he grabbed his backpack and swung it over his shoulder, walking away from her and right past me.

Without even noticing me standing there.

It had been almost two weeks since Griffin kissed me. And it had been about a week and a half since I'd seen him standing in front of his locker with that girl. I kept wondering what they were talking about and why he'd never reached out to me after our kiss. The pieces didn't fit, and the ones that did were ones I didn't want to think about. The picture was twisting into something else when I wanted it to stay just me and Griffin, in my backyard, in the rain, our lips meeting.

It wasn't until I was working at Scoops! that I saw him again. I was sitting behind the counter, slouching in a metal chair with an old, dog-eared copy of a magazine, the air warm and sticky. Even though it was October, it was *hot*. I had rubber-banded a small, mechanical fan to another chair and aimed it in my direction.

Scoops! was a smaller parlor, with only three booths in the corner, each with cracks like spiderwebs across their vinyl covers. Fuchsia-and-white checkered tiles stretched out over the floor.

All the tables and counters were painted teal, and abstract art-work from the owner's daughter decorated the walls.

"If the parlor was only for scoops of ice cream, why isn't it called that? Instead it's called 'Scoops!' Like, as in scoops of frozen yogurt." I looked over my shoulder at Bex, who was standing at the counter with an ice cream scooper in her hand and a pained expression on her face. She'd just informed a red-faced woman that we did *not* serve frozen yogurt. Twice.

I could tell Bex was stifling the urge to critique her logic before gesturing to the selection of ice cream tubs in front of her. "I'm sorry, but we still only sell ice cream here. And cones, if you want those."

"Who wants an ice cream cone without the ice cream?!"

I was beginning to wonder if I should interject when he came in. A bell rang above his head as he ambled inside, flip-flops smacking against the tiles. When I realized it was him, Griffin, the sound of my heart beating in my ears drowned out the mechanical fans and the huffs of the angry woman.

I approached the counter as he looked down at the ice cream selection. Some of the shallow metal tubs were nearly empty, scraped so that you could see the glint of silver at the bottom. He smiled and said, "Hey," as if his heart was just beating normally instead of going into arrhythmia like mine.

"Hey." I wasn't sure what to do with my hands, so I reached for an ice cream scooper, shaking off the water and acutely aware that Griffin Tomlin was watching me the entire time.

"I didn't know you worked here," he said, turning to the fish-bowl we had on the counter, which was filled with strips of folded paper. A pen with a little notepad sat beside it. We had a draw for a free ice cream cone every week. He picked up the pen, but instead of writing down his name and phone number, he tossed it up in the air and caught it.

"Yeah." I nodded. "Since the beginning of the summer."

"It was a pleasant surprise," he said, still looking at the pen, but then he brought his gaze back to me, ocean blue and all. I found myself smiling back because, to Griffin Tomlin, I was a *pleasant surprise.*

And that wasn't something you said to girls you didn't want to see after kissing them, right?

"Thanks," I said, and there was something in my voice that sounded almost *flirty.* Not the kind of flirty Bex or Emily were capable of, but something more awkward that seemed to be *working* because Griffin laughed, like I'd said something funny. "So are you going to put your name in? Winner gets a free ice cream cone."

"A free ice cream cone, huh?"

I suddenly felt brazen, the same rush I'd had when we were in my backyard together, leaning close, radiating through me. "If you want . . ." He looked away from the fishbowl, eyebrows raised, and my heart seized for a split second before I continued. "I mean, if you want, I could put your name in twice."

"Isn't there a law against that or something?" Griffin whispered, glancing quickly at Bex.

"No, there's not." I took in a breath, heart hammering, going on. "If you win, someone—and by someone, I-I mean *me*—will call you to let you know." When he stared at me, still smiling but not saying anything, I added quickly, "Or we could email you. Whichever."

I hadn't realized my glasses had slid down my nose until Griffin reached over the counter and pushed them up with his fingertip.

31

"Or," he said, reaching for my hand and turning it palm-up before uncapping the pen with his teeth, "I could just give you my new number and skip the free ice cream."

He started to write the first digit, a seven, the tip of the pen tickling against my hand, and I had to resist the urge to wiggle away from it. I was both eager and terrified. "No one really turns down free ice cream around here."

Griffin laughed as he wrote the next number, a two, his thumb stroking the back of my hand as he wrote. "My old phone died," he explained. "That's why I haven't texted or anything."

I smiled, hoping my relief wasn't as obvious as it felt, bursting through my chest. But then, just over Griffin's shoulder, I noticed someone standing behind the front window of the parlor. A hoodie was pulled over her face, but I recognized my sister's strawberry blond hair, the same color as mine, draped over her chest. Her green painted nails were knocking softly on the window, over the painted Scoops! sign.

Griffin had just written the dash over my palm when I slowly withdrew my hand. "Griffin, c-can you wait just a minute? Please."

I tried to ignore the slightest trace of hurt flashing over his face as he nodded, capping the pen. "Sure, no problem."

I walked around the counter and headed outside, catching a glimpse of the first half of his phone number on my palm when I turned to Emily and threw up my hands, asking, "What?"

She was sniffling as she grabbed the back of the hoodie, yanking it down and away from her face. I let out a gasp as the sunlight fell over her eye, the skin around it swollen and dark, glistening from her tears. Her chin was trembling as she asked me, quietly with a shuddering voice, "Can you take me somewhere? Please, Clara."

I reached a hand out to her, but she took a step away from me, almost cowering. "What happened? Emily, seriously. What happened?"

She shook her head, crossing her arms. "Please let's just go, okay? Please. Clara."

I hesitated before I reached over and pulled open the front door, calling out, "Bex, I have to go!"

Emily scurried toward the Mini Cooper and yanked open the passenger side door. For a moment, I just stood there, unsure of what to do. Even though I knew she probably couldn't hear me, I asked, "Do you want me to call Mom?"

Instead of responding, she got into the car and slammed the door.

I looked behind me, my gaze penetrating through the painted glass of the window and into the ice cream parlor. Griffin was still leaning over the counter, and I remembered half of his phone number was written on my palm. He stared out at me, confused, the pen still in his hand. Behind me, Emily tapped on the horn.

I sighed, pressing my fingers into the number, and mouthed to Griffin, *Sorry.*

He nodded, setting the pen back down in front of the fishbowl.

Sorry, I wanted to say again, and again, and again.

Sorry.

We drove around for nearly forty minutes, taking turns I had never taken before and pulling onto roads I had never driven before. I rolled down the front windows so the rushing of the air would drown out Emily's sniffling, her breath hiccupping as if she just couldn't catch it.

"Where are we going?" I finally asked.

"Just keep going," she told me, before reaching forward and pressing play on the CD player, the chords of country music filling the car.

So I did.

Eventually, after almost two hours of just driving, I pulled into a roadside gas station. "If we're going to keep driving around, I don't want to run out of gas in the middle of nowhere," I told her as I parked alongside a pump—but really, I wanted out of that car with Carrie Underwood crooning through the speakers in the back seat, and Emily's sniffling and bruised eye. It felt confining, like the air was being sucked out through the open windows.

I pumped in a little gas before jogging into the convenience. I got us some cherry and coke slushies, a bag of mini peanut butter cups, and a box of bandages. I didn't really think you were supposed to put a bandage over a bruise, but all of the ice packs were warm, and I couldn't think of anything else.

We sat in the parking lot for a few minutes and quietly sipped our slushies, occasionally grabbing a handful of peanut butter cups from the console between us. She had pulled her hood down, the glow of the convenience store's sign falling over her features. The greenish hue made the bruise look even worse. Sometimes she would lift the slushie to the side of her face and close her eyes, the evening air ruffling her hair.

"Emily," I said. "What happened? Did you hit your head or something?"

I knew this wasn't it, but there was a part of me that wanted to believe this was all somehow an accident. That my thoughts were worse than what had actually happened, even though I knew that couldn't possibly be true.

"Wilson," she said. "We got into a fight, a *stupid* fight. It was over this girl, one of his friends' sisters, I don't know. I saw a picture of them together on his phone, doing this really *stupid* looking selfie." She grabbed another handful of candies and rolled her eyes—or one of them anyway. The other one was too swollen to tell. "And I got mad. I mean, my boyfriend takes a picture with a slut, I can get mad, right?"

I nodded, somewhat slowly. I felt a little thrown hearing her use the word *slut*, practically spitting it out of her mouth like it had a bitter taste.

"He thought I was being unreasonable, and he was, like, *You're always doing this. You're always asking me if I'm with other girls when I'm not.* And then I brought up this other time a few months ago because I was trying to prove to him it wasn't my fault I was saying this stuff! You know, maybe if he kept it in his pants, then I wouldn't always be asking him if he was sleeping around."

She laughed ruefully around a mouthful of peanut butter cups. Then her face softened slightly, the tremble creasing her chin again.

"But he got angry. Like, really angry. And the next thing I know . . ." She gestured vaguely to her face, to her swollen eye. A thick teardrop slid over her purplish bruise as it went down her cheek. "He just hit me."

"Emily," I whispered.

"But then he got really apologetic, you know? He said he was sorry so many times, and then he started crying." She reached for her slushy and brought it back to her bruise, closing her eyes as she sighed shakily. "I just wanted to get away. So I did."

I wasn't sure of what else to say, so instead I just murmured,

"Emily," again as the neon lights from the convenience store sign flickered over her face, reflecting against her glistening cheeks, and she nodded back. Like she didn't know what else to say either.

chapter six

I was sitting in the cafeteria, stabbing my fork at the salad on my plate, when I felt a whoosh of air against my face as someone plopped down in the seat across from me, and heard the rattling clank of their tray smacking against the table.

"Hey, is this seat free?"

It was the girl who was using my sister's old locker. I took in her pink T-shirt (with darker pink letters spelling out *Let's Taco About It* over a cartoon taco), pink eye shadow, and pink tattoo choker. There was just so much *pink*.

"It isn't now because I'm sitting here but if you had a friend here, I'd move, but I was pretty sure you didn't, because I kind of watched you for a minute. In a totally not creepy way! And whoops, it looks like I've skipped the name part of the introductions, I'm Aniston. You know, like Jennifer Aniston? Apparently, my mom was really into *Friends* and thought naming me Jennifer would be just too kind."

I frowned, confused.

She blinked, waited, and then blurted out, "And you don't have to tell me your name, because I already know it. Clara, which is really pretty. Like *The Nutcracker*." She exhaled loudly, as if she were exhausted from talking so much. "And again, in a totally not creepy way. Knowing your name, I mean! It's just . . . you know—I'm not a creep or anything."

"Okay," I said slowly.

She—Aniston, not Jennifer, apparently—grinned, as if she were so relieved by one simple word and then opened her mini bag of chips. "Great!" she said around the food in her mouth, using the back of her wrist to hide the sight of her chewing.

I looked around the cafeteria, half-expecting there to be a group of equally pink other girls giggling over this or something. It had to be some kind of joke.

"So I'm with the *Madison Register*, the school newspaper. You know, the one no one reads. I'm writing an article and I thought since I was just assigned your sister's old locker that maybe . . ." I felt the color drain from my face and my heart began to pound in my ears: *thump, thump, thump.* I dropped my fork, but instead of landing on the tray, it clattered to the floor and underneath the table.

I grabbed my tray and stood up so quickly I nearly tripped on the table leg. Aniston stood up too, although much more gracefully.

"I'm sorry! I shouldn't have led with that. It's just, well, I thought maybe—"

"It's whatever. It's fine."

It was *fine* that she was snooping around Emily and Griffin just so she could write an article for a high school newspaper only five people read. It was just a mystery most people were suckers for. It wasn't like my sister was in jail or Griffin was dead or that it all was because of me.

Aniston's chirpy and apologetic voice was still ringing in my ears on the way home as I clutched the steering wheel, embarrassed that I felt like crying because someone at school wanted to do what dozens of reporters and bloggers already had.

Focusing on the wind whipping snowflakes against the windshield, I noticed a black blur in the corner of my eye, a quick jerk of movement. There was Kolby Rutledge, in his vest, on his tailbone after slipping on a patch of ice on the sidewalk. Rolling up to the stop sign, I watched as he attempted to hoist himself up, cautiously, so as not to slip again.

I was about to drive away, let him walk the rest of the way home, when I decided not to. I didn't because I remembered the morning after the Tomlins' Super Bowl party, how he had kept his promise to me.

"Kolby?" I called, rolling down my window and leaning my head out. "Are you okay?"

"I'm all right," he replied. He stuffed his hands into his pockets and then nodded at me before turning away and continuing to walk down the icy concrete. His nose and ears were red, his breath visible puffs in front of him, and I remembered him standing on the porch almost a year ago, kind of freaked out and concerned all at once.

"Kolby," I shouted, flicking my eyes to the rearview mirror to make sure no one was behind me. "Do you . . ." I hesitated, not completely sure I should be doing this. "Do you need a ride home, maybe?"

"I'm okay, thanks."

I idled by the side of the road, then started driving slowly alongside him, unsure if I should just head off or if I should push the issue. I paused, inhaling to fill my lungs with the crisp, chilled air before blurting out, "You were right."

Kolby stopped and turned to face me. I pulled over to the side of the road again as he took a step closer to the curb and hunched down at the window. "About?"

"About me. About me lying to you. To everyone, basically."

He nodded and stepped off the curb, going around the front bumper. He didn't seem to be especially surprised by this or anything, but acted like it was a fact he already knew. Which made it even more unsettling when he got into the car and said, "Keep going straight. I'll tell you when you have to turn."

For the first few minutes, the car was quiet. He didn't say anything, didn't ask me to explain why I had lied or what I'd lied about, and also didn't tell me to turn. He just sat there, eyes directed at the road in front of us.

"You aren't going to ask me anything?" I said after a moment, not used to riding in the Mini Cooper with someone else without a Carrie Underwood soundtrack to fill the silence.

He looked at me. "What did you lie about?"

"I don't know why my sister did that—to him. I don't," I told him, wondering if my sputtered lies were as obvious to him as they were to me, jumbled up bits of untruths dangling between us. But if they were, he didn't let it show. "And I didn't know she was going over there that night," I continued, grateful at least *this* was true. "But before the police arrested her, I . . . knew."

"That she'd killed him," Kolby clarified.

I sighed unsteadily, clenching and unclenching my fingers around the steering wheel. "Yeah," I breathed. "That."

Kolby processed this for a moment before turning his gaze back to the road and motioning to the left. "Turn here." As I flipped on the turn signal, I couldn't decide if his voice was his own quiet version of anger or if that was his normal tone when giving directions. "How did you know?"

"She told me. The night of his funeral. I guess she felt guilty or something, I don't know. I didn't really believe her until—until she showed me her clothes." I coughed, wishing my voice didn't sound so small and that he would tell me to make another turn so I could focus on something else. "She kept them in a plastic bag . . . I don't know why she would even keep those."

Kolby was quiet for a moment. I wondered if he already knew about that, had seen it on the news or read it in an article. The police suspected she'd kept them as trophies of what she'd done, but I knew that wasn't true. Maybe she didn't know what to do with them. Maybe she was trying to figure that out when they arrested her.

"Why didn't you tell anyone?"

"Because," I said. I felt so *stupid*, sitting in my sister's car and driving the best friend of her *murder victim* home while trying to *explain* this to him. I remembered how after the Super Bowl party, I could barely catch my breath when I asked him to promise me he would never tell, and how this would be the second time I lost it in front of Kolby Rutledge. "I didn't know what to do. It kind of felt like not deciding was my decision. I mean, it was *Emily*."

"Turn here. My house is just up the street. The brown one with the bike in the yard." Then he tilted his head down slightly and

41

said, "I know you think a lot of people blame you, and that might be true, but if it is, I'm not one of them."

I felt my breath hitch in my throat. "What?"

"Just because you're her sister doesn't mean that you could've changed anything that happened."

I pulled into the driveway of the brown house with the parts of a bicycle visible beneath a blanket of fresh, powdery snow. "Yeah, well." My voice was thick and struggled to escape around the lump in my throat. "I'm not so sure about that," I told him. It felt like the truest thing I'd said since the Super Bowl party.

Kolby shoved open the passenger door and grabbed his backpack, but instead of getting out of the car, he turned to look at me and smiled. Like, actually *smiled*, in a way that looked both totally weird and totally amazing.

"I am," he said. "Thanks for the ride, Clara."

I watched as he trudged through the snow on his lawn up to his porch, fumbling around in his pocket for a moment before pulling out a set of keys. After unlocking the front door, he gave me a wave over his shoulder before stepping inside.

My father was late coming home for dinner. We were already sitting down when we heard the rumble of his car pulling into the driveway. My mother nibbled at her salad, glancing at the front door down the hallway, but quickly turned her gaze back to me as I picked at my chicken.

"I saw a poster for the school's spring musical at the grocery store," she mentioned cheerfully. It seemed like she was about to go on, but she paused at the muffled slam of the car door outside.

She turned back to her salad, continuing, her voice now strained, "I think you would make an excellent Fiona, sweetheart. And it's been"—she paused again when my father opened the front door and proceeded to stomp his shoes on the floor mat, his back turned to us—"it's been so long since we've been to see one of your plays."

When my father walked into the kitchen, my mother pointed to the counter, where a cold plate of dried-out chicken sat. "If you'd called and told me you were going to be late, I would've kept it warm for you."

He only nodded in response, loosening his tie as he yanked open a drawer to grab a fork and knife, then came over to join us at the table. When my mother resumed talking about musicals, he interrupted to rattle on about some facts he'd garnered from his latest meeting with the lawyer, how they were trying to prove a crime-scene tech who processed the scene abused protocol. And, as he usually did, he mentioned Emily's bail hearing from several months ago and how bail had been denied. According to the defense attorney, that was normal for murder cases, but to my father, it was an outrage.

"Where is she going to go?" he said then and now, as his fork stabbed at the plate. "Put an ankle monitor on her and let her come home."

My mother glanced across at him, eyes narrowing into slits as she said in a low voice, "Not now." Then she smiled at me, in a way that was almost too sweet, and took another bite of her salad. "So, are auditions coming up soon? I could help you practice if you want."

My father stood up from the table then, the chair screeching loudly against the floor, before stalking into the kitchen. He dropped his half-finished plate into the sink with a deafening crash as he glowered at the back of my mother's head. "I have work to do," he muttered, heading back around the table and into the hallway.

I glanced over my shoulder, noticing the glint of a beer bottle between his fingers as he disappeared upstairs.

I was sitting at one of the tables in the local library doing my homework, my backpack in the chair beside me. I'd tried doing it at home in my room, but it wasn't long after dinner before my parents started arguing in my father's office down the hall. Once I heard my mother bring up the plea bargain Emily refused last month, I grabbed my homework and left, sending my mom a quick text to let her know.

Since my sister's arrest, there had been several points of contention between my parents, including that my mother hadn't been to see Emily since she'd learned she had confessed to me about the murder—which my sister now denied—but the plea bargain was one of the sorest. Emily had been offered a plea bargain for a reduced sentence in exchange for a guilty plea and a written confession, but my father was against it, even though the defense attorney advised she take it. When my mother had admitted she thought Emily should accept the plea bargain, that was when the tension really set in between them.

My father believed in Emily's innocence.

And my mother didn't.

It wasn't until I heard keyboard keys clacking that I noticed Aniston—dressed in pretty much all pink again, though it *almost* seemed to work for her. I'd only had one conversation with her, but now it seemed impossible to picture her wearing a color that wasn't some shade of peach, fuchsia, or coral.

She was speedily typing something into a search engine. I was about to look away when I noticed something—some*one*—appear on the results. She wasn't researching a class assignment, or stores that sold exclusively pink clothing. She was researching Emily.

A picture of her was in the corner of the screen. Her stringy hair was draped over her shoulders, the straps of her yellow tank top visible, with white tan-lines streaking across her skin beside them. There were dark circles under her eyes as she looked into the camera, standing in front of a gray background. Her mugshot. I had seen it before, but I still couldn't understand how Emily—*my* Emily—could have left our house looking like her usual self, then looked like that a few hours later.

Then there was a picture of Griffin, his blue eyes also staring into the camera. The photo was familiar: him sitting on the grass of his backyard—the very place where he would be murdered months later—sunglasses hanging by the collar of his shirt. He was grinning and tanned and looked so *normal*. He looked like the guy I'd seen at barbecues or in school and wondered if he liked me back, but that boy was gone. I saw something else in those eyes now, a storm lurking in the depths of his irises, just waiting to wreak havoc.

That wasn't Emily in her picture.

And that wasn't Griffin in his.

I sat there for a moment, looking at those two misleading photos on a local crime blog. Aniston scrolled down the screen and a video appeared, surrounded by words too small to read.

The thumbnail was of Detective Marsh—the one who'd arrested Emily months ago—his mouth open as he spoke about a boy and a girl he didn't even know, pretending as if he did. *We believe the murder was premeditated,* his tinny voice said through the computer speakers.

Aniston pulled her phone out and started typing.

> We believe Emily Porterfield approached Griffin Tomlin in his backyard in the early hours of September the third. Text messages recovered from his phone, from Ms. Porterfield, show that she arranged a meeting with the victim beforehand. We believe the murder occurred shortly after she arrived, which was when she struck Griffin Tomlin on the back of the head with one of his mother's decorative garden stones. He fell into their inground pool, and due to his loss of consciousness, drowned.
>
> We believe Ms. Porterfield's motivations were sexual. There was evidence of sexual assault to his body, which would've taken place prior to his death.

I grabbed my notebooks and shoved them into my backpack at this, the last piece of truth we'd held on to, the detail no one else had known until now, when he'd announced it to the world. Aniston turned around at the sound of my backpack unzipping, quickly pausing the video. The detective on the screen was holding up his palm as if he, too, was trying to tell her to stop.

"Clara," she said as I crammed my pencils and highlighters into the front pocket of my bag. I wanted to get away: from the detective on the screen, from Aniston and her ambition to solve a murder for a high school newspaper article. From Griffin and his stormy eyes. From the Emily my sister had become, staring blankly from her mugshot.

I wanted to get away.

"Clara, I am so sorry. I didn't see you there and I just—Clara, no, wait!"

"Shh!" a librarian hissed from behind the front desk.

"Clara, please, just wait!" she called out anyway, ignoring the librarian, but none of that mattered to me.

I just wanted to get *away*.

I pushed open the library door, feeling the bitter windchill against my face as I hurried down the concrete steps. My backpack was slung over my shoulder, my coat draped over my arm because I'd been so frantic to leave before I heard any more of what Detective Marsh would say, or any more of Aniston's babbled apologies.

My bag was still unzipped, my notebooks slipping out, and I kept hearing the clicking of items falling and landing on the sidewalk. I didn't care if I was basically leaving a trail of stationery items like breadcrumbs for someone to follow me with. I felt tired of constantly picking up pieces, stuffing them into places they didn't belong, pretending as if it wasn't getting harder and harder to keep going.

My eyes started to water as I walked. I was so angry with her—angry she'd done *that* to him, angry she was in jail right now awaiting a murder trial, angry that she should've been away from home at a university right now instead, thinking about midterms and not guilty verdicts.

I was also angry no one had told me Detective Marsh was

doing *another* press conference, one where he exposed the details we had been able to keep to ourselves until then. Everyone knew how Griffin had died, but no one knew about what had happened in the moments before.

And I was angry with myself—so angry—because I gave Emily a reason to kill him.

Crash!

I felt my notebooks, my textbooks, my phone, *everything* left in my backpack, slump to the side and hit the ground. One of my notebooks landed in a snowbank, the remainder of my pencils rolled off the sidewalk and onto the side of the road, and my textbook was lying, open, facedown on the pavement. I groaned, a tear burning its way down my cheek, before I shrugged off my empty bag and threw it on the snow.

My sister was a murderer and here I was, crying because my backpack had spilled on the sidewalk.

I had squeezed my eyes so tightly shut I felt them boiling under my eyelids with pathetic, unshed tears, when I heard them: footsteps softly pounding against the concrete, slowing once they noticed me standing there, eyes closed, with school supplies scattered around me. I opened my eyes, glancing over, and of course—*of course*—it was Kolby Rutledge. Of course it was him. He was there the morning after the Super Bowl party, so obviously he would see me now, crying and looking ridiculous.

"Hey," Kolby said, somewhat hesitantly. "Did the zipper on your backpack break?" He leaned down and picked up a pencil.

"No," I said softly. "I . . . there's this girl in the library—she's writing an article for the paper about Emily."

He grabbed my textbook before it was completely sodden, shaking out the pages and wiping the slush from them. Bits of gravel stuck to his fingers. "Aniston, right? She emailed me a couple of times about it. Not even sure how she got my email."

He grabbed a highlighter from the ground. I hesitated, watching as he retrieved a couple of pencils from the cracks in the sidewalk. It didn't quite feel right, just letting him do that, so I picked up a notebook. "I left and I was hurrying and now my things are ... a mess." I laughed, bitterly and quietly, kicking the snowbank beside me. "Kind of like my life, huh?"

He reached down and retrieved my backpack from the snowbank, laying it against his shins and depositing my stationery supplies inside. "Messes can be cleaned up."

Kolby swung my backpack over his shoulder and followed me as I walked home. He didn't say anything about my flushed cheeks or watering eyes, or Aniston and her stupid article. Instead he was quiet and pressed the buttons for the crosswalks.

"Do you have anywhere you need to be?" I said. He glanced at me as he shook his head. "You don't have to walk me home if you do. Or if you don't. I mean, if there's something else you wanted to do, I don't want to keep you."

"I'm good. Besides, it's getting kind of dark out," he replied. Then he hesitated after I nodded uncertainly. "You get it."

"What?"

"You get it," he repeated, stopping abruptly before shifting to face me. "No one around here gets it. All my mom wants to do is talk about it and my dad just wants to take me out to hockey games and hope I forget about it. But you," he said, his voice softening, pointing the index finger curled around my backpack strap at me, "I think you get it. At least better than everyone else."

"My mom wants to forget all about it and my dad wants everyone to drop everything until we fix it. Like it's something that we can even fix. I don't even know what that would mean now," I said.

"See," he told me, his faint little smile growing a little less faint. "You get it."

chapter seven

It was almost eleven at night when I heard the familiar sputtering of Wilson Westbrooke's engine from outside my bedroom window. I was sprawled on my bed, an opened textbook with a highlighter lodged between the pages beside me. I had already completely forgotten what I'd highlighted when my phone pinged with a text from Griffin.

He was at the Red Panda with his family for their Friday night dinner, telling me how he was thinking about saving me a couple of sweet and sour chicken nuggets from his plate. He teased me about the one time, when our parents threw an Academy Awards party and ordered Chinese food, he'd seen me take a whole container of sweet and sour chicken for myself.

I was smiling down at my phone—both embarrassed and kind of thrilled he'd remembered something I barely even recalled, like maybe throughout the years he'd been paying as much attention to me as I had to him—when I heard Wilson's van. I looked out the window, just barely glimpsing the bright shade of Emily's hair as she sat in the passenger seat, her face turned away from me.

It had been almost two months since Wilson Westbrooke had given her a black eye—one she'd explained to our parents was from accidentally getting smacked in the face at cheerleading practice—but she hadn't broken up with him. She'd ignored his texts and phone calls at first, but her eyes had drifted back to her phone with less and less reserve, until the last football game of the season, when she had spotted him sitting in the first row of bleachers.

She told me dreamily that he was smiling while he watched her cheer, even when he didn't know she was looking. He found her after the game and they drove thirty minutes away to find cherry snow cones at a gas station, and he told her how sorry he was.

And somehow bleachers and cherry snow cones and an apology were all she'd needed to forget about everything else. She told me she really felt he was actually sorry about what had happened, and that he was always sweet and romantic with her the rest of the time. I felt like I should've said something, but I was afraid she would get angry at me if I did. For whatever reason, my sister loved Wilson Westbrooke so much, too much, and I was scared if I did or said something that took him away from her, she wouldn't forgive me for it.

From below, I heard the creaking hinges of the van door opening, the muffled pulsating beat of music increasing now. I looked back through the window when loud voices started to accompany it.

Emily was halfway out of the van, the toe of her boot pressed against the pavement, and her hand was gripping the door handle, but she was still sitting inside.

Another text message came in from Griffin, but I was too preoccupied with the tone of my sister's voice. She was yelling, angrily, her words distorted by the music blaring through the speakers and the window's thick glass.

I thought of the last fight she'd had with Wilson, and I slipped my feet into a pair of slippers and headed for the stairs. When I got outside, snow immediately soaking through to my bare feet, Emily was standing on the road, still holding the door with her hand, her hair a curtain in front of her face.

"Stop," she ordered, her voice sharp and loud. She was holding her coat over her arm. "Stop, seriously. Stop lying to me. That's not your sister's name. Just admit some slut is texting you!"

She stared at Wilson for a moment—only his shoulder was visible from where I stood on the front porch—before she reached back into the van in a jerking movement and slapped her hand against the radio, everything suddenly going quiet. Without the pulsating beat of an indie rap song, everything felt piercingly still. For a second, all I could hear was the engine running and the windshield wipers screeching against the pane.

His response came, grumbled from inside the van. "Gemma. That's my sister. *Gemma.*"

Emily scoffed, shaking her head. "Your sister's name is Isabella!"

"I have more than one," he retorted.

I could hear the aggravation twisting and sharpening his words. I took the steps down from the porch and when I reached the bottom, I caught a glimpse into the van.

Wilson was behind the steering wheel slouching against the

seat, its cracked leather held together with duct tape. He was looking away from her, but when he glanced back, he noticed me standing there.

Something shifted in his expression then. Almost like embarrassment was pooling into his eyes. "Speaking of sisters," he said, nodding to me, "yours is right over there."

She shot a look over her shoulder, but her face was a blur against her hair, and she looked away as soon as she saw me.

"Don't *even*," she spat. "You know, you're a freaking sex addict, Wilson. You're a sex addict. You literally can't ever not notice other women. And of course you have a sister I've never heard of before. *Of course!*"

"You *have* heard of her."

She slammed the van's door, her coat nearly slipping from over her arm, the sleeve now dragging in the snow as she stormed away from him. "Don't gaslight me!" she yelled.

Suddenly she was beside me, her fingers gripping hard around my elbow, her nails digging into my skin as she dragged me backward to the porch steps. I caught one last glimpse of Wilson inside the van, leaned over the console, the seat belt tugging against his hoodie, and his eyes found mine for the slightest second. But then he looked away, adjusting the gearshift before pulling away from the curb.

"Did you just break up?" I asked her.

As the sputtering of his engine grew fainter, she let go of my elbow and reached for the front door. "I hate him," she said, instead of answering.

The Tomlins' house smelled like the greasy pizza stacked on the island in the kitchen, still in its cardboard delivery boxes alongside opened bags of chips and bowls of dip. There was cheering coming from the living room, the low murmur of chatter accompanying it.

My father shed his coat and shoes and headed right in, since the Super Bowl was starting. My mother had brought a veggie platter and was moving aside some of the chips to make room for it on the countertop. Emily waved to Mrs. Tomlin before she went downstairs to the basement, where her friends were waiting for her.

I stood there for a moment as my mother chatted with Mrs. Tomlin and a few other neighbors. I grabbed a slice of pizza, scanning the room and doorways for Griffin. When I realized he was probably in the living room with everyone else, I reached for a bottle of soda. Then, just as I was about to pour it into a cup, olive-toned hands fell over mine.

"Whoa, there, let me help you with that," Griffin said, grinning at me as he took the soda bottle. His hair was damp, like he just had showered. "Did you guys just get here? I was looking around for you." He poured the soda for me, and I watched it fizz up.

He was looking around for me. I nodded, reaching for the cup. The tips of our fingers brushed together. "Yeah, a couple of minutes ago." When I wasn't sure of what else to say, I looked down at the stack of themed paper plates on the counter beside the pizza. "Which team are you rooting for?"

He shrugged. "Doesn't really matter to me. I'm not really paying attention this year."

I kept switching my cup from hand to hand, even though I hadn't drunk from it yet. "How come?"

"I think you know why, Cinderella."

I resisted the urge to grin at this. At the thought that maybe after almost six months of Cinderella whispers, backyard kisses, and interruptions, everything would fall into place. Moments would be finished, second kisses would be had, and Griffin Tomlin would be with *me*.

So when he leaned in close and whispered to me that fateful question—the question that turned my life into a series of befores and afters, that would cause his death in seven months—I smiled. Then I murmured the seal to everything, locking it all into place.

"Okay."

I was lying awake in my bed, listening for the sound of snow crunching under tires as he pulled out of his parents' driveway. My heart fluttered in my chest, as if it had sprouted wings, because I just couldn't believe it. I couldn't believe it when he'd asked me earlier, and I couldn't believe it every time I'd glanced at him throughout the night, glancing back at me. He would smile while still doing whatever he was already doing, like talking or grabbing another slice of pizza.

I thought it was really cute.

A couple of hours before, I'd gone through my closet for something that felt more *Cinderella* and less me. I settled on a white sweater that exposed my shoulders, which wasn't actually mine but a hand-me-down of Emily's, and a pair of dark jeans with fraying holes in the knees. While Emily was in the bathroom, I stole a pair of her heels from her closet.

I spent the next hour doing and perfecting my makeup. I wore my hair down because I thought, embarrassingly, maybe Griffin would run his hands through it. I turned off my bedroom light and crawled into bed, occasionally checking the clock and waiting for one. I wondered if he was looking at the clock too, with a heart fluttering like mine.

Sixteen minutes after one o'clock, I heard the Tomlins' front door discreetly creaking open. Grabbing Emily's shoes, I walked, softly but swiftly, through my bedroom door, hearing his engine purring from his driveway.

There was a bluish glow coming from the back seat as I approached the car, regretting that I'd forgotten to bring a coat but at the same time feeling glad because maybe Griffin would give me his. When I pulled open the passenger door, the first thing I heard was a robotic but enthusiastic voice saying, *All right, you have ten seconds to guess the answer. Here we go!*

Griffin smiled at me, not seeming to notice my surprise, since when he'd asked me earlier if I wanted to go out to a party later, I hadn't expected Kolby Rutledge to be coming along. But there he was, in the back seat, playing a game on his phone.

"So," I said, deciding to ignore this situation, and essentially Kolby Rutledge, "where's the party?"

In the rearview mirror, Kolby looked up from his phone. Then the game buzzed and the enthusiastic voice chimed in soon after: *Oh no. You ran out of time! Too bad.*

"Crap," Kolby muttered, glancing back down at the screen.

I wasn't sure if he said that because he'd lost or because Griffin had kept certain details about tonight from him too.

Through the windshield of Griffin's car, I could already see people lingering on the front porch of the house, despite the fact that it was snowing and February. They weren't dancing or groping each other like I'd imagined from the movies or TV. Instead they were just smoking and drinking, stagnant, engaged in casual conversation.

"Nervous?" Griffin asked as he parked along the curb in front of the house. His hand reached out for mine, thumb smoothing over the ridges of my knuckles, and he gave it a squeeze before leaving the car without waiting for an answer, although I wasn't really sure what kind of an answer I could give him.

My heart was in my throat and my palms felt clammy now that he wasn't holding my hand. I was almost feeling like I was going to throw up when a seat belt unbuckled behind me. *Are you sure you want to quit?* a tinny voice asked.

"It's not that bad," Kolby said. "Just loud."

I forced a smile in his direction, feeling as if my lips were curving into my skin, and then reached for the door handle. What I couldn't tell Kolby was that it wasn't really the party, or even getting caught by my parents, that frightened me. It was Griffin. After years of dreaming and wondering what it would be like to be someone Griffin actually *noticed*, the moment was finally here. Uninterrupted by neighbors out after dark or sisters showing up unannounced. Being with Griffin—*really* being with him—was right in front of me, standing at the hood of the car, looking through the windshield as if to say, *Are you coming?*

I took in a breath and brought one foot onto the pavement, nodding.

Yeah.

The hardwood floor stuck slightly to my heels inside the house.

Kolby was already reaching for his phone as he motioned something to Griffin, who nodded in response. As I watched Kolby wander away from us, Griffin's hand found mine. A guy clapped Griffin on the shoulder and said something to him I didn't catch, and Griffin waved to someone else, but he never introduced me to anyone. He'd told me earlier this was his friend's house, someone on his baseball team, but he never pointed his friend out to me. I didn't even recognize anyone from his team here or from school, actually. Everyone looked older, but I thought maybe the dark made them look that way, maybe they were just from other schools.

His breath warmed my ear as he leaned in close. "Let's get something to drink." His fingers loosened and slipped away—I wondered if he had let go because my hands were so clammy they felt gross in his confident grip—and then I felt his hand around my side, over my hip. Griffin Tomlin was walking with his arm around my waist, as if I were someone to him. Not just the girl at block parties, taking too long to scoop veggie dip onto her plate when he was standing nearby, but actually *someone*.

As if I mattered as much to him as he did to me.

The kitchen smelled like beer, pizza, and cigarette smoke. There were cans, opened and unopened, scattered across the counter, pools of amber liquid seeping into the cracks between the tiles, old pizza crusts left on paper plates. Everything in the grungy room made me hesitate in the doorframe, afraid to move or touch anything.

But Griffin seemed to be totally at ease, maneuvering around the puddles and grabbing two unopened beers from inside the fridge. He was smiling as he turned to me, as if none of this seemed weird or gross or anything to him, and handed me a bottle.

"Here. It'll help you loosen up," he said.

I took the beer from him without bringing it to my lips. I didn't want to say anything, but I'd never had a drink before. Griffin was taking long gulps and looking at me. I could feel my Cinderella facade beginning to crack, my nervousness shining through and contrasting with his confidence, so I took a small sip. It was bitter on my tongue and warm, but Griffin leaned in close, kissing me.

"How's it taste?"

"Good," I lied, before I took another sip, still as bitter as before. "I like it."

He let out a laugh and took another gulp from his beer. "Here," he said, motioning for me to have another sip before taking the beer from me and setting it down. "I want to show you something." He kissed me again, his mouth tasting like beer and spearmint.

"What?"

His lips touched my neck for the slightest of seconds, and I couldn't think straight, my thoughts scrambled. "Trust me, you're going to love it."

And then he led me away.

chapter eight

"Clara."

As usual, I never saw her coming. I was beginning to believe that Aniston Hale materialized at will, arriving wherever in a sparkling cloud of pink smoke as her rushed words burst through the haze. Although this was her second time approaching me in the cafeteria, so maybe a pattern was emerging. Today, however, she was panting as she set her lunch tray on the table, though she didn't move to sit down.

"I had PE," she explained, as if I'd asked. "It normally takes me until Government to breathe again. I hate exercising and, obviously, the feeling is mutual. Unless it's punishing me for never exercising. Either way, I'm still not exercising outside of PE because then *it* wins." She smiled at me, as if we were friends who usually did this, eat lunch and complain about PE. Then she furrowed her brow. "Why am I here?"

I wasn't sure what I was supposed to say—if I was supposed to start offering up ideas for her or something. Then, just as I was reaching for an almond from my lunch, Aniston slapped the table excitedly, startling me. "Oh right!" she exclaimed, then hesitated when she realized I'd dropped my almond on the floor when I'd jumped. "Sorry! Sorry," she said, getting down on her knees, pushing one of the chairs away to pick it up. I sighed, glancing down and, sure enough, she was under the table. "Okay, there is way too much gum stuck to the bottom of this table," she commented.

I pulled my legs closer under my chair. "You really don't have to—"

"Found it!" Aniston announced. She stood up and placed the almond on her tray. "Don't worry, I'll throw it out for you. Anyway, the whole reason I'm here is because I wanted to apologize for the other day. I didn't think you were going to be there—not that I think you don't read or anything—but that's no excuse, so I'm sorry."

"It's fine." It wasn't, really, but this wasn't something I wanted to discuss with *Aniston Hale.*

"It's just, don't you want to know? I mean, I know I'm a teenage reporter for a high school newspaper, and if detectives can't figure out why a perfectly normal, happy girl would want to kill someone, then how can I? But, I don't know, I still want to try."

I wasn't sure how I felt about this, although I was sort of annoyed. This was Aniston, a girl incapable of wearing anything that wasn't pink, but there was still a discomforting unease in my chest. I could see something in her brown eyes, as if the flecks of gold inside them were really small flames. It almost made me think maybe she *could* figure it out, maybe she was that good.

"Clara?" Kolby was standing in front of the table, holding his tray. Aniston looked much smaller now, standing next to him and his large frame. But if she felt intimidated by his size, or the fact that he'd basically snuck up behind her, she didn't let it show as she took him in. And if Kolby noticed she was staring at him, analyzing him, then he didn't let that show either. Instead he stepped around her and set his tray on the table.

"Could you give me a ride after school? I have to work and I think my boss is considering paying me less than minimum wage if I'm late again."

I realized after a beat what he was doing. Rescuing me from Aniston.

"Sure, yeah, I can drive you."

"Thanks," he said, grabbing the back of the chair beside Aniston and pulling it out. "Excuse me."

Aniston nodded, quickly leaping out of his way. "Of course. I should probably get going. Got a test I should study for, so I'll probably go do that." She lingered a moment longer, as if she was waiting for me to look up and finally accept the apology I knew her eyes were probably extending. When I didn't, she left in a pink blur.

"Thanks for that." I watched Aniston long enough to see her leave the cafeteria and head for the quad before finding a seat at one of the concrete benches, alone. I almost felt bad for her. There was something about a friendly girl sitting alone that somehow seemed sadder than if it were anyone else.

I thought Kolby would grab his tray and leave for wherever he normally sat, but instead, he reached for his soda. "I was serious about my boss, though. He's *mad*."

He laughed around the last word, something I realized I had never really heard from him before, and the way he laughed made me want to smile back. I grabbed my bag of almonds and pushed it into the center of the table between us, and did just that.

~

It turned out Kolby Rutledge had a job at the local mall working in a soft pretzel restaurant in the food court. I pulled into a parking space, the radio turned down low, and said, "If I'm going to pay six dollars for a pretzel, it has to be the *best* pretzel. Not one that's overpriced *and* stale *and* undersalted."

He opened his door. "Trust me, our pretzels are worth it."

"For six dollars a pretzel, it has be more than just worth it. It has to go above and beyond the normal expectations of a soft pretzel. It should be able to clean my room or something."

He made a face. "I think you expect a little too much from your pretzels."

I was about to argue this when I noticed a girl with short blond hair emerge from the mall, walking with a guy with longish hair who slouched and wasn't wearing a coat. His arm was around her shoulders.

I wasn't sure what made me lean forward, but I did. That was when I realized the girl was Bex. And that the guy was Wilson Westbrooke.

I stared at them, together: her with him, him with her. I could hear the echo of her laughter at something he said as she tilted her body against his side.

"Clara?" Kolby leaned down, poking his head back into the car. "What's up?"

Wilson grabbed a set of keys from his pocket and went around to the driver's side of his van. Bex moved to the passenger side, biting down on her lip as she smiled, watching through the tinted windows as he unlocked the door.

"That's Wilson Westbrooke."

Kolby looked over to where I'd nodded, watching them for a moment before turning back to me, confused. "Who's he?"

"He was Emily's boyfriend."

He looked back over at them for a moment, then glanced down at the ground. "People move on, Clara," he said, as the familiar sound of Wilson's engine echoed through the parking lot.

For a second, I thought about telling him about that afternoon in October almost a year and a half ago, when Emily told me Wilson hit her. Or that the girl in the passenger seat used to be my best friend. But then the van pulled out of the mall parking lot and disappeared.

"Thanks for the ride," Kolby said.

My father was in his office, and my mother was washing the dishes downstairs. I was in my bedroom, preparing for an English test and trying to drown out my father's voice as he talked on the phone, the words *prison* and *convicted* drifting through the walls.

I was about to put on some music when my phone started vibrating. For some reason, I almost wanted it to be Kolby. I told myself that was only because he was the closest thing I had to a friend right now. Either way, I was curious, so I answered the call from an unknown number.

"Hello?" I answered. I heard chewing on the other end. "Hello?"

"What? *What?* Hang on," I heard a girl saying. "Okay, okay, I'm here. Clara! It's me . . . Aniston. Please don't hang up! I want to talk to you. Not over the phone, though. I mean, if that's the only way you'll talk to me, fine. But whenever someone is about to say something super important in a TV show, they always say *not over the phone*, but then they normally get shot by a sniper. Anyway! Will you meet me? Please? I'll buy you a cupcake?"

"Aniston, I don't think—"

"I'm at Spring's Diner. You know, by that Red Panda place? The one that saves red pandas. Anyway, I . . ." she continued, "I need to talk to you. And *not* to apologize this time! I'm just not sure who else to talk to right now and I really, *really* need to talk to someone."

"Why?"

"Because I think I know why Emily did it. And it's totally freaking me out and the waitress is kind of giving me a funny look. I need something deep-fried and will you *please* just meet me?"

I heard her take in another breath, this one slower and calmer, and she mumbled something to the waitress about needing another minute, she was so sorry, she loved the pink crayon behind her ear . . .

"Look, Clara. I know you want to know what happened that night too. I mean, sure, we really haven't talked about it, and I kind of get the feeling you know more than I do. Which I am totally not judging you for, by the way, but I know you don't know *everything*. I think if, maybe, we . . . I don't know . . . teamed up or something, we could figure it out. I mean, what happened totally turned your world upside down! Don't you think you deserve to know the whole why?"

I sighed, slowly unclenching my fingers from the edges of my phone. "I'll be there in fifteen minutes."

"I'm going out to meet a friend," I yelled as I ran down the stairs to the front door.

"Okay!" Mom's voice was muffled, somewhat drowned out by the clanking of dishes under water. I had just pulled open the door when the phone started to ring in the living room. "Can you get that before you go? My hands are all wet!"

Leaving the front door ajar, I went into the living room and grabbed the phone. "Hello—" I was interrupted by a recording of a woman's voice.

"This is a collect call from an inmate of the Roosevelt Womens' Prison. This phone call may be recorded. Do you accept the charges?"

"Wait." I turned around to see my mother standing in the doorway, her blouse splattered with dishwater as she smiled at me, reaching for the phone, soap suds still clinging to her fingers. All I could do was stand there, frozen, as I realized who the call was coming from.

Emily.

Emily had been in the Roosevelt Womens' Prison since October, almost four months, and not once had she called our house.

My mother's arm was still extended to take the receiver but I couldn't move. I couldn't hand the phone to her, even as her brow creased with each second I hesitated. I couldn't tell the automated voice on the other end I didn't want to accept the charges. I didn't want to speak to an inmate from Roosevelt Womens' Prison. I didn't want to hear Emily's voice in my ear.

I wordlessly handed the phone to my mother, the receiver nearly slipping through her hand. I stepped around her as she fumbled with the phone, catching it before it hit the carpet.

She looked over her shoulder as I stepped out onto the porch and closed the door behind me. Then she said a confused hello and paused, before tentatively answering yes. A moment later, I heard the muffled sound of her voice, cautious and maybe even scared, asking, "Emily? Honey, is that you?"

I walked off the porch, unlocked the car door, and jerked it forcefully open. So Emily was calling us now. Each time our phone rang would be a reminder of her, of where she was, of what she knew.

I knew exactly why she was calling. What she wanted from us, from me.

She wanted to tell the judge about the Super Bowl.

She wanted to tell everyone why she *really* murdered Griffin Tomlin that night.

chapter *nine*

Griffin led me to the second story of the house.

"It's fine. I know the guy who lives here. He'll be cool with it," he assured me when I hesitated on the stairs. I hadn't gone to a party like this before. At the couple of chaperoned parties I'd attended, it was an automatic assumption that the upstairs was off limits to everyone.

The noise from the crowd grew quieter as we reached the hallway. It was dark except for the glow of streetlights coming through a window. Griffin extended his free hand, grabbed a doorknob, and twisted it open, peeking his head through for a second before turning to me.

My heart pounded in my chest, my body trembling. He leisurely ambled into the room, as if this was all normal. Focused on his hand wrapped around my own, I followed him. He fumbled to find the light switch, and then the room was lit up so brightly it burned my eyes. Then I realized where Griffin had taken me: a bedroom.

The room had the smell of artificial cinnamon. A bed was pressed against the center of the wall, decorative pillows lined up together against its headboard, an afghan folded at the foot. I swallowed as I stared at the bed, hearing the soft click of the door closing behind us.

Griffin walked back to me, and I caught a brief glimpse of his face before he pressed his lips against mine, roughly. I made a noise of surprise as my feet were forced backward, and I stumbled. He wrapped his arm around my waist, our chests pressed together. And as he stepped forward, and the backs of my knees hit the mattress, it became so dauntingly clear what he wanted, so hard, so fast, that it shattered everything.

Me.

"Griffin," I murmured. He moaned in response as he kissed me, his tongue slithering into my mouth and finding mine. I kept trying to pull away, but he brought me closer, his grasp against my back growing stronger.

"Griffin, wait." I tried to wriggle away from him, pressing my hands against his chest. His hand lifted from my lower back and found one of my wrists, gripping it until his fingers met and my bones ached.

Hormones.

I pressed my hands harder against his chest, trying to move away from the bed, my legs trapped between the mattress and Griffin. I kept repeating that simple word in my mind as I tried to twist my wrist from his grasp. It had to be hormones—this had to be normal. He was just so into this, into me, that he couldn't hear me saying his name against his lips. He wasn't like Wilson Westbrooke, violent and unyielding. He was Griffin Tomlin, gentle and slow.

My nerves tensed and prickled as his tongue slid deeper into my mouth, thick and wet, making me almost gag. I tried to edge myself to the side, toward the corner of the bed, thinking if I wasn't restricted between him and the mattress, if I could separate our bodies, then Griffin would realize what was happening.

He would blink, realizing we were in a stranger's bedroom, that he was hurting my wrist, and then apologize, maybe ask if I wanted to go home. He would tell Kolby we were leaving and that he'd come back for him later because he just wanted it to be the two of us in the front seat. He would be embarrassed and try to apologize again when he'd park in his driveway. I would tell him that it was okay because it would be. Everything would be okay.

Because this had to be just hormones.

Griffin wasn't Wilson Westbrooke.

"Griffin," I repeated as he pushed forward, his legs jamming against my knees until they were sandwiched between his, and I wasn't able to edge myself farther away from him. Again I pushed against his chest, but he remained steady, looming over me, his mouth directly over mine as I tried to speak.

"Griffin, Griffin, wait. Okay? Okay, let's just—"

My protests shattered in my throat as he brought his forearm between us, thrusting it against my chest, forcing my legs out from under me. I fell onto the foot of the bed, the back of my head slamming roughly into the mattress.

Griffin loomed over me, gripping my thighs as he spread them apart and around his hips. Some part of me still hoped this was normal as his hands slowly slid up and under my sweater, fingers crawling over the bare skin of my stomach until he found my bra.

I hoped he would notice how I didn't want this, hoped there was some reason why he couldn't see my hands grasped around his forearms, feel my fingernails burrowing into his skin. Maybe all of this was still somehow *okay*. Maybe I was just too inexperienced to realize that this was how it was supposed to go. Maybe this was how passion was supposed to be.

"Griffin—"

His fingers slid underneath the wiring of my bra as he crawled onto the bed, his knees on either side of my hips, his torso leaning heavily over my body as I tried to wriggle free. I gasped when he clutched my breasts, kissing me again, his teeth biting my lips. My eyes burned, watering, when I realized what was happening. That none of this was normal or okay.

His mouth gravitated away from my face and roamed down my neck as he ran his tongue over my skin. And then, lowering himself onto my body, he brought his lips to my chest and bit my breast, *hard*, over my shirt. I screamed when I felt his teeth embedding into my skin, but not just because it was painful—because I was terrified. Griffin Tomlin, the boy I had been in love with since I was six, was on top of me, biting me and holding me down.

"Stop—!"

And then he did, and I thought that was enough. Maybe my scream was enough. Enough to make him stop. Enough so he would get off me and I could go home.

Instead he moved away from my breasts and lingered over my face for a moment, his ocean-blue eyes darkening into a storm. I furiously blinked back the tears that glided out of the corners of my eyes and into my hair. He leaned in close, close enough that his breath was burning my skin and his voice vibrated against my chest. "Don't do that again."

I turned my head, gulping in air as he lowered himself even farther, his body crushing mine. He curled his fingers around my chin, fingernails digging into my skin as he tilted my face back, forcing me to look at him.

"If you do that again, I'm going to kill you."

His voice was calm, controlled, slow, so it didn't seem possible he could be saying those words to me. Griffin Tomlin was threatening to kill me as he held me down on a mattress.

I nodded, my chin trembling and my breath coming out in choked gasps. His fingers uncurled from my chin. It throbbed from the scratches his nails had left.

Then his hands reached for the zipper of my jeans.

My wrists were behind me, tied together with a severed electrical cord he'd made by yanking a lamp from an outlet in the wall, and sawing at the wire with a pocketknife until it was detached.

He'd torn off my clothes, littering them throughout the room, and used the knife to cut through my bra, leaving a jagged cut along the side of my breast I knew would scar. Then he used the attachments of the pocketknife—the corkscrew, the nail scraper and the actual *blade*— against my rib cage, pressing them into the creases between my bones. He placed his hand over my mouth whenever he did this, tasting like salt and dirt on my tongue, when I gasped at the metal burying deeper into my skin.

Grabbing me by my hair, he forced me to turn onto my stomach, his palm pressing down on the back of my head, nails protruding into my skin. Every time I thought he was finished, he got angry with me for crying, spitting out that I wanted this, he knew I did, I was always staring at him like a little whore. Then he would start again.

When he finally released his grip on the back of my head, a throbbing pain radiated in my chin, my nose. The bones around my eyes ached from the weight pressed against my glasses into the pillow, wet from my sobbing.

"You're going to keep quiet about this, right?"

His voice sounded *altered*, rougher, and so unlike the voice that used to give me a flutter whenever he said my name. I watched him zipping his pants in the mirror on the wall above the headboard before he, slowly and horrifyingly, reached down near the corner of the bed, grasping something white and slipping it into his pocket. I realized a moment later it was my underwear.

He stole my underwear.

I nodded on the bed, too afraid to vocally respond.

He touched the back of my calf and I flinched. The touch almost reminded me of who Griffin used to be—or, at least, who I'd thought he was—but something lingered. He slowly retracted into the boy I'd known before, but there was still part of *him* in his pupils as he looked at me. Maybe it had always been there. Maybe I had never noticed it until now, but it was there and it was never going to disappear.

"If you tell anyone about this, you know they're not going to believe you." He took his hand from my calf and I exhaled into the sheets. He edged away from me, buckling his belt, smoothing his shirt, straightening his hair. He walked backward, as if he wasn't quite sure he wanted to turn away from this, from me, bound and naked on the bed. "If you try, I'll know, and I'll be back and I'll finish this. You understand, Cinderella?"

"I won't tell anyone," I whispered.

"Good." He reached into the pocket of his jeans, the red handle of his pocketknife gleaming as he tossed it across the room, landing on my back with a dull twinge. "See if you can cut your-self out of that, huh?"

And then, just like that, he left.

By the time I managed to slip one of my raw, bruised wrists out from the knotted electrical cord and untie myself, it was almost six in the morning. I grabbed my sweater from where he had thrown it and used my foot to drag my jeans—the zipper still undone and droplets of blood near the crotch—out from underneath the bed.

I felt too unsteady and sore to wear the heels, so I walked barefoot to the adjoining bathroom, glancing in the mirror and taking in the dark circles under my eyes, bloodshot from crying, the redness on my cheek from him forcing my face against the mattress. I tried to smooth out my hair, which was tangled and knotted, especially in the back, so I looked more like I'd had a rough night of partying instead of what had actually happened.

As I stepped out of the bathroom, my heart pounded at the sight of the crumpled duvet lying on the floor near the foot of the bed. The pillows were askew, the sheets marked with spots of blood so small they looked more like period stains than anything else. And on the floor was the pocketknife Griffin had left, the blade protruding. It would look too suspicious to leave it there, smeared with my blood, so I grabbed it when I walked out of the bedroom, praying that Griffin and Kolby had left hours ago. But as I quietly nudged my way downstairs, the lower half of my body throbbing and sore, I heard him. His laughter, the laughter I remembered always wanting to hear.

And now it terrified me.

I quickened my pace down the stairs, holding Emily's heels in my hand. I heard the muffled sound of Kolby's deeper voice saying something and Griffin responding with another laugh. The scent of coffee drifted up the stairs. It seemed so *normal*. Griffin had just held me down, buried my face in the mattress, threatened me, and then stole my underwear, and now he was having coffee with Kolby Rutledge. Maybe Kolby knew. Maybe this was some sort of arrangement they had. Maybe he had breakfast waiting for him for when he was done with me. Maybe that's why they were laughing. Laughing at me, at how I looked naked, laughing at how I barely even tried to get him to stop. Laughing at how I was crying even though I wanted it.

After all, Griffin said I was always staring at him like a little whore.

I tiptoed to the front door, glancing over my shoulder. My breath hitched in my throat as I saw him standing in the doorway of the kitchen, smiling as he looked at me, and I realized he had been *waiting* for me for hours.

His arms were crossed over his chest and he waved at me, a slow waggle of his fingers over his elbow as he grinned. He pushed himself off the doorframe and walked back into the kitchen, already saying something to Kolby, as if none of this had happened.

Bile rose in my throat as I reached the front door, a blast of chilled air blowing against my face when I stumbled outside. The porch was cold beneath my bare feet and I staggered across the icy lawn toward the mailbox before leaning over and vomiting into the snow. My eyes burned, and I wasn't sure if this was because of vomiting or because I was crying again.

I heaved one last time into the snowbank beside the curb, and when I opened my eyes, I saw tears had wet the lenses of my glasses. They were slightly bent from my head being shoved against the mattress, and slipping down the bridge of my nose. Smudges from his fingers clouded the glass. I had just taken them off when the front door opened, and a panic seized my chest that it was him.

But it wasn't him. It was Kolby Rutledge, stepping outside in his socks, holding a set of car keys out. I realized he was trying to start Griffin's car to turn the heat on.

"Clara?" he said. "Griffin told me you'd left."

I swallowed, the nasty taste of vomit still strong in my mouth. "I'm leaving now."

He hesitated. "Aren't we your ride?" When I couldn't think of a response to this, he looked over his shoulder, back at the house for a second, before turning back to me. "Are you . . . are you okay? Do you want me to get Grif—?"

I shook my head, fear lurching in my chest. "No," I told him, my voice choked. "No, I'm fine, just . . ." I exhaled shakily, trying to regain my composure. "Please don't tell anyone you saw me, okay? My parents don't know I was here. I don't want to get into trouble. If you guys drive me home, they'll notice."

"I won't tell anyone," he promised after a moment, nodding slowly, then added hesitantly, "Clara. Are you sure you're okay?"

I took in the blushed-pink nose and ears, the fogged breaths, his voice asking if I was okay. His eyes shone with uncertainty, bashfulness, and something almost like benevolence. I knew then that he didn't know. He was oblivious to who his best friend really was or what he had done earlier that night. I realized Kolby Rutledge was nothing like Griffin Tomlin.

77

I forced a wavering smile, my lips aching from the motion, and told him, "I'm okay, really. Thanks anyway, though."

He went back inside a moment later, after observing me for another few seconds and finally turning Griffin's car on. I heard the engine start somewhere along the curb down the road.

I pulled out my phone and scrolled down my contacts. My thumb hovered over Emily's name on the screen for a second before I pressed Bex's name instead.

When Bex finally came to pick me up, her hair was wet, damp splotches marked her sweatshirt around her shoulders, and it looked like I'd caught her in the middle of her makeup routine— her foundation was applied but her eyelashes and lips were bare and pale.

"If Griffin brought you last night, why couldn't *he* bring you home?" she asked, looking at her reflection in the rearview mirror and wincing. Then, seeming as if she were about to add to this, she looked over as I gingerly crawled into the car. "Hey, are you okay? Why are you getting in like that?"

I curled the sleeves of the sweater over my fingers so she wouldn't see my wrists. "I slipped on the ice. It's no big deal."

She nodded, turning back to the windshield as she started to drive. "So," she said, grinning slyly, "Did he kiss you again? Are you guys like actually *together* now?"

My heart clenched in my chest at the thought, but I tried to shrug casually in front of her. "I don't think I'm that into him anymore," I told her, struggling to keep my voice steady.

"Wait, what? Just like that?" She looked at me out of the corner of her eye, and I nodded. "You're totally over Griffin Tomlin, the guy you've been in freaking *love* with for, like, ten years?"

I nodded. Just like that, I was over Griffin Tomlin.

chapter ten

Spring's Diner smelled like fried food, coffee, and pastries as I
nudged open the heavy front door, the sound of muffled conver-
sations from the booths greeting me. A girl stood in front of a
table, wiping down menus, when she spotted me standing there,
scanning the restaurant for a burst of pink. She tossed down the
crumpled cloth, which was alarmingly dirty, and approached me.
The name tag pinned to her shirt read *Amanda*.

"Can I help you?"

"I'm here to meet someone," I said. "Her name's Aniston?
Hale." When she looked at me, confused, I realized her unusual
name was probably not what would identify Aniston best. "She
wears a lot of pink," I added.

The waitress nodded knowingly and motioned for me to follow her as she walked across the dining area, leading me to a bar.
But instead of bottles of alcohol behind the counter, there were
doughnuts, mini-cakes, and cookies lined up neatly in a glass

case. And sitting on a barstool, in an oversized pink sweater, was Aniston, nibbling at a powdered doughnut.

"Do you want a doughnut?" she asked. "I mean, you don't have to have a *doughnut*. You could have a cupcake or a cookie or something. They're so good, seriously."

I hoisted myself onto the barstool beside her, glancing at the waitress, Amanda, who looked expectantly at me. "I just ate."

"Okay, let me know if you girls need anything."

"That's a shame. I should've called before dinner," Aniston murmured, shaking her head disapprovingly. "But since I'm *pretty* sure you're a straight shooter, let me get to my point. I think I know why your—she, Emily did it. Killed Griffin, I mean. Which you knew, obviously, because I told you on the phone and you actually came down here, so I'm assuming you want to know what *I* know—"

"Aniston," I interrupted dryly, even though my blood was beginning to run cold in my veins. It wasn't like it mattered anyway if she really did know why my sister had killed Griffin, since Emily was on the phone with Mom right now. Probably telling her all about the Super Bowl party and everything that had happened after.

"Right," Aniston replied, nodding. "I think Griffin was . . . Well, but he's dead. You know that already, but it feels weird saying bad things about dead people, even the ones who deserved it but—right, I know, I know. Get to the point, Aniston," she said hurriedly. "I think Griffin was becoming a serial killer."

"Why would—" I stared at her, incredulous. "Why would you think that? No one died, Aniston." I exhaled, shrugging. "Except for him, anyway."

"I know, I know," she replied. "But that's why I said *becoming*. Okay, look. Everyone says they loved Griffin, *adored* him. Literally no one had a bad thing to say about him. At first, I thought it was because he was dead. No one wants to talk crap about a *murdered* kid, right? But then, a couple weeks ago, it was like a lightbulb went off! *Ding!*" She smiled faintly as she mimicked yanking on a lightbulb chain. "No one said anything bad about him because no one *knew* anything bad about him, and that's got to mean that he was hiding something *big*. The nicest guys always turn out to be the meanest."

"Naturally," I said sardonically.

"So I did some digging on him, prior to the whole, you know, murder thing. And I discovered the Tomlins had a puppy. You might remember him. Champion? Stupid name but the pooch did *not* deserve what was coming to him because Griffin—this is so beyond devastating—dismembered the poor thing."

I shook my head. "Aniston—"

"Hear me out! Okay, in an old newspaper article in the library, there is a picture of the Tomlins at a local Fourth of July fireworks display with Champion. Then I discovered a website the Tomlins set up a few months later about their missing puppy. Luckily, they never shut down the website. Anyway, I was looking through more of the newspaper articles and one was about the dismembered paw of a young dog, the same breed as Champion—yellow lab, by the way—found on a farmer's lawn. It had to be Griffin! Torturing animals is part of the serial killer triad!"

I looked away from her, slowly feeling the erratic thumping of my heartbeat decelerating as I realized that Aniston *didn't* know why Emily killed Griffin.

"Aniston," I said with a sigh. "I don't know." Griffin was only a kid when they had that puppy. He couldn't have always been sick like that. It was something I told myself he'd developed, like an allergy or an illness, a change that had happened over time.

I couldn't have fallen in love with a guy who was always . . . *evil*.

"I know you don't," she replied. "But I do! Griffin wasn't who everyone thought he was and, somehow, Emily found out! I mean, she killed him. That kind of sends a pretty powerful message, don't you think?"

"You can't just accuse a dead guy of being a serial killer, after *he* was murdered, because of a dead puppy."

"*Becoming* a serial killer!"

Amanda appeared from behind me, smiling, although somewhat hesitant. "Is there anything else I can get for either of you?"

Aniston—who didn't seem to be particularly bothered that Amanda had probably heard her last sentence—shook her head. "I should probably cap it off at three doughnuts. Wait, do you actually do that here? Like, cap people off for pastries? Because that should be a thing. Also, Clara will have a cookie."

I turned to her. "What?" Then I looked at Amanda, shaking my head. "It's fine. I'm good."

"She'll take it to go. White chocolate chip, please." Aniston nudged me on the shoulder as Amanda nodded, still a little uncertain, before wandering back to the kitchen. "Trust me, they're delicious and you do want one. Plus, Amanda's going out with the cook, so she'll bring you one of the fresh ones."

"You're trying to distract me because you know you've got no *proof*."

"I know I need more evidence. Which is why I'm spending every waking moment at the library reading old newspaper articles and going on crime websites. And, well," she added tentatively, before giving me a sheepish look, "trying to find a way to get ahold of Griffin's computer."

"What?"

She flinched, her gaze almost pleading. "I know it sounds crazy, I really *do*! But that will tell me more than old articles will and sounds a whole lot easier than getting ahold of police records, which teen dramas make look way easier than it actually is." Her gaze softened. "The police gave it back to his parents and if I could just get my hands on it, I could find something that will prove Griffin was evil! Or at least a not-very-nice person who tortured puppies, which in my mind *does* equate to evil but—"

"And I guess the police just totally missed all of the virtual evidence that he was a budding serial killer? Come on, Aniston."

"They weren't trying to prove his guilt! They were trying to prove Emily's!"

"Are you seriously thinking of breaking into their house to get his computer? They're going to notice it's missing. And who says they even kept it?"

"No one's stealing anything! Just going into his room, taking a few photos of his search history, maybe his downloaded files, and then leaving. And I'm not breaking in either."

I shot her a look. "You care *this* much for an article? Are you just trying to use it to beef up your college applications?"

For a moment, she almost looked hurt as she stared at me. Then her gaze drifted down to the plate in front of her, still dusted with powdered sugar. "It's not just about the article. I mean, I would be lying if I said I wasn't planning on still writing it, but it's not really about that anymore. It's about the fact that I know there's more to this and no one else seems to care! No one wonders why a sweet girl like Emily Porterfield would want to kill the school's golden boy. They just assume that she was crazy and killed him when he rejected her." She slumped against the counter. "If Griffin really was just the greatest guy ever, then his family deserves to know why he died. And if he wasn't . . . then everyone else—*you*—deserve to know why Emily did it."

I stared at her for a moment before bracing my elbows on the counter and lightly bumping mine against hers. I wasn't agreeing to anything—certainly not sneaking into the Tomlins' house to take pictures of their dead son's laptop—but there was a slight part of me, for the first time since Emily told me she'd killed Griffin, that wondered if I really *did* know everything about what happened.

Maybe Emily knew more about Griffin than I did.

"And," Aniston continued, "I think I know of a way to *sort of* get us closer to proving everything. And all I need is five minutes, alone, with a phone in Griffin's bedroom. And Kolby Rutledge."

"What do you need Kolby for?"

"I'm pretty sure he's the only one the Tomlins will actually let *in* their house. Because they obviously won't let you in. Sorry, it's true. And they probably won't let me in because, well, let's just say I'm probably one email away from a restraining order."

"You emailed them about this?"

"No! I just wanted to see if I could schedule an interview. I know it seems insensitive and all, and I totally respected their privacy, but then they went on TV, so I thought they were willing to open up and tell the world their son's story. Or at least Madison High School. Evidently, they were not. At least not to a seventeen year old who may have written an article about Brandon Tomlin sneaking under-age kids in to R-rated movies." She sighed. "I guess they're still kind of ticked about that one."

"It was just his cousins," I pointed out.

"Look, all we need Kolby to do is go into the house, chat for a few minutes, and then ask if he can go see Griffin's room for old time's sake—or go to the bathroom, it doesn't really matter. Then he can head to his room, go on his computer, take as many pictures as he can, and then get out. We'll even tell him to call us and leave his phone in his pocket so we can hear what's going on. It's low-tech but it'll work."

"And what exactly are *we* going to tell him?"

Aniston shrugged, undeterred and totally nonchalant as she said, as if the answer were totally obvious, "The truth."

"You can't do that," I said quickly, my voice sounding somewhat strangled. "You can't just tell him you think his *best friend*, who was *murdered*, was a serial killer and that you actually want *him* to help you prove it! Kolby is never going to do that."

"I know it sounds kind of mean, but you and Kolby . . . you're *close*, right?" she said, her voice lowering in pitch as the word *close* rolled off her tongue. I frowned, shaking my head as she nudged her elbow against my side. "And if we're right, then we finally know why he died! Don't you think Kolby deserves to know just as much as everyone else?"

Unease lurched in my stomach. If Kolby believed her about him, then maybe he would start to put the pieces together, connect what happened to Griffin with the morning after the Super Bowl. And that petrified me.

Aniston exhaled, shrugging reluctantly. "Look, if you think we should ease him into this, I guess we could sugarcoat it a little? Say that we're just trying to find out if he and Emily interacted online or whatever, but if we're right—"

"If *you're* right. I'm still not convinced."

"I'm right. Point is, if we find something *huge* that proves us—me—right, then are we just going to keep it a secret from everyone? I mean, if we're right, Clara, this could reduce your sister's sentence!"

I hesitated, remembering the phone call right before I left. It didn't seem like Emily needed my help for that anymore.

"I know you're not really into the whole article thing, which I get. But we should probably discuss what exactly we're going to do if we actually find anything. Right now, though, let's just focus on getting onto Griffin's laptop and recruiting Kolby Rutledge . . . which shouldn't be that difficult."

"Why's that?" I asked as Amanda returned, holding a mint green to-go bag.

Aniston rolled her eyes, then informed me, "Because he likes you."

Somehow it seemed Mrs. Foley had convinced Kolby to ask me about auditioning for *Shrek the Musical*.

"You like the drama department," he said the day before the auditions, while we were eating lunch. "And you're good at it, really good. Why don't you just do it?"

My cheeks warmed at Kolby thinking I was good—*really good*—at performing. I remembered him in the audience when I was in *Into the Woods*, sitting next to Griffin, and then him standing in the lobby of the school. He'd told me I was really good then too, but the memory felt submerged in something else, in a flutter, in Griffin with his arms around my waist.

"Ashley Warden will be happier if I don't. She's been wanting a lead for, like, a few years."

"Who cares about Ashley Warden? If she's so talented, she'll get the lead anyway. But you know she won't, so that means she must *suck*."

"She doesn't suck. She's actually really nice."

He rolled his eyes as he took a bite of his burger. "Whatever. The point is you want to do it, but you're coming up with a bunch of excuses, like Ashley Warden."

To postpone responding, I took a bite of my sandwich. Kolby probably realized what I was doing and thought it was pathetic, which it was, but I wasn't going to perform anymore. Not because I didn't like it—I *loved* it—but because it felt tied to something else, *someone* else. The last time I'd performed, I was thinking of Griffin in the audience, realizing for the first time ever that I had his attention.

"When Griffin practically dragged me to that one play—the one with Cinderella and the wolf and the giant—you were the first person onstage, except for the narrator, anyway. And when you started singing, something changed in your face. It was kind of like you were exactly where you belonged. It would just be nice to see you like that again."

I thought back to what Aniston had told me a few nights earlier—about how Kolby Rutledge *liked* me, as if it were obvious and clear, not completely misguided—and I repeated to myself that it couldn't possibly be true. There was no way Kolby could like me.

My sister had murdered his best friend after pushing his unconscious body into the same pool his parents had hosted summertime pool parties at. The same pool I had seen Kolby and Griffin swimming in countless times, jumping off the diving board or dunking each other underwater. Griffin had drowned in that pool, and my sister had watched.

Kolby couldn't like me.

There was no way.

"Kolby, can I ask you a favor?" I said, trying to focus on something else. "Maybe. If you want to do it, I mean. Aniston is working on this article for the school paper. She wants to figure out why Emily did what she did, so she was hoping that you could maybe . . ."

His brow furrowed slightly. "Talk to her?"

"No," I told him slowly. "She wants you to go on Griffin's computer and take pictures of his search history. Just to see if he and Emily had chatted online or something. I don't know. I told her it sounds stupid, but she's like a dog with a bone."

"You want me to go into his house and creep through his computer?" he said. A beat later, he let out a heavy exhale. "Okay."

"What?"

"I want to know what happened too," he said.

And right then in that moment, I almost felt like telling him. Like saying all the things I never thought I would, and to Kolby Rutledge of all people. But I couldn't.

I couldn't because it would mean Kolby would lose his friend all over again—his memories of him tainted with an ominous undertone—but also because I was terrified. A little less since I'd come home the other night and realized Emily hadn't said anything about Griffin or me or any of it on the phone, but still. Terrified.

Even from six feet under, Griffin was murmuring in my ear not to say a word.

~

"But why do I have to keep you on the line?" Kolby asked.

The three of us were crammed into the minivan Aniston had borrowed from her mother, the scent of cigarette smoke, sugary perfume, and old French fries clinging to the seats. There were stacks of ancient yellowing newspapers in the back seat beside me, food crumbs on the floor. The back doors were jammed, so I'd had to crawl over the console from the passenger seat to get inside. When she'd pulled into my driveway at nine in the morning that Saturday, grinning and waving, I'd realized she wasn't wearing pink but instead all black.

"As much as I adore pink, it's too obvious. Today, Clara, we are *spies* and spies wear black. I think," she explained. "So how do I get to Kolby's house?"

Now the minivan was parked down the street from the Tomlins' house as Kolby went on, his brow furrowing, "I'm just talking to Lisa."

I noticed this wasn't the first time he'd referred to one of Griffin's parents by their first name. I guess Mr. or Mrs. became too formal after so many summers spent practically living in their house. But he'd also mentioned that he hadn't really spoken to any of the Tomlins since the funeral.

Aniston shifted around in her seat to grab her phone from her back pocket. "What if she gets suspicious or says something interesting? And anyway, I want you to video chat me when you get to his computer. I don't want to miss anything."

Kolby looked over his shoulder at me. Out of the corner of my eye, I saw Aniston glance up from her phone in the rearview mirror. I shrugged, looking down at a headline on one of the newspapers beside me: Frankenstorm Hits in Time for Halloween.

After a beat, he told her, "All right."

A moment later, Kolby left the minivan, placing his phone into the pocket of his vest, and walked up to the Tomlins' house. I climbed into the front passenger seat. Aniston's phone was on the console, resting on expired coupons. She set it to speaker as we waited, the sound of his vest rubbing against the phone loud in the minivan.

Then there were three muffled thuds. Aniston focused intently on her phone, as if she were willing someone to open the front door, the answers to all the questions seemingly—at least to her and maybe even Kolby—lying behind it, pressed against the walls so as not to be seen from the outside.

"Kolby?"

The voice was faint and fragile, and not just because we were listening through the thick material of his vest. My heart clenched as I thought of Lisa Tomlin. She'd let us use the pool during the summer, had given me my first bottle of perfume for my twelfth birthday.

"I didn't . . . Hello, Kolby. It's nice to see you again."

"I know. I wanted to talk to you." There was a pause, an uncomfortable silence filling the car, and panic ignited in Aniston's eyes for a second. "His birthday is coming up and I wanted to . . ."

There was a soft sigh. "I know. Do you want to come in?"

After about twenty minutes of small talk over a couple of cups of coffee, Kolby finally managed to concoct an excuse to let himself upstairs into Griffin's bedroom. I could tell he felt uncomfortable lying to Griffin's mom. His voice sounded uneasy and slightly strained as he asked, "Do you mind if I go upstairs, to his room?

I can't find this Sabres hat my dad gave me and we're going to a game this week. I think I might have left it there? I'll just run up real quick . . ."

"Okay," she replied, her voice growing fainter and more distant as the phone jostled in his pocket while he jogged up the stairs. "After you find it, I want to ask you about something. And don't make a mess!"

Don't disrupt the illusion that Griffin will come back.

A moment later, a door closed in the background, then Kolby's voice filled the crammed interior of the minivan again. "Okay. I'm in his room. Man, she hasn't even touched any of this stuff," he whispered, exhaling. "All right, what do I do?"

"Video chat me! And don't lollygag!" I gave her a look as she hung up. "What?"

"Lollygag?" I asked flatly.

"It's a cute word!" she laughed. Something flashed on her phone, and I could just barely make out the blue color of Griffin's bedroom walls on the screen.

"*Lollygag?*" Kolby whispered in lieu of a greeting.

He had the camera directed away from him, the image shaky and pointed partially at the floor. I had a feeling he was still glancing around the room. The things that had once seemed familiar now strange and uncomfortable.

The bed was messily made, a black duvet crumpled and pushed to the side, bedsheets exposed, as if Griffin had just slept in it the night before. The clock radio on the desk was knocked askew, its time fourteen minutes ahead. Notebooks and textbooks were stacked together, and one was open, lying facedown. Beside it was his laptop.

"Am I just supposed to . . . open it or something?"

"Yes, please," Aniston replied.

I watched as he cautiously opened the computer, revealing a dark screen. I could just barely make out the reflection of Kolby's phone and his face behind it, a look of discomfort contorting his features as he pressed the On button.

After the desktop had loaded, too bright and blurred on Aniston's phone, Kolby brought up Griffin's home page, then shifted the mouse to his search history icon, a series of links appearing. The mouse lingered over one of the links, but I couldn't make it out.

"What?" she asked, her eyes narrowing as she stared attentively. "Did his computer freeze?"

He tapped a finger against the touch pad, clicking on one of the links, and an article headline filled the screen, above a picture. The photograph was indistinct on Aniston's phone but large enough for me to realize that it was of a girl around our age with strawberry blond hair, like me.

"That's Ella Dillard," Aniston said, eyes wide and excited. "She was murdered almost ten years ago. The case was all over the news—went national, I think. A guy confessed a few years ago. They never found her whole body, just a piece of her leg." She leaned over the console, her thumb pressed against the receiver so Kolby wouldn't hear. "That guy was a serial killer. He killed seven girls in New York and Pennsylvania. Serial killers look up to each other! Griffin was searching a Shiloh murdering legend because he wanted to *be* like him!"

I shot her a look as I heard Kolby murmur, "She looks just like you, Clara."

Aniston turned to look at me, eyes widening slightly as if she were realizing something. My breath hitched in my throat as I looked away, from both the phone and her.

"Why would Griffin look up stuff like this?" Kolby asked.

Aniston flicked my arm and mouthed: *Tell him.* I shook my head as Kolby left the website and started looking over the other links, snapping pictures of them with his phone.

"He was probably curious," I said. "Ella Dillard is kind of a local legend. Everyone's looked her up."

Now Aniston shot me a look, unamused. "Yep. Everyone. Everyone looks up this sort of stuff. Humans are all about that morbid curiosity," she replied, her tone dripping with sarcasm.

I pressed a finger to the receiver. "*You* do!" I hissed.

"And I'm creepy! If I weren't just a happy, bubbly person with a great *Mamá*, I would totally be a serial killer!"

I looked down at the phone, still unsteadily focused on the bright laptop monitor. "Please?" I whispered, hating how desperate I sounded.

Griffin Tomlin wasn't the boy Kolby thought he was—and maybe he was the boy Aniston seemed to *know* he was—but Griffin was dead and Kolby was grieving. Griffin seemed like the only real friend Kolby had, and now it seemed like Kolby was the only real friend I had. I was too scared that the truth, or Aniston's version of it, would change that. To Kolby Rutledge, Griffin needed to be a good person, even if he wasn't.

Aniston's expression softened, albeit somewhat reluctantly. *Fine,* she mouthed.

Kolby took a few more pictures of Griffin's search history before exiting the browser. We heard chair wheels rolling against the floor as he stood up, slapping down the screen of the computer. The camera jostled as he whispered, "I should go back before she comes looking for me or something."

The screen went black.

"Would the police have found that stuff on his search history after he was murdered?" I asked.

She nodded. "Yeah. They probably either brushed it off as the same lie you told Kolby, or they're holding back information about the case. It's not impossible, considering they're getting ready for the trial right now." She leaned back against the headrest, tilting her head to look over at me. "Also, he doesn't believe you."

"What?"

"Kolby," she told me. "He knows something's up."

Kolby emerged from the house a few moments later, waving over his shoulder with the Sabres hat he'd hidden under his vest clutched in one hand. I was in the process of climbing over the console and into the back seat to make room for Kolby when I spotted Mrs. Tomlin jogging down the sidewalk after him.

"Kolby!" Her blond hair whipped across her face in the wind as she clutched a cardigan tightly around herself and approached him, only a foot away from the minivan. She seemed smaller than when I'd last seen her at the funeral, her face bare and etched with creases. My chest ached at seeing her looking so unlike the elegant woman I remembered.

"Kolby!" she called again. "I almost forgot. I wanted to get your opinion on something. You remember his birthday is on the eighth next month."

"Yeah," he said, nodding.

"Well, it's just—after eighteen years of celebrating it, it seems *wrong* not to do anything. Even if he's . . . we wanted to have a get together for him. Maybe turn it into a benefit. I don't want another family to have to go through this. And there are *so* many organizations dedicated to protecting women but almost none for young men."

Kolby's jaw muscles tensed, his fingers clenching tightly around the bill of the Sabres hat.

"And I was just wondering if you thought that was a good idea." She hesitated, her chin beginning to tremble. "I just don't want him to be forgotten."

Kolby nodded, his gaze now trained on the ground. "It's . . ." His voice was low and thick as he began to reply, and he nodded again before offering her a fleeting smile. It looked a bit like Mrs. Tomlin's, broken and barely holding on. "It's a good idea."

She looked at him for a moment longer, with glistening eyes that reminded me of Griffin's—his dazzling ocean-blue eyes before they turned dark—as she mustered a thin smile. It almost looked real, like it wasn't shattered fragments slipping from her grasp. Then she looked past him, into the minivan, and spotted me.

My heart skipped a beat as I stared back at her, her hair whipping across her face, eyes watering, smile now gone. Out of the corner of my eye, Kolby followed her gaze, his shoulders sinking as he exhaled. I looked away. Somehow, not knowing what she thought of seeing me there was worse than knowing she hated me. My chin throbbed as I tried to stop it from trembling.

"Well," she said, her voice hoarse, "it was nice seeing you again, Kolby."

A moment later, after Mrs. Tomlin had turned around and started walking up the sidewalk, Aniston let out a breath. "That was so awkward," she moaned. She rolled down the window to get Kolby's attention. "Okay, get in before it gets worse," she said.

He was just stepping toward us when a car sped by, veering past the minivan. It was a black sedan with a local community college bumper sticker on the trunk—one of Mr. Tomlin's old cars, with Brandon Tomlin behind the wheel. Kolby watched it pass, then jogged over and got in.

"Was that his brother? Brandon?" Aniston asked, peering through the windshield.

Kolby nodded, glancing over his shoulder. "Yeah," he replied. "He's . . . strange. I don't know. Last year I thought I saw him with this girl and she just looked . . . off. He was taking her upstairs at this party and I thought she was drunk or something. It didn't really look right."

My heart was hammering so loudly in my ears when he said this I barely heard Aniston quietly murmuring, "Interesting."

chapter eleven

The first card came the day before Valentine's Day, eleven days after the Super Bowl party. Sealed in a red envelope, without a return address, with my name in the center.

"It was in the mailbox," Mom said, smiling and pausing as she clipped coupons at the kitchen counter. She'd left the envelope pinned to the refrigerator with a magnet. "It looks like you've got a secret admirer."

I had never really been on a date—it wasn't that no one had asked me or anything, but I'd only wanted *him*, not anyone else— and I had never had a boyfriend. As far as she knew, I hadn't even been kissed outside of school musicals. And now there was a red envelope on the fridge, with the promise of a boyfriend for lonely Clara Porterfield inside. At least to my mother, anyway.

I really didn't think it would be from him. I thought he was done, finished with me. A toy he'd tossed aside after he got bored.

Once the wounds on my ribs had healed, I'd thought I could move on because no one knew, and somehow, that meant it hadn't happened. I convinced myself, as I re-bandaged the gashes between the ridges of my bones and slathered on antibacterial cream every day, that everything would go back to normal once they healed. I would join the spring musical, spend every weekend at the movies with Bex, go shopping with Emily and buy all new clothes. Ones Griffin hadn't looked at me in, never wanted me in.

Everything would go back to normal once I stopped bandaging the wounds, when the soreness between my legs went away. The ache was the only reminder, I told myself. And without a reminder, without a souvenir etched into my skin or forcing me to shift in the way I sat down, I just wouldn't remember at all. Or that's what I'd thought.

But then the card came.

I took it up to my bedroom, tearing open the red envelope and sliding the pink card out from inside. There was a painted white lace pattern around the border, and in the center was a black moustache.

I MOUSTACHE YOU A QUESTION . . .
WILL YOU BE MY VALENTINE?

Below that, written in blue ink, was:

I love you so much, baby. So glad to be spending V-Day with you. Can't wait to see you later. P.S. You're going to love what I got you.

Griffin

~

The next day at school I halfheartedly scribbled down the answers to questions I barely understood, the words as foreign to me as Griffin Tomlin suddenly was, and scanned the cafeteria for him even though I knew he should've been in gym. He wasn't there, or in the hallways between classes, almost like he might have been avoiding me as much as I was trying to avoid him. I was hopeful this meant maybe he was afraid of my telling people what he'd done, and the card was a way to scare me, and that was it.

But that wasn't it. Because just when I reached Emily's car, slumping against the door and letting my backpack fall on the snow-covered ground as I waited for her, there he was. Standing in front of his car, hands stuffed into his pockets, with his head tilted as he looked at me, a slight smile on his face. For a moment, he almost looked like the boy I had known ever since his family moved into the house across from ours.

But he wasn't, and the dull, throbbing ache across my ribs reminded me of that as I stared back at him.

I hoped to catch a glimpse of Emily through the glass school doors, thinking of the car keys in her coat pocket, wishing she would come out instead of forcing me to wait by the car as she talked to her friends. I heard footsteps in the slush and I hoped he was turning around, but instead the sound became louder and closer.

"Hey, Clara."

My body clenched at the sound of his voice, but I couldn't look away from the school doors, couldn't look at *him*.

"I haven't seen you in a while. You're not avoiding me, are you?" He cocked his elbow out slightly, his hand still in his pocket, like he was joking, teasing me. Like that night had never happened. Like he was genuinely flirting with me.

"Look," he said. I took a small step back, closer to the passenger door, until my spine was arched against it, but I still wouldn't look at him. Instead I kept my eyes focused on the school doors. "I know last week, things got a little tense. And I'm sorry about that. You just have this way of making me lose it. But tomorrow is Valentine's Day, and I don't want *this* to ruin that. If it takes an apology to fix this, then fine, I'll apologize."

I turned my head to look at him before I realized what I was doing. He was actually serious. He still wanted us to be together. The card in the mail that morning wasn't a threat or a reminder. It was an actual, sincere *valentine*. And somehow all of this terrified me more than when I'd thought it was meant to scare me into keeping quiet.

"I need to—Emily, she's—"

His fingers wrapped around my wrist as I tried to edge away from him, my hip colliding with the side-view mirror. His grip wasn't gentle but it wasn't forceful either.

"Wait," he murmured, his voice almost pleading in a way that made me want to squirm as I stood, cornered between the cold metal of the car and his body. I looked back at the doors, but she still wasn't there. "Clara, I don't want us to be like this. Look."

He used his free hand to search the inside of his pocket. I almost tried to twist my wrist free and shove him away before running back into the school, finding Emily, and asking her the same question she'd asked me outside of Scoops!.

But the ache between my legs reminded me of who he was and what he could do, so I held my breath as his hand pulled out a velvet box and he let go of my wrist to open it.

He looked down at the necklace inside, a chain glinting in the afternoon light. Dangling from it was a charm in the shape of a gold slipper. Like the ones Cinderella wore to the festival.

"I had it made," he explained as he unclasped it. "Thanks to you, I won't be able to look at Cinderella the same way again." He reached out and fastened it around my neck. The metal chain felt cold against my skin. Then his hands carefully pulled my hair out from underneath the necklace. "There. Happy Valentine's Day, babe."

He pressed a hard kiss against my mouth, lips like rubber, and the taste of mint was overwhelming. Fear tensed my shoulders before he finally pulled back, leaning his forehead against my own.

"You," he whispered. His breath burned against my skin. And then he murmured the three words I had been waiting and longing for since before I even knew what they really meant. "I love you."

My stomach churned, and I bit my lip to stop myself from retching. A second later, he was gone, retreating back to his car. As he pulled out of the parking lot, he honked the horn before disappearing onto the highway. Leaving me there, numbly slumped against the car, the feel of his lips still on mine.

I grabbed the golden slipper and pulled it away from my skin, breaking the clasp. I ran across the parking lot and dropped it into the snow, behind a tree, burying it so he wouldn't see I had thrown it away. Then I puked a few feet away.

A moment later Emily finally jogged out of the school and apologized, explaining something I felt too nauseated to actually listen to. I crawled inside the car, the bitter taste of bile swirling in my mouth.

"Why didn't you just come inside? It's, like, twenty degrees out."

I forced my shoulders to shrug in response. "I was fine," I lied.

chapter twelve

Aniston dropped Kolby off and then she drove me home. After I waved good-bye, I turned and noticed the trunk of my father's car, parked beside Emily's in the driveway, was open. Our front door was ajar, and even from where I stood on the front lawn, I could hear footsteps pounding down the staircase and something clanking against the floorboards in the front hall.

When I nudged the door open, I saw two bulging suitcases at the bottom of the stairs. A second later, my father appeared in the doorway, his white button-down shirt untucked and sloppily hanging over his pants, his dark hair tousled, like he had been raking his fingers through it all afternoon. He stared back at me with bloodshot eyes, a dazed expression on his face, holding a photograph—one that was bent and creased, like he had struggled to get it out of the frame—in one hand. A beer bottle was in the other.

"Are you going somewhere?" I asked softly.

He reached down and partially unzipped one of the suitcases.

I realized the photograph was of Emily, an old school picture from her freshman year.

"Clara. Your mother and I . . ." He laughed bitterly and lifted the beer to his lips, gulping it down. It made an awkward suctioning sound as he pulled it away. "We see things *very* differently. Your mother, for example, she likes to pretend everything is so *great*. She wants to live in this suburban la-la land. What kind of mother do you think that makes her, Clara?"

The uneasy feeling in my chest expanded and morphed into a panic that coiled around my heart and lungs. Everything reminded me too much of another moment when I'd felt the same panic twisting its knobby fingers around me. I hoped to hear my mother's footsteps upstairs or a toilet flushing—*something* to indicate it wasn't just me and him.

"I don't know," I said after a moment of him staring at me with agitated eyes, my voice thick and unsure.

But if my father noticed my nervousness, then he didn't let it show. He turned back to his suitcase, the beer in his hand sloshing over the glass and spilling onto the floor.

"Exactly," he grumbled. "But me? I'm actually *doing* something about it! I believe in my daughter. She said she didn't kill that boy, so she didn't! But your mother just can't *get* that, can she?" He stumbled as he took a step, his foot landing in the puddle of beer, and he glanced down. "What the . . . ?"

I looked away from him because I knew that the reason my mother didn't believe Emily was because she'd believed me when I told her that she confessed after his funeral. I even told the police about the bag of clothing she'd shown me in her closet. Although he never actually said it to me, I knew he didn't believe me about her confession. And although my dad never said this either, I knew he still hadn't forgiven me for saying it in the first place.

It was probably one of the reasons he was always gone, even when he was at home, out of sight in his office.

And one of the reasons he was leaving right now, suitcases packed, with only Emily's picture clutched in his hand.

I could feel the weight of Emily's keys in my coat pocket as my father stumbled into the kitchen after downing what remained of his beer. I heard the pop and hiss of him opening another bottle in the next room and decided to slip out of the house.

When I'd started the engine and pulled out of the driveway, no one bothered to glance out the front door to see that I was leaving.

It was nearing six o'clock in the evening and I was still driving around aimlessly throughout Shiloh, too afraid to go back home and see if my father's car was still in the driveway. I'd stopped at the mall a few hours earlier, buying a couple of sweaters and a *Ten Second Trivia* board game I'd spotted in a gaming store. It was a version of the game Kolby was always playing on his phone and I wondered what he would do if he saw it. A moment later, I was grabbing the box, hoping it wouldn't seem too weird if I gave it to him.

My headlights beamed against pavement as I drove, my phone quiet since I'd left, and I was both relieved and disappointed no one had tried to call me. I wondered, as I spotted the cemetery farther down the road, if my dad had left yet or if Mom even knew he was going. If she'd found the puddle of beer soaking into the rug or the bottle cap on the kitchen floor, and had to realize he was gone through what was missing. An empty picture frame pointing the finger as to exactly why he'd left.

Passing by the cemetery, I noticed something familiar and hesitated just for a moment to look again. There, standing behind a row of headstones, was Kolby Rutledge in his black puffer vest. He was so still, and even from the road I could see the snowflakes in his dark hair, his nose pink and his cheeks flushed.

I remembered Kolby stepping outside the morning after the party, asking if I was okay as I tried—and failed—not to cry in front of him. Or how he'd found me outside the library, the contents of my backpack spilled on the sidewalk, telling me messes could be cleaned up.

A second later, I was pulling over. Because now it was my turn to be there for him, like he had been for me.

The soft sound of my feet crunching on the inches of freshly fallen snow echoed beneath the bare branches of the trees as I approached him, his back turned to me. A light layer of snow dusted the top of Griffin's headstone, a bouquet of wilting flowers against the granite obscuring the date he'd died. I wondered if this was purposely done by whomever had left them there.

If he heard my footsteps, then he didn't react to them as he stood there, hands buried in his pockets. I hesitated, lingering a few feet behind Kolby and wondering if I'd made a mistake. Maybe he didn't want me out here, intruding on a moment I didn't belong in. But then I heard him exhaling deeply, his shoulders rising and then falling and, with my heart hammering in my chest, I took a chance that maybe he needed me as much as I realized I needed him.

I took a step closer to him, slipping my arm around his, our shoulders brushing against each other.

The muscles of his bicep tensed slightly as I cautiously rested my palm against it, and he glanced down at me. His nose and the tips of his ears were bright red, his cheeks pale in comparison. Then his muscles relaxed against my hand. "Hey, you're really warm," he murmured.

I leaned my head against his shoulder. A moment later, I felt his cold cheek resting against the top of my head. "You're really cold," I said, rubbing his forearm with my hand, the swishing sound of my palm against his sleeve echoing in the quiet cemetery. So many hearts in this small space, but ours were the only two still beating.

He chuckled, gave a slight nod against my head, and it was quiet as we just stood there, together. But there was something about it that felt tranquil and okay, and so natural too, as if this was a rhythm we both knew the steps to.

We kept our arms linked together as we sidestepped and maneuvered around the headstones. Every few seconds he sniffled, his pink nose wrinkling. I leaned my cheek against his arm, cold and firm beneath my skin.

"Clara," Kolby said, his voice vibrating against my cheek. "You and Griffin—were you . . ." Our footsteps in the powder-like snow quieted as we stopped, and I turned to face him. "Did you like him?" He laughed, softly and awkwardly, his ashen cheeks becoming as red as the tips of his ears. "I mean, I *know* you liked him but did you ever really date him?"

"Griffin and I—" I sighed, not completely sure of what to

say, and embarrassed I was talking about it at all, especially to him. "We spun around in circles but we never dated. I mean, you know how those old neon signs flicker and blink but they're not constant? That was us. We blinked and we flickered and then we burned out."

I glanced up at him, noticing he was stifling a smile, biting it back with his teeth. I nudged my elbow against his ribs, a blush creeping beneath my cheeks, but I didn't feel embarrassed anymore. "Shut up, I'm trying to be deep here."

"I didn't say anything."

I tugged him toward my car, a light dusting of snow now over its windshield. "Come on," I told him. "You're freezing."

It wasn't until we got into the car that he started shivering, the vibrations trembling under my shoes as we left Griffin behind with the wilted flowers. I saw he placed his hands between his thighs to warm them, and I could hear his teeth chattering together, almost painfully.

"Sorry, the heat doesn't work," I apologized.

He shrugged, his smile jumping. "It's okay," he told me, even though by the time we reached a nearby a gas station, the shivering hadn't stopped, his shoulders still bouncing under his vest.

"How long were you out there?" I asked as we walked inside the convenience store, our shoes squeaking against the tiles in the otherwise quiet place, with only the constant low hum of the refrigerators echoing through the aisles. His hands were trembling as he reached for a cup stacked beside the coffee station.

"A while, I guess," he said, the steam from the coffee drifting toward his face as he poured. "I don't know. You want one?"

I shook my head before wandering down to the candy aisle. I grabbed a package of trail mix and a box of hot cinnamon candy because I sort of remembered Kolby eating them at lunch once and thought maybe the spiciness would help warm him up.

After I paid and we walked out to the parking lot, I looked over at Kolby as he took a sip from his coffee, watching it shake in his hand. I smiled when he caught my eye, raising his eyebrows. Then, before I realized what I was doing, I grabbed him by the elbow.

"Okay," I said, moving my hand away as he glanced down at it. "Do you have a fever or something?"

I stood on the tips of my toes and brushed my fingers beneath the strands of his hair, feeling his forehead against my hand. It took me a moment to realize that he was looking at me—not staring, not watching, but *looking* at me—and his brown eyes resembled the color of amber. I hadn't realized I was standing so close, or that my face was closer to his than it had ever been before, my chest actually *touching* his arm.

Not again, a small frightened voice whispered within me as I took my hand away. *Not again, not again, not again, not again.*

"Clara." Something laced his voice as he said my name, something I couldn't understand, maybe didn't want to. I took a step back, away from him. An icy panic filled my veins, my heart hammering against the rib bones Griffin had scarred, and I almost wanted to say that I didn't mean it. I didn't mean *that*. I didn't mean for him look at me like that, like I was something he couldn't quite fathom but wanted to. Like I was beautiful and mysterious to him. I just wanted to make him laugh, not *look* at me. "Do you—"

"My dad left," I blurted, before he could finish. "When I came home this afternoon, he was packing his stuff into suitcases and drunk." I shrugged, realizing he had stopped shivering. "I guess they're getting a divorce now."

"That sucks," he told me, and I nodded. "I'm sorry."

I smiled wanly, then gestured to the parked Mini Cooper with my bag of trail mix. "Come on. Before you start shivering again. You really should buy an actual coat."

He laughed. "I'll keep that in mind."

The next morning, I found my mother in the kitchen holding a box of pancake mix, her reading glasses on the bridge of her nose as she read from the instructions. She glanced up, noticing me in the doorway, and smiled. It almost made me wonder if that meant my father was back, upstairs sleeping off his hangover or something, but when I looked at the frame on the wall, I saw the picture of Emily was still missing.

"We're having pancakes this morning!" my mother's forcefully cheerful voice announced. "I thought we could spend Sunday together, just the two of us. Shopping, go out to lunch, maybe watch a movie or something. It's been so long since we've talked or done anything fun together."

"Sure, okay," I told her hesitantly.

"Great!" She grinned, setting down the pancake mix. "Now do you want chocolate chips or blueberries? Or both?"

After she bought me a new perfume, a winter coat she thought looked warmer than the one I already had, and an infinity scarf she said brought out my green eyes, she took me to Spring's Diner for dinner. When we'd finished eating, she ordered us both cupcakes with at least three inches of buttercream frosting and sprinkles. They were in front of us on a small dessert plate when my mother laced her fingers together and drew in a breath.

"Sweetheart," she began. "Dad's going to stay at a hotel for a little while. Your father and I have been having some problems lately."

I peeled back the wrapper on one of the cupcakes. "I know."

She sighed, looking down at the table. "We see things so differently, Clara. It's like your father lives in this world where everything is just so simple when it's not. I feel like he's in denial and doesn't understand the gravity of the situation."

"You mean he doesn't believe me about her confession," I clarified.

Her expression softened, but her eyes looked pained at this. "Your father loves you, very much. And I shouldn't be talking about this to you. He's your father and he's a good man. There's just not much room for understanding in that black-and-white world of his."

I looked down at the cupcake, still untouched, my voice quiet as I asked her, "Do you believe me about it?"

She hesitated, then reached out and grasped my hand. "Of course, honey. I know you wouldn't lie about something like that."

I nodded, forcing a small smile for her. I would never tell her the whole truth about what happened, but I liked knowing she believed the small part she did know.

Three days later my father called and apologized for leaving, for being drunk that night, not calling sooner. "I'm staying at a hotel about twenty minutes away. I was thinking we should have breakfast sometime before you go to school? Remember that one diner you like, with the omelets?"

He was basically saying the same thing Mom had as she'd stirred the pancake batter days earlier—*It's been so long since we've talked, I feel like I hardly see you anymore, I think it would be nice if we could do something.* Except, even through the phone, I could feel his attention slipping away from me and turning back to Emily.

"Sure," I said anyway, because that was easier than saying anything else. "Omelets sound good."

Beneath Bex's hair were scribbles in thick, somewhat faded black ink on the back of her neck. As she looked down, I caught a better glimpse of the writing, forming a sentence that made me clench my teeth together: Property of Wilson Westbrooke.

I wondered if she'd thought that was funny when he wrote it on her neck, giggling at the felt tip against her skin. Then I wondered if she'd let him write that because she was too afraid to tell him no.

"Is it just me, or does she have a contract on her neck?" Aniston strode up beside me, on her phone, appearing suddenly as she always did. "Do you think I should go over there and tell her possession isn't romantic?"

"Aniston," I said after Bex rounded a corner and slipped out of view. "If you knew someone wasn't good for someone else, would you say anything to her? Or him?"

"That's a whole lot of *someones* in that sentence." She gave me a pointed look, but I feigned an innocent shrug, to which she rolled her eyes. "Is this about Bex and her newfound relationship status with your sister's abusive ex?"

"How did you—?"

"It's a long explanation about my suspicions based on your sister's black eye a year and a half ago, and the fact that she was a junior dating a twenty-three-year-old. Huh, I guess that wasn't really that long. Anyway, I've been trying to call Bex to give her a heads-up that her boyfriend might be a loser and not in the cute, endearing kind of way, but she's ignoring me. I guess love is blind and, apparently, deaf. And deleting my voicemails."

My mind drifted away as Aniston started rambling about her phone battery, thinking back to Emily slipping out of her bedroom window that night, barefoot, and into Griffin's backyard. Maybe she'd known better than to try and convince me to tell someone. Maybe she'd known the only way to stop someone was to confront *them*. Not their confused, clueless girlfriends.

She'd stopped Griffin that night in September, and now it was my turn to return the favor.

His beat-up brown van was idling in the back of the school parking lot after school ended. He was probably waiting for Bex while she was in the auditorium with Mrs. Foley and the other students cast in *Shrek the Musical*. As I approached, the pulsating beat of deafeningly loud rap music emanated from inside.

Wilson wore a gray beanie, fraying around the hem, blond strands of his shoulder-length hair spilling out from underneath.

The dashboard was littered with crumpled, grease-stained paper bags from fast food places, empty bottles of energy drinks missing their lids, and at least three lighters.

It wasn't until I rapped my knuckles against the smudged window that he noticed me. My heart rate quickened as he glanced up from his severely cracked phone screen and turned my way. I expected some sort of reaction from him, but all he did was shout over the music, his voice muffled through the window he hadn't bothered to roll down: "What?"

"Hey," I said. He leaned forward, closer to the glass, and I weakly gestured for him to open the window. He just stared at me blankly, like he didn't even recognize me. "I'm—I know Bex. Your girlfriend? And I just wanted to say I think you should stop seeing her. Because you're not . . . she deserves better than a guy who—"

"You're Emily's sister, right?" he asked, continuing before I could answer, turning down the music. "You've been hanging out with that fat kid too, right? Giving him rides and—"

"He's not fat," I interjected.

But Wilson went on, undeterred by my interruption. "Wasn't he friends with that guy she killed a couple of months ago? You know, I wouldn't have thought the two of you would hit it off."

I tried not to look away from him. "I didn't have anything to do with what happened to Griffin. Kolby knows that."

There was something in the way Wilson looked at me then—a shift in his eyes, a shade of blue lighter than Griffin's—that almost seemed *knowing*. "So Emily murders the guy you had a thing for, for years, and it has *nothing* to do with you?"

My heart clenched. "I—"

"Save it. I don't rat people out. You can thank me by leaving us alone."

And then, just like that, he reached for the volume knob, spinning it until I felt the tremors resume beneath my feet. I just stood there, dumbfounded for a moment, before turning away. Panic swelled in my chest as I saw Kolby emerging from the school, Bex a few steps behind him.

I took one last glance at Wilson Westbrooke, but he had already turned away.

chapter thirteen

before

I stayed home on Valentine's Day, pretending I'd caught the stomach flu. I kept pretending I was sick for days afterward until my mom started to get worried and considered calling the doctor. After that, I was forced to make a miraculous recovery and start attending school again.

Now it had been twenty-three days since the night of the Super Bowl party, and I actually did feel like I had the flu when I walked into the kitchen, the smell of cooked bacon and pancakes filling the air. *Twenty-three days* kept filtering through my mind. It was something that terrified me almost as much as hearing his laughter in the school hallways like thunder rolling in a dark, turbulent sky.

It had been five days since I was supposed to get my period.

~

I told myself the constant feeling of wanting to vomit was because I always saw *him*, everywhere. In the hallways at school, in the parking lot, everywhere. He was even at home, just across the street from my house.

It wasn't until my period was almost a week late that I considered a possible explanation. It had plagued the back of my mind but I'd pushed it aside because that was easier than admitting what I was beginning to think could be true.

That I was pregnant with Griffin Tomlin's baby.

On the last day of February, I finally decided to do something about it, asking Emily for the keys to her car by feigning a craving for frozen yogurt and offering to grab her one too—wondering if, eventually, saying things about craving frozen yogurt wouldn't be lies anymore but frightening truths.

I parked on the side of the road near Bex's house, grabbing a handful of stones from her gravel driveway before finding her bedroom window. I hesitated, the thought of a pregnancy test—a positive one—reverberating through my mind again. I told myself that wasn't going to happen. I wasn't going to take a pregnancy test to find out if I was pregnant. I was going to take it for peace of mind, to be assured I *wasn't*.

After I threw the first couple of pebbles, I saw the flicker of her shadow against the wall in her bedroom on the second floor. I took a quick glance around her dark neighborhood as she opened the window.

"Clare! Thank goodness you came!" she whisper-yelled down to me. "My wicked mother has left to gather the ingredients for hazelnut soup, so now, my prince, we can be alone! Halt, while I let down my luscious golden hair, which is never dirty, even though it's almost as long as the Empire State Building."

"Bex," I whispered.

She started to sing one of the songs from *Into the Woods*, about the prince's agonizing love for Rapunzel. I felt myself panicking as her voice grew louder, looking over my shoulder at the houses across the street.

"I'm late," I blurted out while she was mid-lyric. Then I said something that felt too real, and too big for anywhere other than the starless expanse of that night. "I think I might be pregnant."

We drove out of town, even though Bex had pointed to a Walgreens ten minutes earlier. "We could just go there," she told me. "No one would recognize you."

I shook my head. I was too afraid of him finding out, that I would step into line with a pregnancy test in hand and glance over my shoulder to see him, browsing discount Valentine's Day candy or something. I was afraid of what he might do, if he would get the same look in his eyes he'd had that night and find me again. Or if he would act like he had that afternoon after school and pretend to be my boyfriend. Maybe he would say he would be there, no matter what. That I wasn't in this alone.

I wasn't sure which side of him made me feel sicker.

We stopped at a Good Greens two towns over after Bex finally convinced me no one would recognize me there and that we really couldn't go any farther and make it back in time for curfew. Once inside, I cautiously approached the hygiene aisle. As the pregnancy test boxes came into view, I became all too aware of the fact that I might actually be pregnant.

I stopped, unable to force my feet to move any farther. I would have to tell my parents, my sister, the few friends I still had. I would have to lie in a paper gown, sedation coursing through my veins, and something inserting itself, like it had that night, except now it was to take away what he'd left. Or I would have to take vitamins, cut out deli meat, and feel a part of him squirming inside even when he wasn't there, and then either have to love it or give it away.

And I wanted none of it. I felt so angry that I was so terrified when this had never been a choice I'd made. He'd ripped something away from me, and now I was staring at the display of pregnancy tests from a distance, thinking how all of this was too real and too close.

I went over to the snack aisle and stood there for nearly five minutes, shaking my head whenever Bex tried to persuade me to keep going, until she finally decided to grab the test for me. She found me a few minutes later with a plastic bag around her wrist and took my hand, saying nothing as she led me to a family restroom and locked the door behind us.

The plastic bag rustled as she grabbed the test, skimming over the instructions on the back. "Okay," she said, tearing open the box, "it says to hold the test in a *downward stream* at a ninety-degree angle for . . . five seconds. Then stand by for three minutes and await your answer."

I slumped against the wall.

She pulled out a slender package from inside the box. "Do you remember what a ninety-degree angle looks like? Does it really matter? Like, don't these things test for hormones? How does the direction of your pee change that?"

"Bex." My voice sounded hoarse, unused, and scared.

"It says *first morning's urine* is best, but isn't that just another way of saying after you haven't peed in a while? So, like, the hormone can be soaked up or something?" She glanced up from the box, her brow unfurrowing slightly. "When was the last time you peed?"

"I can't do it," I whispered.

"You kind of have to," she told me

I shook my head. Earlier I'd wanted to know. But now, with the test right in front of me, waiting for me to take it, I didn't want to know. Knowing was worse, I decided as I slid down to the floor, my knees pulled close to my chest and my fingers threading into my hair. Knowing meant I actually had to do something much harder than pee on a test.

"You're probably not pregnant, Clare. You're just late, and freaking. And if you're freaking out, then everything makes you feel like you're pregnant. You probably just feel sick because you're so worried about this."

I didn't say anything, letting out a slow and shaky exhale. My heart thrashed around in my chest like it desperately wanted a way out, just like me.

"Clare . . . *Clara.*" I glanced up as she said my real name, the name she never called me. Her expression softened as she set the test down on the back of the toilet. "Who's the father?" She hesitated before speaking again, quieter this time. "Is it Griffin?"

My heart, still erratically pounding, suddenly stopped and dropped into my stomach when I heard his name. "What?"

"I mean, you've only had a crush on him forever. And you guys have been doing this dance since he kissed you." I swallowed, desperately trying to control my breathing as I closed my eyes. "So, is it him?"

I nodded slowly against the wall, my voice cracking as I whispered, "Yeah."

She paused after I said this, and my eyelids fluttered open just as she nodded, holding the test out to me again. Her warm hand found mine and I felt the smooth packaging against my palm.

"Take the test, Clare." Her thumb brushed away a tear on my cheek, and she smiled. Even though she didn't say it, her eyes were scared and anxious, but her features were determined and braced. "I hope you remember what a ninety-degree angle looks like."

It was negative. I wasn't pregnant. But I wasn't relieved either.

"So," Bex finally said after ten minutes of us sitting in the car after leaving Good Greens and finding a frozen yogurt place. "Now that we know you're not pregnant, I think I'm going to need a few details. Why didn't you tell me you guys did it?! Also next time, rubber up, okay? So spill. What made Griffin Tomlin realize what he was missing?"

"It wasn't really like that. Not at all, really."

She took a bite of her cake-batter-flavored yogurt. "That's just the first time, Clare. The more you do it, the better it gets. And sex isn't always as passionate as it is in the movies, especially with high school boys. They have *no idea* what they're doing."

"It wasn't that," I mumbled. It seemed almost safe there, with the flickering lights from the frozen yogurt shop against her cheek, filtering in through the windshield. Like I could say anything, and wasn't that what you were supposed to do, anyway? It was what I had seen encouraged by hotline advertisements and school counselors before, posters in doctors' offices too. Maybe you were supposed to speak up, even when you were threatened not to.

"He . . . I think he kind of—I don't know." Bex blinked at me, her brow furrowing, as I stumbled over my words. I had no idea how to say any of it out loud. "I mean, he didn't drug me or anything but he, like, tied me up and . . ."

And then I heard it, the bubble of awkward laughter I would always remember. In some ways, it was more of a warning than his threats in my ear.

"Clare," she said, her voice almost forcefully nonchalant. "That's just kinky stuff. It's normal. It's what some guys like. You're just, you know, new to it. Just tell him you don't like that kind of thing." She scooped a large spoonful of yogurt into her mouth. "I mean, it's *Griffin Tomlin*."

It was Griffin Tomlin.

And, somehow, that was enough.

chapter fourteen

Bex passed me in the hallway at school, her neck free of any dec-
larations from Wilson Westbrooke. Earlier I'd seen the school's
casting sheet tacked to a billboard. She had been cast as Princess
Fiona in the spring musical.

I wondered what she saw in Wilson. A guy who slept until
noon, always smelled a little bit like body odor, and smoked cigarettes he could somehow afford despite being unemployed. She
knew he was Emily's ex-boyfriend, and she also knew I'd never
liked him. She'd laughed at the jokes I made about him finally
discovering shampoo, but maybe she liked him even then. Maybe
at all the block parties I invited her to, I was so focused on Griffin
that I never noticed she was focused on Wilson.

Now, in the hallway, she slowed when she noticed me near my
locker. "Hey," she said. "I saw you talking to Wilson yesterday."

"Yeah."

"I know you don't like him," she told me. "He can be a little hard to get to know, but he's actually really nice. Maybe what you didn't like about him was that he didn't *fit* with Emily."

"I think what I didn't like about him was that he doesn't shower and says a lot of stupid stuff, plus I'm *pretty* sure I saw him pee in one of my mom's bushes. But you're right, they didn't really fit well together."

She made a face. "He was just trying to be funny! He does stuff without thinking sometimes, but honestly he's just trying to make you laugh! I think he feels bad that we're, you know, going out, because he dated your sister."

I scoffed. "I don't think Wilson Westbrooke feels bad about anything. You know, you're the second high school girl he's dated, and he's in his twenties. Don't you think that says something?"

"Clare, I'm eighteen. I'm not a minor anymore."

"By, like, two months," I pointed out.

She glanced away for a moment. "Yeah, it was a really awesome birthday," she remarked sarcastically, but also softly. Not for the first time, I felt sort of guilty for not responding to her text message—the first one she'd sent in months—asking if I wanted to come to her birthday party. I still wouldn't have, but sometimes I felt like I should've at least said that instead of just leaving the message as *read*. "I know we're not—I mean, do you want to hang out sometime? Forget everything about Griffin and your sister, and just move on? Who else am I going to run lines with?"

She cracked a small, anxious smile, but I still remembered her in the parking lot of the frozen yogurt store, licking the back of her spoon as she told me *It's Griffin Tomlin*.

"I know the past few months have been rough for you. You didn't even audition for the spring musical and now you're hanging out with that weird girl from the paper who keeps blowing up my phone. I'm worried about you. You seem kind of lost, Clare."

I shot her a look, now no longer feeling guilty but annoyed. "The only reason Aniston is *blowing up* your phone is because she's trying to warn you about Wilson. She thinks he was abusive to Emily."

I wouldn't tell her I *knew* he was. That was Emily's secret, her own night left alone with a boy she thought she knew, one she trusted. But I would tell her Aniston suspected it, hoping that would be enough.

"Well, then it's a good thing it's Aniston Hale saying those things," she said. "She takes the paper too seriously, like it's an actual job. She'll say anything to write a juicy story."

"I don't think that what she wants is a good story, Bex."

She rolled her eyes. "You know, this is like the first time we've talked in months, so can't we talk about something actually important?" She looked around the hallway before taking a step closer to me, lowering her voice. "Like Grif—?"

"You deserve better than Wilson," I interrupted, not wanting to hear whatever she was going to say next. I stifled the urge to groan when she let out an exasperated sigh and started walking away, shaking her head. "He's not a good person. Bex. Bex!"

But even when I called her name, she kept walking away from me until she rounded a corner and disappeared out of sight.

I found Mrs. Foley sitting at her desk, glasses sliding off the bridge of her nose as she squinted, the computer screen reflected in her lenses. On the monitor, I saw a message telling her she'd misspelled her password. "*No*, that is my password. I only have one password, for everything!"

"Mrs. Foley?"

She looked away from the screen, her gaze lifting over her frames. "Clara!" she exclaimed, motioning for me to come in. "I wasn't expecting to see you here! It feels like forever and a half since we've talked! How are you?"

I nodded, like this was somehow a response to her question, but it was one I was used to dodging because the answer was never meant to be the truth. Otherwise it wouldn't be asked so lightheartedly.

"I know you already cast everyone, but I was wondering . . ." I thought of the black ink on Bex's neck, the brown van idling in the school parking lot, and I decided I wasn't going to be like her. I wasn't going to awkwardly laugh and change the subject, pretending like I hadn't heard. And I wasn't going to let Bex become me. ". . . If maybe I could still be a part of the musical? In the background, even? I really want to get back into theater again. Be, you know, *normal* again."

She crossed her arms over her chest, and her lipstick smeared against her skin as she pressed her lips together. "All of the roles are taken. And I don't think it would be fair to ask someone to give up their part just because you've changed your mind. But we could always use an extra." She smiled warmly, patting my arm. "We'll just add another fairy-tale character. Toss in a line or two. How's another sugarplum fairy sound?"

I nodded. "Fine. Thanks, Mrs. Foley."

"This is going to be so good for you, honey! And you'll get to spend some more time with that boy." She attempted to wink at me, but her eyes blinked instead.

"What boy?"

"Well, Kolby! Kolby Rutledge? You two always eat lunch together, don't you?"

"Yeah," I said slowly, confused. "But he's not in the musical . . . right?"

She nodded, turning back and squinting at the computer screen as she pressed the backspace button. "Yes, he is. He's our pianist."

"The—wait, he knows how to play—?"

"Clara!"

A pink blur darted into the classroom, boots squeaking against the floor. Mrs. Foley, seeming to be undeterred by this, looked up from her keyboard and smiled at Aniston before returning to retyping her password.

Aniston waved as she took in a breath. I thought back to what Bex had said about her, that she took the paper too seriously, and I knew I'd thought the same thing when I first met her. But now, as she almost jumped with excitement, waving her phone at me, I wasn't sure if that was what I still saw when I looked at her.

"Clara, I need to show you something. Like, right now." Then she looked at Mrs. Foley, even though she was still focused on her computer. "Nothing serious, though. Just can't decide what scarf to wear."

"Scarves?" I asked after she'd ushered me into a girls' bathroom, then bent down to look underneath each stall. "Really? Of all the excuses, you went with scarves? Why did you even need an excuse?"

"*Look!*" She thrust her phone in front of me. On the screen, there was a picture of a girl smiling into the camera, beside a news article. The background was dark behind her, a midnight sky, with the glow of a streetlamp in the far corner. Her teeth were slightly crooked and acne was scattered over her chin. Then I read the headline.

POLICE DEEM MISSING GIRL, ELIZABETH
MONNER, 17, A RUNAWAY

"Look at the dates! She went missing three weeks before Griffin died! And look, she had strawberry blond hair, like Ella Dillard! That must be Griffin's type, I'm *telling* you."

"Aniston," I murmured, but when I tried to find something else to say, I couldn't. I was too focused on the date she went missing. *August 19*, two days after my birthday.

Happy birthday, dear Clara. Happy birthday to you.

"The police ruled she was a runaway because she used to do drugs and ran away once when she was thirteen. Last August, she got into a fight with her boyfriend and called her mom saying she was going to be home later that afternoon, but never showed up! Because Griffin took her! She lived in Buffalo, so I didn't find this until now, but it makes perfect sense! I know it sounds crazy, but what if Griffin wasn't just *becoming* a serial killer? What if he already *was* one? Or at least a lot closer to being one than I thought."

"You really think he killed her? That she didn't just . . . run away, like the police said?"

She shrugged. "I don't know. I mean, I guess it's possible, but so is Griffin doing something to her. Maybe on purpose, or by accident, I don't know, but I feel like it had to be him."

I realized then as I looked at her, at her pleading desperation, that if I finally admitted the truth about what had really happened between Griffin and me, she would believe me. Aniston was the only person who saw the same Griffin I did—not the one who mowed church lawns or played Marco Polo with little kids at his family's pool parties. But who he really was.

Now it was my turn to believe in what she saw. "It's worth looking into."

She grinned at me. "Yay! Now, do you have any plans this weekend?"

It was snowing as Kolby and I trudged through the school parking lot later that afternoon. My teeth clenched together as we passed a familiar van with rap music blaring through the windows. Ten minutes later, I pulled into Kolby's driveway. A dog barked from inside the house, a curtain shifting in the window.

Kolby had grabbed his backpack and rested his other hand on the door handle, but besides that, he hadn't moved since I'd pulled in.

"So . . ." he laughed, kind of quietly and awkwardly under his breath. "You've been driving me to work, and here, a lot, and I feel bad about not paying you back or anything—"

I waved my hand dismissively through the air with a small smile, because I thought he was going to try to pay me back for gas or something.

"So I was wondering if I could make it up to you, on Saturday. See a movie or something? I could borrow my dad's car."

"Kolby." I looked down at my hands curled in my lap. "I'm actually going to be kind of busy this weekend. My mom's forcing me to go see my dad, and then I'm going to Buffalo with Aniston."

He nodded, smiling in that way people do when they don't feel like smiling, when their lips and their disappointed eyes convey two different messages. I felt a pang in my chest, one that made me interrupt him as he began to say something, probably that it was all right, another time, even though we both knew there wouldn't be one.

"There's this girl who used to live there, in Buffalo, named Elizabeth. She went missing a couple months ago and Aniston thinks it has something to do with Griffin's murder."

"Why would a missing girl in Buffalo have anything to do with Griffin?" He hesitated, then asked, "Are there things you haven't told me about? About Griffin and Emily?"

I was quiet for a moment, then nodded.

"Are you ever going to tell me about them?"

I shook my head, my eyes following the glimmers of the midwinter snowfall, because he couldn't know. He couldn't look at me as the girl his best friend had touched, hurt, tainted. He couldn't decide that he didn't believe me.

"Not right now, but maybe someday," I told him, even though *maybe* and *someday* were just words leaving my lips, not promises. "It'll make things different. I'm not ready for that."

He seemed to consider this for a moment before nodding. "Okay," he replied softly, glancing over his shoulder at me before opening the door, letting in a gust of cold air and snowflakes. He smiled. "See you tomorrow, Clara."

I stared at him as he waved back at me while walking up his driveway a moment later. Somewhat stunned, I opened my door, Kolby stopping and waiting as I got out. "Wait, that's just . . . it? *Okay*?" I walked up beside him.

"Yeah," he said, like it was clear. "It's . . . you. And for now, that's enough for me."

The bitter cold wind brushed against my fingers as he nudged them with the side of his hand, a warmth that somehow spread up into my chest as I looked at him. "And does that mean something to you?"

"It . . ." His smile grew faintly as he exhaled, looking past me for a moment before his eyes found their way back to me. He looked at me in a way that made me want to take a step forward and a step back, all at once. "It means a lot to me. *You* mean a lot to me."

That was when it happened: when he took that one step forward I was too reluctant to take. I tilted my chin up to look at him, and maybe he saw that as something else, something that made his mouth touch mine, warm and tentative. His lips tasted of coffee and they were just barely closed as he kissed me.

I knew I was too still, my lips unmoving under his, but I couldn't. The last boy who'd kissed me was dead. The last boy who'd kissed me wormed his tongue into my mouth and slid it around until I almost gagged.

Kolby wasn't Griffin Tomlin.

Griffin wasn't Wilson Westbrooke.

That was something I'd believed too, and I'd believed it until one night in February proved I was wrong.

I couldn't be wrong again.

So I pulled away.

I took a step back as he said my name, softly and only once. When I went back to the car and slid behind the wheel, he was on the porch. Even from where I was, I could hear him groan loudly as he leaned forward and bumped his forehead against the wall, repeatedly. Then he stood there for another second before banging his head one last time and then unlocking the front door.

It wasn't until he disappeared inside that I realized I was almost, nearly, *maybe* smiling.

chapter fifteen

before

Since taking the pregnancy test and telling Bex about what had happened at the Super Bowl after party—and her saying I was *just, you know, new to it* since it *was Griffin Tomlin*—I had started avoiding her around school. I stopped going to drama practices and ate lunch in the school library, and since Scoops! was closed for the winter, I didn't have to think about seeing her there either.

She was still sending me text messages, though, regardless of how hard I tried to dodge her at school. Sometimes she called me and left voicemails when I didn't answer, but I never listened to them, even though I kind of wanted to. In her text messages, she asked me if something was up, if anything was going on. I almost wanted to reply that she knew what was going on. She'd just totally dismissed it because it was Griffin Tomlin.

I managed to evade her in person for almost two weeks before she approached me at my locker, surprising me since I knew she was supposed to be in class.

"Hey," she said, sounding a little too casual to actually be casual. "What's up? You haven't answered my calls. I thought we were going to go to the movies last weekend."

I grabbed a textbook from my locker. "I didn't really feel like going anymore."

"Why couldn't you have just told me that? You know, one of the many times I called or texted you?" She laughed, but again, it felt too forced to be sincere.

"I didn't feel like talking."

"That's why they invented texting. Do you want to go to the movies this weekend? Or do something else, like go shopping or whatever?"

I scratched my thumbnail down the spine of my textbook. "Not really."

"What's up with you? Why are you acting so weird?"

I shrugged, tucking my textbook under my arm and closing my locker. When I walked around her, she followed me. It was something we would've normally done, but now it felt awkward, like we were out of step with one another. "I don't really want to hang out. Ask someone else to go shopping."

"Hey, hey, wait." She reached out for my arm, grasping my wrist as she sped up to stand in front of me. I tried not to flinch at the touch of her hand on my skin. "Is this about Griffin? I've been trying to talk to you because—"

I moved out of her reach, suddenly very aware that we were in a *public* high school hallway. "It isn't about anyone, okay? I just don't want to hang out with you." I lowered my voice as I glanced around us, assuring myself he wasn't there to have heard what she'd said. "Please just leave me alone, okay?"

Hurt flashed across her eyes before I walked away from her, clutching my textbook so tightly that the tips of my fingers were numb by the time I finally made it around the corner.

Dear Clara,

Here is a blown glass pumpkin carriage I found on the internet. I thought it was cool how it was a combination of the glass slipper and the pumpkin. You were such a perfect Cinderella. I remember not even wanting to go to the play, but my parents wanted to support you and made me go with them. Then you were onstage and it was like everything else was gone. Like how even when the lights around you turned off, I could still kind of see you. You were so beautiful, even with the dust and the messy hair. I knew I had been missing out on something my whole life. You're my perfect Cinderella princess.

Love, Griffin

Dear Clara,

I saw you at school today. You had your hair in a bun and all I could think about was reaching over and undoing it for you, watching your hair fall everywhere. I love your hair. It's kind of like the color of a sunset when there's more orange in it than pink. I tried to tell you how beautiful I thought you were, but you walked away without even looking at me. Didn't you see me there?

Love, Griffin

Dear Clara,

I found this CD for Into the Woods. *I'm not sure if you have a CD player or not, but I could find one for you if you don't. I wanted you to listen to it and hear how much better you are as Cinderella than anyone else. I listened to a few songs but they don't sound as good without you. Every time I hear them, I think of you, but I don't hear you, so it feels wrong.*

Love, Griffin

P.S. Why haven't you written me back?

Clara,

I saw you at school today, talking to one of the guys from the football team. Like you were flirting with him. You

smiled at him, but you haven't smiled at me in months.
Is it because you're hiding something from me? Are you
screwing the guys on the football team now? What about
the guy teachers? I see you staring at them. Is that why you
haven't responded to any of my letters or even thanked
me for the gifts I sent you? Do you think it's easy to find a
glass pumpkin carriage? But I looked for it and bought it
for you because I love you. I'm starting to think you don't
love me, which I can't understand. You're this nobody.
You blend in with everyone else because there's nothing
about you that stands out, nothing special. You're liter-
ally like every girl at this school. There's nothing attrac-
tive about you. Your body looks like a middle-schooler's.
You think that because you sang in a school musical,
you're pretty and talented, when you're not. No one was
even paying attention when you were onstage.

Griffin

P.S. Are you ever going to write me back? Why don't you
wear the necklace I bought you?

After the first letter, I started bringing in the mail, scanning for
envelopes with no return addresses. I threw the letters away after
tearing them into shreds of disturbed and twisted sentences that
made my skin crawl. I'd stuff them into pad wrappers before
shoving them into grocery bags I'd toss in the garbage cans outside on garbage night.

The letters came for weeks that turned into months. I shredded each one, but I always felt as if the ink from his words—words that were loving, caring, but terrifying, as if instead of telling me he loved me, he was telling me he hated me, and instead of telling me he thought I was beautiful, he was telling me he wanted to kill me—lingered on my fingertips, stained and tainted them. Just like the rest of me, no matter how many times I scrubbed, I couldn't get them clean.

While we were at school he normally kept his distance, even though I always felt his eyes on me. Every time I heard his laughter ricocheting against the walls and looked up, I would see him, over someone's shoulder or behind a locker. His lips would be moving, speaking to someone else, but his eyes would be on me.

It wasn't until April that the letters started to change, become more desperate, asking why I never wrote him back or why I never wore the necklace he'd given me months ago. He questioned why I was always staring at our male teachers, or why I'd spoken to Miles Benway the day before when all I'd done was give him directions to the guidance counselor's office. He even asked why I'd smiled at something I overheard a girl saying. He dedicated a whole letter to the fact that he thought I was a *lesbo* after I'd accepted a hug from a graduating senior I knew from drama club. He told me I wanted it so bad, I would probably go to anyone, I was that much of a slut.

Then the next letter would be drenched in compliments, saying he knew I was thinking of him, he couldn't wait to be with me again. And every day, I was afraid he would finally stop observing me like a caged bird and approach me.

When school finally let out in June, I thought that was it, at least until late August anyway. Sure, he still lived across the street, but I wouldn't really have to see him around anywhere. I never reapplied for my job at Scoops!, and he was working as a lifeguard at the community pool most afternoons. I thought it was ironic, that someone like him was being paid to keep people safe.

I expected the letters to still continue, but I thought maybe not seeing each other for two and a half months might simmer everything down.

I really thought I wouldn't see him again until school was back in the fall.

I was wrong.

It was the day before the Fourth of July, and my mom was opening and closing the cupboard doors, shifting soup cans and pasta sauces around. With a pen and notepad in her hand, she added graham crackers, hot dogs, buns, and spicy mustard to the list in her cursive handwriting. She told me it was our turn to host the neighborhood barbecue the next night.

"Are the Tomlins coming?" I asked hesitantly.

She peeked her head out from around the cupboard doors, a bemused smile on her face. "Of course the Tomlins are coming."

Of course.

The next day, I found myself sitting in a lawn chair in the backyard in front of a barely smoldering fire pit. My legs were tucked up to my chest, sweat clinging under my arms and wetting my bra since I was overdressed in my sweatshirt and jeans, but I wanted to be protected from his eyes. The smell of smoke and grilled hamburgers filled the air, dusk barely beginning to settle into the sky as we waited for our neighbors.

I told myself he wouldn't be able to do anything. I was safe here in front of all our families. Safe.

Then the patio door was pulled back, accompanied by the distant sound of my mother laughing from inside the house. I sat there, arms wrapped around my shins, hearing flip-flops smack against the deck behind me.

"Hey, Griffin," my dad greeted. "You can just set that on the table over there."

chapter sixteen

When I arrived at my father's hotel room Saturday morning, the bed was unmade and his suitcase was left open on the table beside the mini-fridge. The television was on and tuned to a weather channel, a reporter mentioning the latest snowstorm headed in our direction.

We'd only just said hello when his phone started ringing. He answered it right away, pointing to it before disappearing into the bathroom, his voice muffled through the walls. It wasn't until almost half an hour later, when I'd seen the same footage of the snowstorm at least three times, that he finally got off the phone and came back into the room.

"Sorry, Clara Bear," he told me, slipping his phone into his back pocket. "Something came up with the lawyer he wants to talk about. You wanna tag along and we can go out after?" He didn't even wait for my response before slipping on his jacket.

"It can't wait until afterward?" I said.

He shook his head. "No, sorry, it really can't. But then we can go out for brunch. That's even better than breakfast, right?"

"It's okay. We can go out another day."

"You sure?"

I nodded, but he barely even glanced over at me as he turned off the television and reached for his keys on the nightstand. "Yeah, sure. No problem."

After Aniston and I ate breakfast—which came from a Tim Hortons drive-through—we left in her mother's minivan to head to Elizabeth Monner's house. After almost an hour of driving, the house number we were searching for appeared on the side of a dented mailbox.

A chain-link fence lined the property, brown patches of grass peeking out from under the snow in the front yard. A chipped ceramic bowl filled with ashes and stubbed cigarettes was on the first step of the front porch and a rusted lawn chair sat near the screen door, which had holes sliced through the mesh, leaving it agape like an unhealed wound. It struck me how that was what the house was. An unhealed wound. Despair seemed to linger in the windows like an uninvited visitor that wouldn't leave, so persistent eventually you just let it be. You assumed it belonged there now, in the place of someone else.

Someone who was gone.

Muffled voices coming from a television drifted from inside the house and out onto the porch as we approached the front door, ringing the doorbell. After a moment, the television grew quiet and I could hear someone grunting, then footsteps thumping toward us. The door behind the screen opened, revealing a woman behind the torn mesh. She was shorter than either one of us, and heavier, with wrinkles tracing out from the corners of her eyes as she blinked at us.

"Mrs. Monner?" Aniston asked. "Hi. We're from Madison High School, in Shiloh. We wanted to ask you a couple of questions about your daughter, Elizabeth, for an article?"

Mrs. Monner set out a package of cookies on the dining room table after letting us inside. She intertwined her fingers as she sat down with an anxious smile. She told us about Elizabeth, how she loved animals, and was on the track team last year until they found the pot in her locker and she was kicked off.

Her eyes were watering as she explained, "I know the drugs weren't okay, but I don't even care about that anymore. I just want her to come home safely."

"Did Elizabeth ever mention knowing someone named Griffin Tomlin?" I asked. "He didn't live here in Buffalo—instead about twenty miles away from here in Shiloh."

She shook her head. "I heard about him in the news a few months ago, but I never heard her talk about him. After she went missing, I went through her phone and all her contacts. He wasn't one of them." She hesitated, glancing between me and Aniston. "Do you think what happened to him is related to Elizabeth?"

I looked over to Aniston, totally unsure of how to respond. "We're obviously not detectives, Mrs. Monner, but we thought it was worth asking, since he died around the time of her disappearance."

"But they caught who killed him, right?"

"They did."

Aniston took a cookie and stood up. "We're really sorry if we wasted your time. And we really hope they find Elizabeth safe."

I wasn't sure what I wanted to hear—that her daughter started receiving letters in the mail or found windows suspiciously left open—but whatever it was, I hadn't heard it. Maybe I'd hoped she knew something, but there was nothing.

I knew what to look for, but I had no idea where to find it.

"We'll be fine," Aniston said after we'd left and gone to a mall for a snack. "I want to say we'll totally crack the case like Columbo or that someone will find Elizabeth Monner eventually, but I'm not really sure of either of those things. I mean, I *think* eventually everything will fall into place, but even if it doesn't, we'll be fine. It's just . . . *new* now, for everyone. But time really does a wonder when it comes to healing, and everything will be fine. Even if we don't crack the case."

"You don't know that."

"Yeah. I do," she said, before reaching into her pocket and taking out her phone, holding it out to me. On the screen was a picture of a man with shaved dark hair and a young girl. "That's my dad, Santino. He died when I was thirteen. Well, he didn't just die. He was killed. The police still don't know who did it. I don't think they really care since he was an immigrant. They told my Mamá it was probably some dispute over drugs, like because he was from Mexico it meant he had to be involved in drug dealing or something. But he wasn't! He hated drugs."

I handed the phone back to her. "You look like him."

She smiled. "For a long time, I thought if I could figure out who did it, it would hurt less. I became obsessed with it, but eventually I had to let it go. All the things I loved to do were getting replaced with trying to find who killed my dad, and I realized just how *outraged* he would be if he found out I was missing school dances or not going to the movies or shopping, just so I could figure out what happened to him. So I stopped. And started wearing pink because that was his favorite color." She laughed, shaking her head. "And then I get obsessed with your sister's case. Believe it or not, I'm actually a lot less obsessive now! I still go to the mall, after all, so it can't be *that* bad or anything."

I smiled, then looked down before telling her the only thing I could've in that moment. "Griffin Tomlin raped me."

"Yeah, I . . . I know, or I figured anyway. I wanted to give you this big, bone-crushing hug when I realized, but I didn't think you wanted me to know. I didn't want to push you away because I always feel like I'm one mistake away from pushing someone away, so I pretended I didn't know, but I did."

"How did you . . . ?"

She seemed to consider something for a moment before saying, "How about we find something to eat? Then I'll spill my guts. Not literally, of course."

"Wait, isn't that what we're doing now?" I asked, pointing to the fries still on our table in the mall's food court.

She waved her hand, shaking her head as she grabbed her purse. "These are too salty, and definitely not worthy of gut-spilling, unless you mean the literal kind. Let's bounce." Then she hesitated. "But first we have to clean this up."

~

Apparently, what Aniston wanted to eat was popcorn, and to be more specific, movie theater popcorn. Which was how I found myself sitting on one of the loveseats near the women's restroom at the cinema, listening to the droning of a hand dryer echo inside. A part of me wondered if the reason she was spending so much time deciding what size popcorn to get was because she was trying to delay an awkward conversation with me.

After she had finally purchased her large popcorn, she plopped herself down onto the seat beside me and placed it between us, already reaching for a handful.

"Okay," she proclaimed. "How did I know? Well, it wasn't really that hard to figure out? I didn't really *know* you until a few weeks ago, but I'd seen you around school. Before last year, you were *different*. Shy, yeah, but not isolated. You wore more makeup, did your hair, you were in drama club. Then last year, you just changed. You started wearing baggier clothes and you were always by yourself, like you didn't want anyone to notice you. And when we found the stuff on Griffin's search history and then Elizabeth Monner, I realized how much you looked like his type. Your crush . . ."—she swallowed, eyes searching mine—"it made you an easy target. But it didn't make it your fault."

I barely glanced over at her, my eyes beginning to water and the muscles in my face going tight. "You knew I had a crush on him?"

"I think everyone kind of knew. But Kolby pretty much confirmed it when I ran into him the other day. He looked really upset, and when I asked why, he basically admitted he felt like an idiot for kissing the girl he already knew liked his best friend."

"It happened after the Super Bowl last year. The . . ."—I made some sort of vague gesture with my hands but she understood it anyway, nodding as she listened—"not Kolby kissing me. Griffin invited me to this party with him and I snuck out to go. And it just *happened*, and I didn't know what to do. So I didn't do anything. I didn't fight or scream, I just let it happen. And maybe I shouldn't have? Maybe someone would've heard me if I'd screamed more."

Aniston dumped the handful of popcorn she was holding back into the bag. "Or he could've done something seriously bad to keep you quiet."

"But then maybe things would be different? It didn't stop after the party. He sent me letters and text messages, always wanting to know where I was or who I was with. And one day, it got really bad," I told her, feeling it in my throat when my voice cracked on the word. "It happened right before Elizabeth Monner went missing, and I think he killed her because he couldn't find me."

I closed my eyes for a moment, feeling tears soak my eyelashes, letting out a shaky breath through my nose.

She leaned over, toppling the bag of popcorn and scattering its contents onto the carpet and across our thighs as her arms wrapped around me. "It wasn't your fault. It really wasn't, Clara."

A few moments later, she pulled away, laughing awkwardly at the mess. We didn't really speak after that, both of us grasping handfuls of greasy popcorn and dumping them back into the bag before leaving the theater. But we didn't need to say anything more.

We'd already said it all.

As we walked out into the parking lot, I noticed a woman dressed in a blue parka with the hood pulled over her face. Standing in front of a telephone pole, a handful of papers clutched in one hand and a stapler in another, she stapled one of the papers to the pole. I realized it was a picture of Elizabeth Monner, the word *Missing* looming over her—her mom was out there in the cold, looking for answers, just like we were.

I knew she'd probably kept her daughter's room the same, like Mrs. Tomlin had, in a state of limbo. A world where she still expected someone to come home and sleep on that unmade bed or wear the clothes left on the floor. If she took them away, then it meant Elizabeth wouldn't need them anymore.

And then I felt myself getting upset with the one person I knew probably wasn't even involved—Emily never even knew about Elizabeth Monner or her disappearance or that I thought Griffin was responsible for it—but I was anyway. I was upset she'd murdered him because if she hadn't, then he would still be here. He could tell Mrs. Monner what he'd done to her daughter. Be arrested for hurting her like he'd hurt me. Spend decades in prison, in a world where no one loved him anymore. He wouldn't be this golden boy everyone still thought he was, but a boy who'd stolen things no one could ever return.

Here, so that if I said something, to anyone, then they could believe me.

It was then, as I watched Elizabeth Monner's mother walk quietly out of the parking lot toward the next telephone pole, that I knew where I had to go.

I had to see Emily.

There was a cool draft coming from one of the vents in the room

147

the correctional officer brought me to, telling me to take a seat. A metal chair sat in front of a wall with a phone attached to it, beside a large window with a chair behind it that I assumed my sister would be sitting in once they brought her in.

Just her. And me.

I heard a door closing in the room behind the glass and saw the correctional officer through the pane. She was in front of him, wearing a beige jumpsuit, handcuffs locked around her wrists connected to a chain that extended around her waist and down to her legs, another set of cuffs around her ankles. Her hair was in a ponytail, swaying behind her as she shuffled into the room, chains clinking together. She almost looked like herself, like the Emily who was kind, sweet, likable. Someone you thought would always do the right thing, even when you didn't.

And then the correctional officer unlocked her handcuffs. I picked up my end of the phone, and she picked up hers.

"Hey." Her voice almost sounded hoarse, but not emotional, more like it wasn't used much anymore. She looked bare and exposed without her makeup on. "I wasn't sure I was going to see you again. I almost thought I accidentally denied you access or something."

"Well, you *are* in prison. It's not like they let you text in here or anything."

She tilted her head back and her eyes widened slightly, but only for a second before she smirked, almost like she thought I'd made a joke. "So what's been going on?"

"Well, Dad left. He and Mom have been arguing so much that he just decided to leave a couple of weeks ago. And Mom is so confused about everything, she can't even live in reality anymore."

"They probably just need some space from each other to cool

off. That's all," she said, like she was trying to reassure me, but all it did was bother me. She was acting like none of their problems were caused by what she'd done, like our parents were a normal couple experiencing normal marital issues. "What else has been going on? Are you in the school musical again?"

I nodded slowly. "I'm one of the background fairies in *Shrek*."

"Not the lead?"

"I missed the deadline."

"You'll probably still blow everyone else out of the water. You can hold those long notes better than anyone. I bet Mrs. Foley will ask you to switch to Fiona in a couple of weeks."

I swallowed around a lump steadily forming in my throat, glancing down at the phone cord against my arm. It seemed so unbelievable to me that we were talking about the high school's musical so casually with a plate of bulletproof glass between us, pretending like it—along with the jumpsuit, clinking chains, and Griffin Tomlin's murder—wasn't even there.

"I doubt it. I don't think anyone really wants to see me front and center onstage."

She frowned at me, like she actually couldn't understand this. "Why?"

I shot her a look, glancing away after my vision started to blur. "Look where you are. What you did." The muscles in my throat tightened, constricting around the words I was going to say. "Why did you have to kill him, Emily?"

"What?"

"What did you think it was going to do, Emily? It didn't fix anything, it made everything so much worse. The Tomlins are planning some *thing* for his birthday because they see *him* as this victim."

"What are you—"

"And you . . ." My shoulders fell as I let out a breath. "You're in jail, and you could go to prison for a really long time. I never wanted that, no matter what Griffin Tomlin did. And now I'm alone, because I'm lying to everyone about what happened."

"I don't know what you're talking about."

"Oh," I said with a laugh, shaking my head. "Right, they're recording this. Can't say anything that could get you convicted, right?"

"Is that what you're trying to do?"

I stared at her, incredulous. "No! But if that's all you care about, then—just . . . whatever." I slammed the phone down on the hook and stood up.

Through the glass, I could still hear her muffled voice. "Hey, Clara. Come on, just hang on a second."

But I didn't.

Instead I left her, alone. Just like she'd left me.

Somehow I ended up at Kolby's, my finger pressed against the doorbell. As the door unlocked, I caught a glimpse of myself, my complexion blotchy and my eyes somewhat swollen, and I wondered if maybe I shouldn't have come straight here from the jailhouse.

But then the front door opened, and that all disappeared as he blinked at me, warm brown eyes holding a look of surprise, before he stepped outside. He wasn't wearing any shoes, just a pair of black socks, like he had the morning he'd found me outside. He looked nervous and uncomfortable but concerned. Concerned for me.

The only person who was. And, suddenly, I knew I wouldn't regret this later.

I perched myself on the toes of my boots, the snow-dusted porch slick beneath my feet, but I didn't care anymore about slipping or even falling, because he was right there, his hand finding its way to the curve of my back. I brought my hands to his face, leaned closer and pressed my lips against his.

A second later, I felt him kiss me back.

chapter seventeen

before

The orange flames of the campfire glowed between us, my gaze numbly tracking the burnt hot dog he held over the fire, skin black and bubbling. My dad clapped him on the shoulder as he passed him, chewing on a bite of his own burnt hot dog. "Now that's how a man likes his hot dogs, burnt to a crisp."

Griffin laughed. "That's just well done!"

I felt his eyes glancing up, away from the fire and across it, to where I sat with a Styrofoam plate holding some pieces of homegrown cucumber I'd barely touched. I'd only grabbed them because my mom had started asking me if I was okay. My fingernails peeled at the green skin and pressed down on the white seeds. Out of the corner of my eye, I caught Kolby staring at my plate, so I stopped and put it on the ground, bringing my knees back to my chest.

He was *there*.

He was *here*.

He reached into a package of jumbo marshmallows, ribbing Kolby about how he liked his s'mores without chocolate, just graham crackers and a burnt marshmallow. "It's just not right," he told him, dramatically acting repulsed as he watched Kolby eating his chocolate-less s'more. It was like he was trying to impress me with how funny he could be. "It's like eating pizza without cheese. You only do it if you're allergic to dairy."

My eyes focused on the flames of the fire, I heard him say my name. I looked up, and bright ocean blue was waiting for me, the flames twirling under his chin. He was smiling and it looked so genuine it hurt, like staring into the sun.

"Clara," he repeated. "Do you want a s'more?" He held up the s'more he'd made earlier, white marshmallow melting off the side and chocolate sticking to the edge of his thumb.

"No, thanks," I said, looking back to the fire. He was quiet then. It wasn't until I looked up that I realized his silence wasn't what I wanted.

No one else would've thought he looked angry—maybe bemused or even concerned, but not angry, not defied—but I did, because I'd seen that look before. That storm settling into the waters, that rush of anger that seemed to come and go like waves lapping onto a shore. Then it slipped back under the tide until he looked normal again, even to me.

I tightened my arms around my legs and held my breath until I finally heard him speak, with a theatrical sense of disgust in his voice as he asked Kolby, "No, seriously. How can you eat that? It's an insult to all humankind. That's just *wrong*."

I got up from my lawn chair and walked over to the cotton candy machine one of our neighbors had brought, watching the cotton-like baby-pink candy spin. Emily was picking a piece off her cotton candy stick when she looked over at me. "What's up with you?"

"Nothing," I said, shrugging. "How's the cotton candy?"

"Good." She took another bite, holding the stick out to me. "Try it. I don't think it actually tastes like bubblegum, though."

I shook my head. "I don't want any. I think I'm probably just going to go inside."

She made a face. "We haven't even set off the illegal fireworks yet!"

"I can see them from inside. Besides, I don't feel like hanging out right now."

"Why not? There's a bunch of food and Griffin Tomlin is right over there," she whispered, winking as she looked over at him, still lamenting Kolby's chocolate-less s'more. I resisted the urge to flinch. "Tonight could be your night to finally make a move."

I looked away, crossing my arms. "I don't want to make a *move*. I just want to go."

She stared at me for a moment, her brow furrowing, before her features suddenly relaxed. "Okay, but please don't." She pouted, her gaze looking out over the backyard brimming with our neighbors—some roasting marshmallows over the campfire, others playing ladder golf, a few more bringing out grocery bags of sparklers. "You're right, this is boring, so please don't leave me here alone with these people. You know the second you leave, everyone's going to start asking, *Where's Clara, oh, she must be going through that sullen teenage girl phase.*"

I sighed, even though I knew she was probably right. My parents would definitely notice if I went inside at only seven in the evening and missed the rest of the barbecue. "Fine, I'll stay." I pinched off a piece of her cotton candy. "You're right. It doesn't taste like bubblegum."

The distant sound of fireworks crackled and exploded in the sky as I spied the occasional burst of red or blue on the dimming horizon over our neighbors' houses. I stood near the fold-out snack table with its checkered tablecloth fluttering in the warm summer night's breeze, held down by pans of hot dogs and bowls of fruit salad.

Griffin was still at the campfire, talking with Emily, relaxed in his lawn chair and nodding at something she was saying while she swatted a mosquito on her leg.

My scars itched as I glanced over at them, and a part of me wanted to come between them. But I remembered the look in his eyes earlier and the threat he'd whispered into my ear that night, and I was afraid. Afraid enough to stay by the table and only watch from afar.

"Hey."

I blinked and turned to see a hand snaking into the bag of potato chips in front of me. Kolby stood behind me with a paper plate in his other hand.

I nodded and took a step back, assuming he just wanted me to move so he could get to the chips.

"You all right?" he asked, his voice low, as he dumped a handful of chips onto his plate. "You're quieter than usual." He said this as if it was an explanation. "And you were doing that thing with the cucumbers."

I shrugged, looking away from his eyes. "I'm fine," I replied.

There was a pause before he responded, "Okay," in a way that sounded barely convinced, a tone specifically designed for when you know someone is lying and you want them to know it too.

I looked over my shoulder and I saw Griffin staring at us, his gaze controlled and narrow, the muscles in his jaw tight. I almost thought maybe the hatred was directed at more than just me, his eyes finding Kolby beside me.

He held that glare until Kolby looked over, his brow furrowing when he saw Griffin staring at us. "What?"

Griffin's eyes softened slightly before he retorted, a slight edge in his voice, "Nothing."

It was nearly midnight before everyone left our house. Everyone except for the Tomlins anyway.

Mr. Tomlin was behind me, helping my father disassemble the ladder golf equipment, and Griffin, Brandon, and Kolby were all gathering lawn chairs, their voices occasionally carrying throughout the yard as they asked which person each chair belonged to. Emily had a trash bag in one hand and was filling it with the garbage scattered in the grass.

I walked away from everyone else, my skin sweaty and hot since I was still in my sweatshirt. I grabbed one of the trash bags slumped against the railing of the deck and headed for the front yard. I felt a hand brush against my elbow and I almost jerked back at the touch.

"Hey, sweetie," my mom said, not seeming to notice my jumpiness. "Thanks for helping clean up." When I just nodded and shot her a tight smile, she frowned somewhat, brushing my hair back behind my ear. "You feeling okay? You barely got up from your chair all night."

I nodded. "Yeah, I'm fine. Just cramps."

"Why didn't you tell me? I would've got you some medicine."

I gave her a look. "Mom, I'm almost seventeen. I don't think I need to ask you anymore."

She smiled, nodding. "I know, I know. Okay, how about you take that out to the curb and then go inside. We can take care of everything else out here." She kissed me on the forehead and then went back to the kitchen to wash dishes.

It wasn't until I reached my mailbox that I heard someone jogging, flip-flops smacking against heels, then on pavement, behind me. I clenched my fingers around the trash bag when the sound stopped.

"Clara," Griffin breathed. "I've been trying to talk to you. Did you get my letters?"

My teeth were gritted so tightly that my jaw ached as I faced away from him, but I didn't say anything, even though a part of me knew I should've. I should've calmed him down with reassurance that I'd got his letters, they were very sweet, thank you. But I couldn't.

"Seriously, what is up with you? You can't even tell me if you got them? Do you know how many girls want to be with me, Clara? Are so jealous of you right now? But you think you're too good for me, don't you? Think Kolby can give it to you like me? Because he can't. The dude doesn't even have his own car. I have to drive his sorry—"

"Clara?" Emily said.

My fists relaxed slowly as I heard her calling out from the side of the house, and his voice stopped, angered and frustrated and now severed.

I dropped the trash bag beside the mailbox and turned around, seeing that Emily was standing by the corner of the house, glancing between us. I realized my lips throbbed from biting them so hard.

"You guys okay?" she asked.

"Yeah, fine."

I slipped inside the house, closing the front door with my back. When it shut, I let out a breath I hadn't realized I was holding.

chapter eighteen

My father called me twice after I'd visited Emily, but I hadn't answered either of the calls. I wasn't sure if he knew about what I'd said to her, or that I'd even visited her, but I wasn't that interested in finding out. He was on Emily's side, always, and it seemed like the more he clung to that, the further away he was from me.

"Maybe you should talk to him," Aniston said as I looked down at my phone, my father's name on the screen as it rang. I pressed the Decline button. "Or not, apparently. Come on. You don't know he's mad. He could just want to check up on you."

"He's mad. He has to be. He wouldn't call if he wasn't."

Aniston rolled her eyes. "Talk. To. Your. Father," she said. "And your mother. And your sister. And your boyfriend. You know what? Talk to everyone. Seriously. You need help. No one keeps this many secrets. It's weird."

I made a face, but I felt somewhat exposed. "I don't keep that many secrets," I said. "Just the standard hidden motives behind the murder my sister committed. Not that many."

"They'll believe you. I did. And your family will too. So could your crush-turned-boyfriend, Kolby Rutledge. Maybe it won't be so hard for him to believe you! What if he knows things he doesn't know he knows? Like, you tell him and then, all of a sudden, all those things that seemed kinda weird to him make sense? And even if they don't, he's dating *you*! And he's desperate to understand everything and you might not think that because he's not going all 'Aniston' on you, but he *is*."

I glanced over to him on the piano bench, practicing one of the music numbers while Mrs. Foley stood behind him, squinting at the sheet music. He'd told me earlier he thought if he joined, then maybe I would consider it too.

"It's not just Kolby," I told Aniston. "It's everyone. They all loved him, even if he didn't deserve it, and now they're suffering for something they probably won't even believe he did."

Griffin told me it was my fault that night, and that would be what everyone else thought too. I'd snuck out of the house to go to a party with him. I'd gone upstairs to a bedroom with him. And when he'd thrust me against the bed, I didn't fight him. So if I'd fought harder or hadn't led him on in the first place, then maybe it wouldn't have happened and he wouldn't have died because of it.

Just then Bex emerged from the corner of the stage, holding a water bottle in her hand. I was waiting for the day she came into the auditorium wearing an oversized sweater, with the cakey look of heavily applied concealer over her eyes.

Aniston saw her too, following my gaze. "If she didn't believe you, then why are you here? I mean, don't get me wrong, she doesn't deserve it, but you did your part. And yet you still joined the school musical, which you were against doing, for her. Why?"

I watched as Bex bit the inside of her cheek, like she did whenever she felt nervous or out of place. "Because," I told her, shrugging. Because I didn't want her to end up like me.

Through my window blinds, I looked to catch a glimpse of a boy I knew from across the street, but this time it wasn't Griffin. Instead of curly black hair and ocean-blue eyes, I was looking for short chestnut hair and earth-brown eyes. I'd seen his dad's car pull into the Tomlins' driveway earlier.

Kolby had arrived there half an hour ago, his eyes finding my house and lingering there for a moment while he waited after knocking on the front door. Then something flickered over the frosted glass panel beside the door and I saw Mrs. Tomlin opening it before inviting him inside. They had met a couple of times recently to discuss the birthday fundraiser for Griffin, but this was the first time I'd seen him go to her house.

A part of me began to worry after twenty minutes that maybe this wasn't just about Griffin's-posthumous-birthday-party-slash-charity-event. Maybe he was asking her the same questions Aniston seemed to think he wanted to ask me.

I remembered what Aniston had said about how he knew so many pieces he didn't realize belonged to the puzzle that would solve everything. Maybe something was beginning to make sense. Griffin and I and our flickering relationship, me standing in the cold after the Super Bowl party, Emily assaulting Griffin before he died.

I was afraid he was beginning to see everything, finally—too many pieces to disregard anymore.

I knew he wouldn't be able to look at me the same way afterward. Something would shift, and he would choose a side. The girl he barely knew or his best friend.

And I knew it wouldn't be my side he found himself on.

It wasn't until almost an hour later that Kolby finally left the house. When I saw him, I went jogging down the stairs, zipping on my coat. He was standing in their driveway, glancing across the street as I came out the front door.

"Hey, more plans?" I asked.

He nodded, squinting slightly as sunlight beamed over his features and he walked toward me. "It's in about two weeks," he groaned. "She's trying to find charities about violence against guys but, as it turns out, there aren't that many of them, so now she's talking about starting one or something. I don't know." He sighed again and then reached for my hand, curling a finger around my pinkie. "Want to grab lunch?"

"It sounds like you're asking me out on a date," I teased.

"Well, yeah," he laughed. "I tried to, like, a couple weeks ago." Then he smiled softly. "Didn't go too well."

I knew then, as I gazed up at him, that Kolby Rutledge wasn't Griffin Tomlin. He never was and never could be. His eyes revealed a nurturing and kindhearted earth, while Griffin's had exposed the violent crashes of a storm at sea. And when I leaned forward, his lips found my own.

I heard it a moment later, the sound that caused him to tense under my touch and his lips to retract from mine. A front door opening. My eyes were so close to his face I could count the number of freckles dotting his nose, but I looked away from him and turned to see my mother, standing on the front porch.

She held the phone in her hand, close to her chest. Her forehead was creased as she glanced between me and Kolby, a frown tugging at the corners of her lips.

Kolby cleared his throat awkwardly and took his hand off my elbow, shoving it into the pocket of his vest.

"Clara," she finally said, her voice tight and strained, as if it was taking everything in her not to say more than just my name, "your father's on the phone. He wants to talk to you."

"I'll call him back later."

"Now, Clara," she told me, her voice lowering in pitch, and I knew she was trying to sound firm, but there was something fraying at the edges, something flustered and confused and even desperate.

I turned to Kolby, without actually looking at him. "I guess I'll see you later."

He just nodded, like he was too afraid to say anything in front of my mother, before going back to his car in the Tomlins' driveway, his cheeks bright red with embarrassment.

I walked back inside and took the phone from my mother, muttering responses to my father's questions as he asked me if I was doing okay, how was school, how were things going at home. I could see my mother's suspicious gaze lingering on me out of the corner of my eye as she sat down on the sofa and quietly pretended to read an old magazine.

A few hours later I found my mother outside, bundled in a thick parka, crouched on the ground in the backyard, using a gloved hand to brush snow away from my father's vegetable garden. The one garden she hadn't touched in months.

Gardening was my mother's solace: planting bulbs, scooping fertilizer, and reading tips on how to keep bugs from eating the leaves. When Emily was arrested, she'd started pulling all the weeds from her garden. My father hadn't understood, had come outside to angrily shout at her between phone calls. But my mother had kept pulling each weed until, finally, my father grabbed a handful and chucked them angrily across the lawn before storming off. But his garden was one neither of them had touched, the remaining vegetable stalks dried and dead and buried beneath snow.

"I just don't see why it has to be *that* boy," she said now, when I tentatively stepped out onto the patio. Her hands worked faster to swipe away the snow, even brushing away some of the dirt that crumbled away from the garden. "There are so many nice boys out there, Clara. So many nice boys you could be happy with. Everything is already complicated enough with dating. Do you honestly think you can have a relationship with him? The kind a young, pretty girl like you should have? No. It's going to be complicated, messy, painful." She heaved out a sigh. "People will talk *so* much, sweetheart. You don't even understand."

I looked up at the pale gray clouds that hid the blue sky away, a secret all to itself. I wished Kolby and I were still like that, a secret kept from everyone, hidden and tucked away, only for us.

"People already talk, Mom," I groaned. "He's, like, one of the only friends I have now. And he doesn't care about it." *It* being that my sister had murdered his best friend. "Can you just come inside? If you're going to lecture me, then we might as well be warm."

She grunted in response, her hands still scratching away at the soil and snow. "You're not seeing things clearly, Clara," she shouted over the wind that blew her hair across her face. "Just because things are fine now doesn't mean they always will be. Things change. *People* change . . . or they start to show you who they really are. But you can't just—"

And then she stopped, her voice abruptly silent within a fraction of a second, as her hand snagged on something in the dirt. I was about to protest when she opened her mouth and screamed. Not words, just a sound that pierced my ears and made me flinch. I skidded on the snow until I stood in front of her. She was gasping, shaking, holding her hands to her chest.

"What?" I asked her, my voice already breathless. "What is it? What?" I looked down at the garden, overgrown with dead weeds and leftover mulch.

That was when I saw it.

I stumbled backward, nearly falling into the snow. It poked through the earth, taunting and unmoving and caked in dirt.

A small human hand.

chapter nineteen

before

I showered after the Tomlins finally left, taking their Tupperware containers and lawn chairs with them. I scrubbed my face and then washed the scent of smoke from my body, feeling as if somehow he was there, his odor touching my skin and lingering in my hair.

I dumped my clothes into the washing machine. He'd never touched me, had barely even spoken to me before I took the trash out to the curb and he'd found me there, but I still felt his fingers scratching at my thighs and his palm pressed against the back of my head. I felt his breath on my neck and his words lodged in my ear and the taste of his tongue in my mouth. He was everywhere, inside and out, and no matter how many times I washed my body or brushed my teeth or tore the letters he wrote me, he was still there. Like a stain that refused to be washed out, a wound that refused to heal.

I decided to run my clothes through the washing cycle one more time, convinced he'd managed to touch me without my noticing. I was pouring a capful of detergent into the machine when I noticed Emily standing in the doorframe, her hair messily tied in a bun, wearing a tank top that showed the white tan lines against her shoulders.

"Those clothes are already clean," she told me.

"They still smell like smoke."

When I tried to walk past her, she crossed her arms and took a step to the side, her bare foot slapping against the tile as she stared at me, green eyes narrowing slightly. "What's going on with you? You're acting all weird, and I mean more than usual. Did you and Griffin—?"

"Emily," I sighed.

"Couples argue, Clara," she told me, as if she had any idea of what a normal, healthy argument between a couple would be like. I stared back at her, willing her to move. I didn't want to hear her talking about Griffin and me like that, like we were a forbidden secret she'd discovered in our driveway. "There is always one way to get a guy to shut up about his insecurities." She smiled and then winked as I felt bile building in my throat.

"We're not together," I said before shouldering my way past her, just as the washing machine started turning behind me. She followed me through the hallway and up the stairs, not saying a word. I was grabbing the doorknob to my bedroom when I felt her fingers clutching the fabric of my sweatshirt.

"Clara, come on."

Her bright blue fingernails with white dots cinched around my sweatshirt, her grip tugging me backward, and I wanted her to let me go. I wanted fingers to stop gripping around me. I wanted hands to stop touching me. I wanted voices to stop saying my name. I wanted eyes to stop staring at me. I wanted whatever it was holding me, bringing me closer and closer, to just let me go.

I turned around and wrenched my arm away from her, watching as she stumbled backward.

"Just leave me alone!" I slammed my bedroom door behind me, and the sound echoed in my ears as I leaned against it, closing my eyes. I heard my father's voice from downstairs.

"Hey, what was that?" he called.

I could still hear my sister breathing outside my door as she hesitated before calling out, "Nothing!"

It was only after I heard her bedroom doorknob turning that I realized my phone was vibrating on my dresser. I opened my eyes, seeing the screen shining its white glow against the wall.

I waited until my sister's bedroom door closed before walking over to my dresser. When I picked up my phone, my eyes followed the trail of text messages that scrolled down the screen. Some of them were in all caps, some of them were questions or demands, some of them threatening, some of them loving.

All of them were from Griffin Tomlin.

    hey, can u talk??
    hello
    clara?
    seriously, u gonna start ignorin me now?
    come on u i kno u c me
    ur thinkin about me
    u were starin @ me all nite just like u used to cuz u want me
    u need me
    kolby can't give it to u like i can

answer me, slut

SLUT

SLUT

SLUTSLUTSLUTSLUTSLUT!!!!!!!

In some of the text messages, he described to me what he would do the next time he saw me. Either in his backyard, sitting on the edge of his pool with my *hairy, ugly, disgusting* legs dangling in the water, or at school with my *ugly, slut crazy eyes* watching him. He would lead me away from everyone, and he could because I wanted him so desperately I'd do *anything* he wanted. He would grab my throat, squeeze until he heard *choking sounds.* Watch me collapse to the ground, gasping for breath. He would use the handle of his pocketknife to punch me in the throat so I couldn't scream after he got sick of the sound, but he would savor it first because one day he'd miss it. Because I would be *dead.*

The phone slipped between my limp fingers as I frantically tried to keep scrolling, even though I could hardly breathe, as if the knife handle he'd mentioned had already collided with my throat. I stumbled against the edge of my bed, the springs creaking. Bile rose in my throat and I vomited on the carpet, coughing and choking, spit stringing from my lips as I realized he could see my window from his house. Even though the blinds were drawn, I still felt as if he could've seen through them and watched me as I heaved onto my bedroom floor, puke splattering onto my phone with his text messages still on the screen.

"Clara? Are you okay?"

Light from the hallway spilled into my darkened bedroom as Emily stood in the doorframe, her hand lingering on the doorknob before she stepped into the room.

"Ew, it's on your phone."

She picked up my phone with the edges of her fingers, carefully, her nose wrinkled and eyes narrowing as she glanced down at it before her revolted gaze softened. The rigidity in her body gave way, her shoulders relaxed, and the bridge of her nose smoothed. She scrolled down the screen quickly, the glow reflected in her dark pupils as she read, swiping through the droplets of vomit, neither noticing nor caring. "Clara."

The bitter taste of bile was still heavy on my tongue. "Can we go somewhere? Anywhere but here."

She went and got some paper towels and helped me clean up the puddle of puke, while explaining to me that if either one of our parents came into my bedroom and found vomit and my bed empty, there would probably be police cars in the driveway whenever we got back. She handed me some fresh clothes and when I changed, I glanced over my shoulder at the blinds dangling in front of my window, in front of where he would've been able to see me if the blinds hadn't prevented him.

We'd driven a couple of towns over when she pulled into the drive-through of a Burger King.

"Greasy food helps everything," she informed me as she pulled up to the illuminated menu on the side of the building. *Everything* apparently included neighboring stalkers.

She ordered two Whoppers and a large onion rings. "I know it's your favorite," she whispered as the tired employee told her through the crackling speaker to pull up to the first window. I nodded, forcing a small smile, but I still tasted the bile in my mouth, and it reminded me of the messages on my phone, currently tucked into the pocket of Emily's shorts. It made eating onion rings the last thing I wanted to do.

After an employee gave her our drinks, she handed one to me. A Sprite. "Take a sip," she instructed me. "It'll get the throw-up taste out of your mouth." The window opened again and they handed a brown paper bag to Emily, starting to tell her to have a good night when she interrupted by asking for ketchup, *lots* of ketchup.

Another one of my favorites.

The smell of the deep-fried food filled the car as my sister drove farther away from home, the grease-stained bag sitting between us as she hummed along to the radio and occasionally lifted a hand off the steering wheel to rummage through the bag for an onion ring.

After nearly twenty minutes, she turned onto a gravel road. The passenger side dipped into a pothole and I almost banged my head on the window, and Emily had to grip the Burger King bag with one hand to stop it from spilling.

I was about to ask her what she was doing when I noticed a building in the dark, finally caught by the headlights, guarded by oak trees and with rows of fruit trees lined up behind it. Its wooden boards were bent inward, as if it were collapsing in on itself, and the doors were agape. Red paint was peeling off the wood, especially around the entrance, and I realized it was an abandoned barn.

I turned to her, watching as she pulled the key from the ignition and the headlights were absorbed by darkness. She smiled. "Welcome to the greatest place no one will ever find," she said to me.

~

Not exactly no one, apparently.

As we approached the barn, Emily using the flashlight app on her phone to light our way, I saw crushed cigarette stubs, dented bottle caps, and small shards of tinted glass in the grass. In the barn, there were a couple of empty beer bottles scattered on the floor, and a fleece blanket with dirt and twigs clinging to it flung over the rails of a stall. Emily grabbed it without hesitation and spread it over the concrete floor, then she set down the Burger King bag and sat, cross-legged, beside it.

When she patted the spot next to her, I wondered if it was a shadow or actual dust that floated through the air. "Come on. Sit already. You're making me nervous."

I slowly inched down onto the blanket after she patted it a second time and reached for a ketchup packet, grasping it by the tip and shaking it. I still didn't feel like eating, but I wanted something to do with my hands.

"When did he start going insane?" she asked around a mouthful of Whopper. "Is that why you were so weird today? Being exceptionally quiet at the barbecue, arguing with him in the driveway, yelling at me . . ."

I knew she was trying to make a joke, but I just stared down at the ketchup packet and said, "Sorry."

"In the texts, he said he wanted to give it to you . . . again. Did you guys sleep together and he got clingy or something?"

"It doesn't matter," I told her. "He probably doesn't even mean it. He saw me flirting with his friend. He's just upset about that. That's it."

"Most guys don't threaten to chop up their girlfriend if she has a conversation with his best friend. Which is what I'm guessing actually went down, since you don't even know how to flirt."

She lifted an onion ring and took a bite, wiping her hand on her bare leg. I tried to shoot her a look, even though she wasn't wrong. "Did he already hurt you?"

"Griffin isn't Wilson Westbrooke," I retorted.

"So that would be a yes," she commented. "What did he do?"

"Emily," I said, shaking the ketchup packet faster.

"What did he do?"

"Nothing," I said forcefully.

"Why are you protecting him?" she asked me incredulously, plopping her burger onto its wrapper, smoothed out over the blanket. She reached across and snatched the ketchup packet from my hand and then launched it over my head. I heard it collide with the wall behind me.

"Did you even read any of those texts? The things he said he wanted to do to you. And yet here you sit, defending his creepy—"

"I'm not defending him!" My voice pierced the quiet of the barn, slicing through her own voice and accusations. I got up from the blanket. "I thought after Wilson, you would just *get* it."

"Clara!"

I stormed out of the barn and found my way back to the car, slumping against the side, my shoulders against the warmed metal of Black Beauty. I felt a lump forming in my throat as I swallowed, the disgusting taste combination of Whopper and vomit lingering in my mouth as peepers croaked somewhere in the distance, beyond the orchard.

The sky was dark and vast, glittering with thousands of stars, and it felt so quiet and so untouched that it was hard to believe that somewhere out there was a boy, waiting for me. I almost understood it here, with the stubbed cigarette butts and cracked beer bottles, in *the greatest place no one would ever find*. It was tempting to stay here, camped out on the old blanket, listening to the distant firecrackers in the starlit sky. Somewhere so quiet and so vast seemed untouchable, even by Griffin Tomlin, as if his legs could just never bring him this far.

Then a second later, I heard Emily's battered flip-flops smacking against her feet, saw her flashlight bobbing my way. I could already see her lips parting, and before she even started, I wanted her to stop.

"Just don't, okay?" I whispered as she grasped the handle of one of the back doors, yanking it open and carelessly tossing the fast food bag against the back seat. I noticed, out of the corner of my eye, the lit screen of my phone in her hand as she stared at me and, somehow, I knew what she was about to say next. I leaned the back of my head against the car and closed my eyes, my eyelashes beginning to wet as I heard her voice.

"He's still texting you," she told me quietly. And then, "He said what happened."

I heard distant fireworks exploding into a series of colored embers, ignited against the darkness of the cloudless sky. She bit down on both of her lips and cast a hesitant glance toward the phone, held in both of her hands, and when I tried to peer over her blue-and-white painted fingernails, she tilted it away from me. I blew out a sigh, turning away as the sound of another crackling firework filled the air, nearly echoing my pulse beating in my ears. I closed my eyes and heard her swallowing, and then her voice, curious and quiet and almost—maybe—betrayed.

"Why didn't you tell me?" Another explosion followed her words.

"You wouldn't believe me," I said, my voice wavering. "I mean, he's Griffin Tomlin. Who would believe that he would ever?"

And for one aching, raw, piercing moment, I felt it again. That same tingling of shock in the places that his lips had forcefully kissed or where his fingers had grabbed too intensely. That same lingering sense of denial, of doubt, that I was too inexperienced to know how sex was really supposed to be. That same betrayal that iced through my heart and poured into my veins when he whispered his threat to kill me, fingernails clawing at my skin as he tore my jeans from my body.

That same earth-shattering knowledge that the boy I had spent so much of my life loving had devastated me in the worst way possible.

"Clara," I heard her say into the heavy, warm midnight air that was causing the skin beneath my arms to dampen with sweat. Another firework exploded behind us, followed by another round of distant laughter and shouts. Beside me, a much softer and more somber voice spoke. "How did it happen?"

"I snuck out of the house," I admitted, "after the Super Bowl. He asked me to go to this party with him, and I thought that . . . I thought I would finally *know*, after months of wondering, if he might have, for some reason, liked me. But when we got there, he just . . . he just told me to drink a bottle of beer and took me upstairs . . . and—and that was it.

"I can't even sleep on my stomach anymore because every time I try, I feel his hand against the back of my head. When I shower, I run the water scalding hot so the mirror will fog before I take my clothes off because I can't look at the scars anymore. And . . . and he sends me gifts. Necklaces and fairy-tale books and an *Into the Woods* CD." And then I heard it, another text message vibrating from my phone within her pocket. "Give me my phone," I mumbled.

"You don't want to," she warned, but I reached forward, my hand snaking around her waist, and gripped the top of my phone before her fingers clenched around my forearm. Her fingernails dug into my skin as I yanked the phone away from her.

"Clara, Clara, seriously. Clara, stop." Blue-and-white fingernails frantically tried to swipe at the phone, her fingers leaving smudges against the screen. I held my phone above her head. As I scrolled through the text messages he'd sent me—his tone softening, and the heart emoji ending almost every one of his recent messages, apologizing, telling me he was drunk, he would never hurt me—I suddenly knew.

He'd never said anything about what had happened. He'd never texted about what he'd done. He'd never mentioned it. Not once.

He said what happened, she told me.

And she lied.

And the next thing I knew, I was shoving past Emily and grabbing the handle of the driver's side door. I reached for the keys on the console and listened to her muffled shouts echoing behind me as I started the engine and drove away.

chapter twenty

A couple of middle-aged investigators brushed away the rest of the dirt, just like my mother had, but gingerly, carefully, methodically, from the body in our back garden. They paused every few minutes for crime-scene photographers to do their work, adorned in their white bodysuits with blue covers over their shoes. Everyone but the detectives and police officers guarding the corners of the yellow crime-scene tape was dressed like that, preserved, almost as if they didn't want one piece of our backyard, of the *crime* scene, to taint them, even though I knew it was the other way around.

My mother kept touching her hand, like she could still feel the fingers there, snagging against hers. We stood there, peering over the crime-scene tape from the street since we weren't allowed in the house, watching as they slowly brought up the body. It took them hours to do, even though I heard one of the officers say it was a shallow grave, just deep enough to not be discovered too easily.

Over the course of seven hours, during which my mother massaged her fingertips compulsively, I managed to overhear the detectives speaking to one another. The hand belonged to a young woman buried, decomposed, and half-clothed. One of them said her femur bone was almost split in half, like whoever had killed her tried to dismember her but gave up halfway through her thigh. *Might not have been strong enough,* the detective speculated. I wondered if he meant physically or emotionally. She didn't have any identification on her, so they called her Jane Doe.

When they finally lifted her out, flashlights pointed at the grave as they worked slowly, carefully, delicately, I caught glimpses of the black decayed skin on bones between the frames of the coroner and his assistants. And then, just as my mother snaked her arms around me, telling me not to watch, I saw it, dangling over their forearms.

Faded strawberry blond hair, matted with dirt, and I knew.

They'd finally found Elizabeth Monner.

My mother and I were sitting together at the police station, her eyes glancing back and forth from the detectives to me. "Do you have an idea of who the young woman we found might be?" one of the detectives asked. I recognized him as Detective Marsh from when Emily was arrested.

I hesitated before answering. "I heard of this girl in Buffalo who went missing. Her name was Elizabeth Monner. My friend is sort of an amateur detective and she was kind of investigating it."

"Do you know why?"

I shook my head. "It's just a hobby of hers. She wants to be a crime journalist, so I guess she's practicing or something."

He nodded. "Okay, did Emily ever mention knowing Elizabeth Monner?"

"No."

"Did Emily ever pay any special attention to your father's vegetable garden? Getting upset whenever anyone touched it or anything?"

"Emily never cared about gardening or anything like that." I watched as he wrote this down. "Why do you think she did it?" I asked him. "Just because the body was buried there doesn't mean she did it. Someone could've snuck into the backyard in the middle of the night and buried her."

The detective just stared at me for a moment. "Do you have any reason to believe someone would do that?"

I hesitated, then shook my head. "No, I don't."

"Well, then, neither do we. So we check out everyone who was living here at the time and rule them out first. If your sister's innocent of this crime, then the evidence will point to that."

I nodded, even though I wasn't convinced. And it didn't look like Detective Marsh was either.

"Should we..." I was pacing in Aniston's bedroom, anxious. "Should we tell them about Griffin? Or do we just let them ... figure it out or something?"

I felt paranoid, as if I had been backed into a corner by him, so many months after his death. He was still terrorizing me, reminding me of what I would've been. A dead girl in my father's vegetable garden. Then I felt like vomiting again, knowing she'd been out there. That he'd left her there for me, like a cat proudly bringing his owner a mangled bird.

"I don't think we should tell them about Griffin. Not yet. We should just see where they go with it. They might find other suspects."

"What other suspects? It has to be Griffin! You said it had to be Griffin when she was missing. She was in my backyard. It has to be him!"

I knew it had to be him. He wanted me to find her body, but he died before I could.

Before he could taunt me with her half-naked and battered corpse and remind me that I was next.

Aniston blinked, her eyes focused on the carpet, before she finally muttered, "Right."

We were staying at Aniston's place until the police released ours the next day, since most of our relatives lived upstate and none of our neighbors were speaking to us anymore. Her mother's minivan had pulled up alongside the crime scene, but this time, her mom was actually driving. She was a short woman, with curly brown hair and a thick accent. Her name was Francisca, we soon learned, after she'd ushered us into the car and finally convinced my mother to come spend the night at her house—and it didn't take long to realize where Aniston got her chattiness from. During the ten-minute ride over, Francisca not only explained that they had changed their last name from Hernandez to Hale after her husband's murder, but that she couldn't get the air conditioner in her car to shut off, and that she had been preparing pozole for dinner.

My father came over later in the evening, to hug me, ask if I was okay. He asked for my mother, but I told him she was asleep—when I really knew she was still awake, her hair damp after her third shower that night. For a moment he looked like he was going to protest but then he shook his head.

"They're going to blame your sister for this," he complained, heading into the kitchen and opening cupboards, shifting around packages of instant oatmeal and peanut butter before grabbing a coffee mug. I thought about saying something—since it wasn't our house—but all I did was watch.

"You don't think Emily killed her, right, Dad?"

"It doesn't really matter if she did or didn't," he said. "She's the only person in Shiloh charged with a violent crime, let alone murder. They could find a body on the other side of town with all sorts of evidence pointing to someone else and they'd still pin it on her."

The scars between the spaces of my ribs stung slightly as I heard this. I nodded, glancing down at the counter and gliding my fingertips over the surface until I realized he'd never answered my question. But before I could consider this, I heard the doorbell ringing.

I didn't hear Aniston or her mom coming, so I ambled out of the kitchen and into the hallway while my dad just stood there, only glancing over his shoulder once before turning back to the coffee maker.

I opened the door, expecting to find a police officer or detective behind it, but instead it was Kolby.

"Hey," he breathed into my ear as his arms wrapped around me and pulled me against his body. His fingers stroked the back of my head, burying into my hair. "Aniston texted me. Are you okay? You weren't—did you find . . . ?"

I shook my head against his chest, his voice vibrating beside my cheek and the steady rhythm of his heartbeat—accelerated, but there, strong and echoing—in my ear as I allowed myself to relax into him. "I was there, but my mom found her." I felt a few strands of his hair, raised in a cowlick on the back of his head, grazing against my knuckles. "She didn't do it, Kolby."

"Clara—"

"I know, I know." I let out a breath, nuzzling my face farther into his chest, waiting until I heard the echo of his heartbeat again. "But she didn't do it."

The floorboards creaked behind me, and my father loudly cleared his throat. Kolby's arms loosened around me, an embarrassed flush coming over his cheeks as he took a step back. "Hi, sir."

I stifled the urge to smile at this. Kolby had never called my father *sir* before in his life.

My father just stood there, steam curling around the rim of his mug and his eyes darting from Kolby to me before he nodded, exhaling, and then returned to the kitchen.

Kolby kissed my forehead before he left, disappearing into his father's car and then—speedily—driving down the street. I watched until the red glare of his taillights faded into the darkness.

I went back to the kitchen, seeing my father standing in front of the kitchen sink, slowly sipping his coffee with his back turned to me. Then he suddenly spoke. "Be careful, Clara Bear."

I didn't know which part of my life he was referring to.

The local news stations and websites heard about the body found in our backyard and started reporting it. By that weekend, it was announced that dental records were able to identify the young female recovered and the police were waiting until the family was notified before making an official statement. The day after, Detective Marsh came to our house and told me I was right. The girl found in my father's garden was Elizabeth Monner.

I pulled into the school parking lot and twisted the keys in the ignition until the rough hum of the engine stopped and the inside of the car went quiet, except for the sound of Kolby's seat-belt buckle clanging against the passenger-side door. I glanced out through the windshield. A few students briefly looked up from their phones or just openly stared, some of their lips moving, asking questions I couldn't hear.

I knew they probably didn't expect to see me today, as if the fact that a dead body had been found in my backyard meant that I would be under house arrest or something.

"They're just going to stare." Kolby's fingers brushed against my knee, giving it a small, reassuring squeeze. "They'll stare and whisper but that's it. You'll be fine." He leaned over the console between us, pressed a quick kiss against my cheek, and then got out of the car.

When I hesitated, he called out, his voice muffled through the windows, "You know they can still see you in the car, right? The only difference is that you'll be *cold*."

I sighed before reluctantly getting out, frowning at him as he smiled, his hand reaching out for mine, threading our fingers together and bringing me forward.

"There you go."

~

Bex smelled like weed, at least according to Aniston during drama practice.

It was something she'd noticed when she was interviewing Bex for an article about the production of *Shrek the Musical* for the school paper. She smelled it on her leather jacket when they'd sat down together in the library, with Bex telling her what it was like to portray such a beloved, strong female character and how itchy the green face paint was.

"You know, he's probably the one giving it to her." She scrunched up her nose, looking up from her phone. "And by *it*, I mean pot. Not anything else, although he's probably giving that to her too, but that's . . . nasty. But I read about it. Guys who hit first and kiss later get their girlfriends hooked on drugs so they become dependent on them. Even if the girl wants to leave him, she can't because he's more than just her boyfriend now. He's her *dealer*. It's kind of ingenious in a really sick, evil, twisted kind of way."

I looked over at her. "Can you even get hooked on pot?"

She shrugged. "I don't know, everyone says something different. The point is, if he supplies her with one drug, he can supply her with another. Like a *really* bad one. Also, it's totally illegal for her to be smoking pot anyway."

Bex stood beside the boy playing Donkey as he laughed at something someone in the orchestra pit said to him. He turned to Bex, maybe to see if she was laughing too, but she was staring down at the floor, her eyes almost dazed. I realized she might have been stoned then. Not just the lingering scent of it clinging to her clothes, but actually *high* at school. Something she never would've done before.

Before she started dating Wilson Westbrooke.

~

I waited for Bex in the hallway outside of the auditorium, leaning against the lockers.

Technically I was waiting for Kolby too, and I felt a sense of uneasiness as I tried to decide what I would tell him if he appeared before she did. I didn't know how to explain to him why her and Wilson Westbrooke's relationship was something I just couldn't force myself to let go of. I couldn't leave her to the boy she thought she knew, who wanted to hurt her more than he wanted to love her.

Bex Underwood was not going to be Clara Porterfield.

Her leather jacket—the one Aniston said smelled like pot— was draped over her forearm as she walked up the worn, carpeted aisle of the auditorium, her green eyes seemingly trained on the scuffed toes of her boots or the lazily tied laces. When she finally looked up and spotted me through the doors, she sighed, and the slow rhythm of her combat boots thudding against the floor stopped.

"Hey, Clara," she said. I ignored the sting of hearing her say my actual name. The name that never felt right coming from her lips. "You going to try and convince me my boyfriend's hitting me again?"

I pushed myself off the lockers, my backpack falling onto the speckled tiles of the floor as she stepped into the hallway.

"It's what he used to do to Emily," I told her. Her eyes avoided me, like if she didn't look at me, then she couldn't hear what I was saying. "She killed a guy who was taller than him, and *stronger*. Don't you think if she were going to kill anyone it would be him? But she didn't because he scared *her* so badly that—"

"Clara, you . . ." She hesitated, her jaw clenched as she looked over her shoulder. "Did you ever think that maybe your sister was the one who scared *him*?"

My mouth opened but no words formed on my tongue.

"She *killed* someone, Clare. You really think that's something a sane, nonviolent person does? She was the one who hit him, the one who scared him. She made him stop hanging out with his friends because she would tell him lies about how they would all try to, like, gang rape her when he wasn't there. Then they would go back to his place and she'd rape him there. She slashed his sister's tires because she was convinced he was sleeping with her."

I stared at her, incredulous, remembering the argument I'd overheard when she was breaking up with him, shouting that the girl he was texting wasn't actually his sister. "Is that what he told you?"

She nodded.

"And you actually believe him?"

Her eyes were fixated on me for a minute, almost in disbelief, and then she laughed humorlessly and shook her head. "Unbelievable," she muttered. "You haven't talked to me in almost a year because you thought I didn't believe you, and now here you are not believing him. You can be such a hypocrite, Clare. I mean, it's what she did to Griffin when she killed him, so why do you think it can't happen to Wilson? Because girls are nice and sweet and innocent and never do anything that awful, and guys are just scumbags who go around defiling young girls, right? Never the other way."

"Bex! I don't believe him because he's a liar, not because he's a guy."

"Bull," she retorted gruffly. "Everything you know about *my* boyfriend comes from a girl who murdered someone in their own backyard." She shook her head. "You know, you and Wilson are a lot more alike than either one of you think. Both of you were banged around by people this sick town loved too much to actually believe either one of you."

She shoved past me, the sound of her combat boots squeaking against the floor, and before I had a chance to say anything in return, I heard Kolby calling out from the auditorium, "Clara! I'll be right there in a minute!"

When I turned back, she was gone and the school doors were swinging shut with a deafening clang.

"Hey," Kolby said as he jogged up to me. "Were you talking to somebody?"

"Yeah. Bex *was* here. But she had to leave."

"She's the girl you brought to all the block parties, right?" I nodded, almost wondering if that was where she'd first met Wilson. Kolby studied my expression as we walked down the hall. "I don't really see you guys hang out anymore. Not even at practices."

"We stopped being friends last year. I don't really want to get into it."

"Okay." For a moment, we both just walked together down the hallway, our shoulders brushing against each other. "So I was thinking. The last, what, two times I've tried to ask you out on a date haven't gone the greatest. But you've already kissed me a couple of times, so if I did ask you out on a date, would you say no again?"

"I don't think so." When he still looked at me, raising his eyebrows, I amended and said, "No. I would not say no."

"Thanks." I almost burst out laughing when he said this, and then he rolled his eyes. "That's not what I—okay, it is but *anyway*. Do you think if I asked you out on a date, your mom would come popping out of one of these lockers or something?"

"It's unlikely."

He nodded. "Okay, so then"—he smiled, reaching for my hand—"want to go see a movie with me tonight?"

I gave his hand a squeeze. "I mean, if you really want to," I teased.

"You look nice, honey."

My mother was standing in front of the kitchen island, a couple of sliced bell peppers grouped together on the corner of her cutting board and a package of mushrooms beside it. Her blond hair was tucked behind her ears, and she was still wearing her scrubs, the ones with cartoon paw prints on the fabric. When I'd first come into the room, she'd looked up and hesitated, and I'd felt somewhat self-conscious, playing with the hemline of the top I'd taken from Emily's closet. I'd almost wanted to hurry back up the stairs to change back into my own personal armor of invisibility.

I tried to remind myself that I had already kind of been on a date with Kolby Rutledge before. But after he'd asked me out on an actual, real date—something not even Griffin had done before the Super Bowl—earlier that afternoon, I'd felt *different*. Like my standard oversized sweater, leggings, and thin layers of mascara and lip gloss weren't enough for that night. A night normal couples had with shared popcorns and armrests. Something other girls would've done.

Something I hadn't done with Griffin.

Something that was completely mine and Kolby's.

And I didn't want to be invisible anymore—not with him anyway.

"Are you going out tonight?" She hadn't mentioned Kolby, or our relationship, since she'd found Elizabeth Monner in the garden a few hours after seeing us together, but I knew she hadn't forgotten about it. I hoped that now, with another murder pinned on Emily, Kolby and I could edge out of her concerns and she'd focus on something that actually deserved her attention.

"Yes," I told her. "I'm just . . . going to wait outside, okay?"

"Clara," she said. "I'm sure that Kolby is a lovely boy, but relationships require more than just attraction. They require work and compromises, and that's just a normal relationship, let alone . . ." She gestured vaguely in the air. "You're just teenagers. Don't you think you both deserve to not have to work so hard at a relationship so young? And it might not be work now but, honey, it will be. Especially when your sister goes to trial."

She sighed as I heard tires slowly crawling up the driveway. "These next few months are going to be tough enough as it is, sweetheart. You don't need to be trying to save your relationship at the same time. It can be too much, even for an adult."

"I know."

I turned around and headed for the front door, listening as the sound of the knife against the cutting board stopped for a moment. She and my father might have chosen their problems over each other, and she thought we were teenage versions of them, but we weren't. We were different. I wasn't going to break us apart out of fear that if I didn't, we'd inevitably find a way to shatter on our own.

~

We'd decided earlier that afternoon to see an action movie. He'd purchased the tickets online, asking if I wanted an aisle or middle seat.

When we entered the warmth of the movie theater, I breathed in the heavy scent of buttered popcorn and reminded myself that this was normal. To walk inside a movie theater with my fingers intertwined with my boyfriend's as his eyes scanned the menu behind the concession stand.

Kolby approached the counter, his hand bringing me with him. "Do you want anything?"

"Just popcorn." I watched as his other hand plucked his wallet from the back pocket of his jeans. "No, put that away," I half-heartedly protested. He ignored me, but I didn't urge any further because a moment later, a deadpan voice spoke to us from across the counter. I recognized it and so did Kolby as he sharply looked up.

"Hey." It was Brandon Tomlin, standing to the side of the cash register, his fingers gripping the edge of the countertop. His eyes, ocean blue just like his younger brother's, took us in, including the fingers laced together at our sides, before he looked back at Kolby.

"What can I get you, Kolby?" he asked, a sigh around his question as Kolby distractedly said *uh* and proceeded to scan the menu again. Even though Brandon wasn't him, I felt a piece of Griffin within him. The curly black hair and the ocean-blue eyes that looked at me, with my shimmery eyeshadow on and my skinny jeans curving to my body—it was as if Griffin were looking at me again. Observing me from across the flickering flames of a campfire or through a crowded hallway at school. And just like that, I regretted agreeing to this, to a date at the movie theater where I knew Brandon Tomlin had worked for years but had forgotten because a boy asked me out.

"I'm . . ." I started to say when I felt both of their eyes on me. My tongue stumbled around the words as I backed up, untangling my hand from his. "I'm going to go . . . find our seats."

I quickly turned around and headed for one of the hallways, the distant but loud soundtracks of other movies ringing in my ears until Kolby's voice hesitantly called out behind me, saying that our movie was playing on the other side of the theater.

Brandon was still working when the movie ended. He was in the carpeted hallway outside of the men's restroom, sweeping up spilled popcorn kernels with a large broom. He glanced over as we walked past him, Kolby offering a small wave, and I looked over my shoulder as Brandon nodded back. I remembered what he'd told me a couple weeks earlier in Aniston's mother's minivan—how he had always felt kind of weird around Brandon, and the time he'd seen him at a party as he led an intoxicated girl from the crowd—and I wondered if maybe that was why his grip around my hand tightened as we walked away.

"Did you get the invitation?" Kolby asked once we'd headed outside.

"What invitation?"

"To his birthday charity thing," he clarified, even though I felt pretty sure I already knew what he meant. When I started to respond, he interjected. "I know, I know, it'll be weird, but it won't be bad. And on the off chance that is it, there'll be a couple of cops from his case there. One stink eye from anyone and those cops will put them in their place. Promise." He smiled at me then, but I looked away as the tires of a truck rolled through slush in front of us, splattering Kolby's pants. He didn't seem to notice.

"Mrs. Tomlin didn't invite me," I told him, and he let out a sigh. "Does she even know you did? I mean, inviting the sister of the girl who killed her son really sounded like a good idea to you?"

"I was thinking more like the girlfriend of the guy whose friend was killed. Completely different."

Maybe he had really convinced himself that all I was now was the girlfriend of the guy whose friend was killed. But I wasn't. And everyone at the party would know it in their bones when they saw me. They wouldn't see what he saw. They would see Emily in me, recognize the color of my hair and the shade of my eyes, and they would never be able to look past my sister. I felt his fingers loosely fitting between mine, gently squeezing, and his lips brushing against my hair as he leaned down and whispered against my skin. His breath warmed my temple as he murmured *please*, the word drifting into my ears.

I thought of him standing in the cemetery, snowflakes in his dark hair, shivering as he looked at the brand-new headstone before I'd threaded my arm through his. It was the one moment that he'd needed me, and now another moment had come.

I closed my eyes and leaned my head against his chest and whispered *okay* into his vest.

chapter twenty-one

before

Griffin was sitting at the table across from us as a waitress delivered a slice of chocolate cake. Peanut butter drizzle oozed over the sponge and a candle pierced the frosting, glowing with a small flame as the waitress held her hand in front of it, singing, "Happy birthday to you . . ."

Soon my parents joined in, and then Emily's mumbled voice echoed the lyrics a second too late. I pretended to smile but it felt like it was about to fall from my lips as I looked over the waitress's arm and found him, sitting with his family and Kolby. Griffin watched me, beaming as he mouthed the ending of the song. *Happy birthday, dear Clara. Happy birthday to you.* And then he quietly clapped along with my family as they told me to blow out my candle.

Make a wish. Don't tell it or else it won't come true.

He disappeared when I closed my eyes. I blew out my candle. Made my wish.

My wish was that I would never see Griffin Tomlin again.

I opened my eyes. It didn't come true.

My mother had spotted them almost half an hour before, sitting at a table across from ours, and she'd waved her hand in the air, grinning, and beckoned them over. Then they'd pushed the tables together, banging the edges and accidentally knocking over a half-empty bottle of soy sauce.

Griffin sat across from me, fumbling comically with his chopsticks before he dropped one and used the other to stab his orange chicken, bringing it to his lips and taking a bite as my father laughed. He was looking at me as he chewed, smiling, and then he said, "Happy birthday, Clara."

"Thanks," I responded quietly, staring down at my cake instead of meeting his eyes.

"Chocolate your favorite flavor?"

I nodded.

He took another bite of his orange chicken, casually speaking around it as it formed a lump under his left cheek. "I hope your wish comes true," he told me, and when I glanced up from the still smoldering candle, gray smoke and the scent of melting wax drifting between us, he winked at me. I could feel the weight of his arms against my waist, lifting me off the ground again, like he had after the musical. I remembered how he'd winked then too, biting off the heel of a Cinderella slipper. How I'd felt suddenly totally different then than I did now.

Emily kept watching him as she swirled the ice in her drink. Sometimes I felt her gaze on me as I used the side of my fork to slice through my cake, even though I knew I wasn't going to eat it. We hadn't really spoken since the night at the barn, after I'd driven back to pick her up a few minutes later. We rode home together in silence and it had lingered over us ever since. Whenever we did speak to each other, it was never about Griffin, but the shared knowledge was still a weight in the air. Unspoken, but hiding behind each of the few words between us. This was the first time we were all together—me, Emily, and Griffin—since she'd found out, and I was almost as scared about what she might do as I was of him.

"Your baby's growing up, Samantha," Mrs. Tomlin said to my mother, smiling over at me. "Soon she's going to be headed off to Julliard or some other prestigious music school to become a big Broadway star."

My mother pretended to cry. "I know, I'm not ready." She touched my cheek with her warm hand, smoothing her thumb over my cheekbone, and smiled softly. Griffin said something as he looked at us, his eyes flickering between my mother and me. I barely heard what it was, but I knew it was about me, to me.

I pulled myself away from my mother and stood up, the back of my chair slamming into one behind me, making a loud and sudden *crack!* Out of the corner of my eye, I saw the gleam of the lights reflecting in an older man's glasses below me as I stood. It was his chair I'd smashed into. He looked up, his brow furrowed and confused. "Sorry," I mumbled. "I have use the restroom."

I awkwardly maneuvered myself between the older man and Kolby as he moved his chair in until his chest bumped against the table, causing one of the drinks to spill. I didn't see whose drink it was or where it started to pool as I tried to resist the urge to run in the opposite direction of Griffin, through the doors and out into the night, and keep running. Run until my legs were about to fall from my hips and my shoes were battered and torn, and Griffin Tomlin was far, far, far away, wondering where I had gone. But I only made it to the fish tank near the entrance of the restaurant, beside the gumball dispenser.

I stared at the air bubbles erupting from the corner of the tank as the fish lazily swam through the synthetic seaweed and coral, while trying to block the sound of Mr. Tomlin laughing at something my dad said.

I noticed a reflection mirrored against the fish tank, its glass smudged with small fingerprints. Soda was dripping from his hand at his side. His face was missing from the reflection, the image only extending to his throat as he looked at me, crouched in front of the tank, tracking the goldfish with the black spots on her scales because I knew she was no one's favorite. Her golden trademark was dotted with darkness, tainted, and I wished that I could be as ignorant as she was to it. Her black spots never bothered her. She was perfectly content to swim through the plastic seaweed and not care. I wondered how a goldfish could do that but not me.

"Clara," Kolby said, and I heard the droplets of soda *plink-plink-plink*-ing onto the plastic mat in front of the doors. "I need to . . ." I looked over my shoulder as he gestured toward the restroom in front of me, the door left ajar. I stepped aside so he could walk in. I tried looking for the black spotted fish again, but she was gone. A moment later, after the deafening sound of the dryer had quieted, Kolby stepped back into the doorframe, wiping his still-damp hands on his jeans.

"My birthday's next week," he remarked quietly once a few seconds had gone by. I tore my eyes away from the tank and looked at him. He looked uncertain, brown eyes gazing into the water and then into me. I wondered if he still remembered that night in February, finding me outside in the snow, and if maybe, after all these months, he was still trying to determine if I was okay.

"Happy birthday, Kolby."

He smiled, glancing down at his hands and then back at me.

"Happy birthday, Clara."

He walked back toward the table, a slight smile lingering on his lips as he made his way through the dining area. When he reached his chair, I saw him sit beside Griffin, who had shifted in his seat. His eyes, as blue as the water I had been fixated on, were now fixated on me. A darkness swirled in them, as if the black of his pupil had begun to bleed and submerge everything else.

And two seats down, my sister's eyes were fixated on him.

I felt the stifling hot air against the inside of my wrist as I stood in front of my opened bedroom door the next night, the sight of the curtain fluttering in the breeze blurred in the corner of my eye. Even though it was silent, it was loud. The sound of an owl crooning, distantly, through the ajar window, the rumble of an engine a couple streets away, a dog barking.

I never left my window open.

I felt him there, even though I couldn't see him. I couldn't hear him. I felt him there, waiting for me, and for a moment, I thought about running or screaming, maybe slapping my hand over the light switch and exposing him, but then I remembered I was alone. My parents were on a double date and my sister had left soon after.

If I ran, he would catch me. If I screamed, he would find me. If I turned on the light, he would grab me. There was nothing there to put between us, and my heart hammered in my chest because I knew, I knew, I knew.

The floorboards creaked under his weight just before a blur of motion rushed toward me from beside the doorframe, slamming my shoulder into the door. His hand clenched around my neck, tight at first and then gentle, delicate, when he had me pinned between him and the door. He whispered words muffled by my hair.

"Clara." His breath was warm against my skin. The stench of beer was all I breathed in. "Why are you always looking at other guys? Are you kidding me? Are you *kidding* me?!"

His hand thrust my head against the door, not hard but I felt the thud reverberating through my bones and out my ears.

"I wasn't looking at other guys," I whispered, too afraid to move anything but my lips, my voice trembling and faint against his ragged breathing.

"You're always staring at Kolby. You're such a slut that you're going after my best friend, huh? Really?"

I felt the muscles in my throat struggling against his hand. "No, I haven't. I haven't, okay? Kolby wished me a happy birthday, that's it. I'm not looking at him. I promise."

His chest pressed hard against my shoulder as he retracted the hand braced against the door by my side and reached into his back pocket, my eye catching a glint of silver.

"You're a such a filthy liar."

Black plastic was clenched in his hand and I knew it was another pocketknife, just like the one he'd used that night and that I'd snuck out with me. He'd bought a new one for tonight.

He was going to do it again.

Then the next thing I knew, my elbow slammed against his

ribs, the bones firm beneath. I whirled around, pushing both of my hands against his chest and watching as he stumbled. He landed against the doorknob of my closet, pain contorting his face for a split-second before it turned to rage.

He lunged for me, the knife pointed. I reached for his forearm, gripped it with my fingers, my nails piercing his skin and leaving angry marks and torn flesh. He started swearing, trying to yank himself away from me.

The knife almost slipped from his fingers as we struggled, his legs forcing me forward until the backs of my shins collided painfully with the bedframe and I gasped at the impact. His eyes appeared pitch black, like a shark's, lurking in the water for prey.

My back collapsed against my mattress, the duvet rumpling around my shoulders as I writhed underneath him. He held the pocketknife in one hand, and I realized there was blood seeping between his fingers. I thought for a second he must have stabbed me somewhere and I couldn't feel it, until I saw it was coming from cuts on his own hand from trying to hold on to the blade.

He climbed on top of me and reached for my face, his fingertips drenched in blood. It was warm and slippery against my cheek and his muscles relaxed against my body until he was almost a dead weight against me, my chest caving in as I tried to breathe.

"Griffin," I wheezed. "Please, okay? Please don't."

"I want to give you your birthday wish," he whispered against my ear, his lips touching my neck. The blood on my skin was starting to smear over his nose. I shook my head beneath his bulk, trying to tilt my face away from his hands.

"Griffin, no, please. You don't have to do this, okay? Please, Griffin, stop."

I couldn't catch my breath, the stiflingly hot air drifting in through the opened window above the bed almost as suffocating as his weight over my lungs. I was so afraid he would reach for the waistband of my pajama bottoms.

I tried to bring my arms from my sides to push against his shoulders, but I couldn't even lift him an inch from my body.

Then, almost as suddenly as the moment he'd appeared in my bedroom, he hesitated. A second later, he was scrambling to hoist himself off me, the mattress rising beneath me. The pocketknife fell against my collarbone as he panicked, leaning his head out the window and searching for what he'd heard—tires rolling up the driveway of my house, then a car door opening—and he glanced over his shoulder at me.

His sun-kissed skin was now washed pale and glistening with sweat, fingernails stained red. He pushed himself through the window, his feet landing with a thump on the overhang. His shoes scratched against the shingles as he scrambled out of view before everything went quiet, only the sound of my parents unlocking the front door downstairs audible.

I lay there for a moment on the edge of my bed, gasping, the weight of the pocketknife slipping from my collarbone and over my throat as I stared up at the ceiling, not completely sure what had just happened.

Then I lifted myself from the bed and closed the window, securing the lock in case he decided to come back. I tugged on my blinds—slightly bent now—before I quickly got in the shower. I washed the blood from my face and took my duvet and poured bleach and cold water onto the small stain of blood he'd left. I was already prepared to tell anyone who asked it was a period stain. I wanted to throw it out, but I knew my parents would notice if my duvet was missing.

Back in my bedroom, I leaned against the wall closest to my bed and watched through the window for him, but he never came back. The house on the opposite side of the street stayed dark until morning, when his father opened his front door with a cup of steaming coffee and craned his neck to see if the paper had arrived yet.

After I watched him retreat back into the house once he realized the paper boy was late again, I crept out into the hallway, quietly knocking on Emily's bedroom door. I listened until I heard her groggily responding, a muffled grunt, and then I opened the door.

She lifted her head from the rumpled pillowcase. Her bleary, squinted eyes closed when she saw me, her head dropping back down onto the pillow. "What?"

"He broke in last night," I whispered. The bed creaked as she hoisted herself up by her forearms at this, her legs moving beneath her duvet, drawing closer to the edge of her bed. "Can we go somewhere, please?"

And then, as she gaped at me, as if her drowsy state created some sort of delay in her mind, I told her what had almost become our signal. Our white flag fluttering in the air. "Anywhere but here."

The barn looked different in the morning, sunlight filtering in through the cracked spaces between the wooden boards of the walls and warming the concrete floor. The straw crunched under my shoes as I walked inside, brushing my fingers alongside its worn planks. The sound of birds chirping outside drifted in, warmth and humidity swelling the barn and causing it to smell of stagnant air and wood.

Emily stood behind me, again clutching bags of fast food and a drink tray with our sodas. She dropped them onto the floor and went into one of the stalls, grabbing an old quilt with little pieces of straw clinging to the fabric. She draped it over the floor before placing the bags and drinks on top, her hand reaching inside a moment later to pull out a handful of grease-stained napkins. She gave me my onion rings and chicken nuggets, tossed me a couple of ketchup packets, and split the large fries between us, pouring the soggy French fries onto the napkins. I tore off pieces of my nuggets and ate them, quietly.

I wanted to say something about him in between onion rings and slurps of diet Coke. But every time my tongue started to form the words, they became almost too frightening to say, as sharp as the knife he'd left in my bedroom. I glanced at the bag I'd brought with me, slumped on the floor beside my thigh. She hadn't asked about it *yet*, but I'd noticed her eyeing it on my lap during the car ride here.

I had it for his pocketknife. I'd used a roll of toilet paper to wipe the blade clean and then flushed the bloody pieces of tissue down the toilet, then placed it in a grocery bag I'd grabbed from one of the kitchen drawers on our way out. I wanted to bury it out here or something. I was too afraid to throw it out—that maybe my parents might find it—or keep it like I had with the last one. Maybe he would remember I had them and realize how they could be incriminating. Maybe he would come back looking for them and decide to dispose of all his evidence.

Eventually the morning turned into afternoon as we quietly ate and slurped our drinks. Emily stretched out on the blanket, stared up at the ceiling, and exhaled. I noticed a piece of hay in her hair.

"So," she breathed after a moment, tilting her head toward me, her cheek almost touching the patches of the quilt, "he broke in last night."

"Yep." I heard Emily say my name quietly, and I hesitated for a moment, my hand still inside the fast food bag. "Yeah, he broke in last night."

She angled her face away from me and gazed back to the ceiling, the shadow of a trapped bird's wings fluttering as it tried to find a way out. I brought my knees close to my chest and watched as it flew into a corner. Something knocked against my shin, the liquid sloshing inside glass louder than the bird chirping. I looked down to see her grasping the neck of an opened beer bottle, and when I met her eyes, she nudged it against my leg again.

I remembered the beer Griffin had given me, the few sips I'd had before he led me away, how it tasted warm and sour. But as I stared at it, I wondered if it would literally take my edge away. The prickling of nervousness I constantly felt. The endless exhaustion that coursed through me whenever I saw him in school in his varsity jacket, reenacting some of his greatest swings, laughing with those who didn't really know him, despite all the pizza slices and baseball games they'd shared.

I took the bottle from her, even though it was almost *hot*, not just room temperature. I wasn't sure how long it had been left here in the barn, but I hesitantly took a sip from it, the pressure of the thick glass against my teeth as I swallowed. The taste was warm on my tongue and it left an aftertaste that made the space between my eyebrows crinkle, but there was almost something comforting in the warmth as it went down my throat.

As I took another sip, Emily reached forward and grabbed the bag from beside my thigh. She grasped the pocketknife by the handle and slid it out of the grocery bag, holding it against the sunlight as it streamed in through the opened doors. The silver glinted against the walls and reflected in my eyes.

"Did he use this?" she asked quietly, although not softly.

I wondered if the ease I felt was because of the beer or because that's what I'd thought it would do, but either way, I held on to it. "Yeah," I told her.

She nodded and placed it down on her opposite side, the one facing the wall and away from me. I took another gulp of the beer, even though it felt like the taste had got worse and nearly made me retch against the bottle.

"That beer's old," she informed me and then hoisted herself up from the ground, straw and crumpled pieces of old leaves clinging to her hair and back. She reached for her keys and smoothed the dirt off her bare knees, telling me, "I'm going to get some more. I got an ID, a fake one."

I took another slurp of the beer, but my heart started to pound again as I heard her say that she was leaving me here, alone. She looked down at me, brushing a lock of hair behind my ear, and smiled. I wondered if it was the beer or her that made it look convincing. "He won't find you here. Remember, greatest place no one will ever find."

"Then why does it look so trashed?"

She just shook her head at me and brought her hand from my face. I closed my eyes as I listened to her flip-flops smacking against the concrete until it went quiet again, then I swallowed the rest of the beer. I lay against the quilt, sun-warmed against my cheek, and the bird continued to chirp in the rafters. I opened my eyes long enough to see it finally find the opened barn doors and fly out into the warmth and freedom of the apple orchard. I smiled as my eyes closed again. The warmth of the beer lulled me to sleep against the quilt in the barn, alone.

Maybe that was why I never noticed that the knife was gone.

The side of my face was hot from the sun when I stirred awake and noticed the barn's weathered ceiling above me. The glare of the mid-afternoon light blinded my sleepy eyes for a minute as I blinked, feeling the dampened strands of my hair against my neck. A taste lingered in my mouth and pieces of hay poked at the exposed skin of my arms and ankles. From the corner of my eye, I noticed a familiar pair of abandoned flip-flops a foot away. Emily was sitting beside me, with a six-pack on the other side of her, two of the bottles missing. She stared at her phone, then looked at me, almost nonchalantly, as if she were expecting me to still be asleep, but when she noticed that I was awake, something shifted in her expression. She adjusted her position on the floor, bringing her knees from her chest and crossing her legs. Her lips formed a smile that didn't quite reach her eyes.

"You've been out forever," she told me. "I got back, like, four hours ago but you were still knocked out. I decided to let you sleep. I got the feeling that you probably didn't do much of that last night with, you know, Griffin . . . breaking in."

I shrugged against the ground, my sleepiness making me feel brave and relaxed even though I knew he was out there somewhere, thoughts of me still in his mind—but I felt so distant that even Griffin Tomlin couldn't touch me.

"Why won't he just go away?" I shook my head. "I want him . . . I want him to step out onto the street a moment too soon and get run over by a bus. And that sounds horrible to say, but it's true. I want him to disappear, but for good." I let out a sigh as I stared up at the ceiling, the sound rattling in my throat. "I want to wear shorts again. And makeup again. I want to do things again without worrying about arousing my rapist neighbor!"

I said, "I want him to get diarrhea so bad that he dies of dehydration."

She hesitated. "He'd poop his pants to death. That would be on his grave."

"Probably not, but I could scratch it in or something."

"I'll buy the laxatives."

I smiled, the saltiness of sweat gathering on my chapped lips. "I'll get the brownie mix."

chapter twenty-two

The Tomlins were hosting the party in the ballroom of an enormous—and expensive, if the marble flooring and ivory pillars were any indication—hotel. Large round tables with white tablecloths were scattered throughout the room. There was a DJ in the corner in a metal folding chair, slouching as he sipped from a can of Coke, casting a bored gaze around the room.

It was filled with women wearing so much hairspray that their hair looked brittle and men clapping each other on the shoulder whenever they glimpsed someone they recognized. Mrs. Tomlin wore black, of course, with a black shawl draped over her shoulders, and her hair was pulled into a tight bun. Her smile was forced as she touched others on the arm while they gazed at the photo montages of Griffin, ranging from a newborn swaddled in a hospital blanket to a couple of months before he died, standing on the beach in front of the ocean. Grains of sand on his chest as he leaned down and smiled into the camera, which was reflected in his sunglasses.

When Mrs. Tomlin saw me walk into the ballroom with my fingers interlocked with Kolby's, she hesitated, her eyes turning steely. She looked to where her husband sat at one of the tables, his lips glued to his champagne glass. His eyes were closed, almost squeezed shut, and I wondered if that was because he'd seen us together, hands joined, and his response was to down the rest of his drink. Brandon was beside him, twisting his glass and puffing out his cheeks with a sigh.

I spent the first half of the party searching for ways to separate myself from Kolby and glancing over my shoulder. Every time I untangled his hand from mine, someone would almost immediately approach him. Sometimes while they spoke to him, he would look over their shoulder at me.

I would feel a twinge of guilt twisting around my insides as I turned around, reminding myself that here, he was Griffin Tomlin's best friend. When others looked at him, that was what they wanted to see. The best friend who was just as devastated as they were over his murder, not the best friend who'd mourned him for a moment and then decided to get together with the sister of the girl who'd caused them all so much pain. I couldn't let them see him like that.

Because the only good thing Griffin Tomlin ever did in his life was befriend Kolby Rutledge.

No one spoke to me, except for Kolby and an elderly woman who probably had no idea who I was when she asked me to pass her a napkin. I idled around the buffet and my table, staring down at my plate whenever someone else sat down, purposely trying not to look at me.

I glanced at the montage of photos on the screen in the corner of the room, wondering if there had been a moment when everything changed. If that little dark-haired boy standing on couch cushions with his fists on his hips was just destined to become a storm or if the waters had ever been calm.

When I'd met Griffin Tomlin, I had just turned six and he was seven. I had been sitting on the front lawn in our turtle sandbox, with its weather-worn smiling lips and eyes, scooping sand with my shovel when I heard the rumbling of a large truck. I looked up to see a moving van driving down our cul-de-sac, barreling past our mailbox, and parking at a house that had been vacant for nearly a year.

The For Sale sign had been pitched on the front lawn for months, but a few weeks ago it had been removed, much to my father's curiosity. He'd noticed it one morning as he was leaving for work and run back into the house, his tie flapping. My mother had glanced over around the opened refrigerator door. "Did you forget something?"

"Hey, did you see?" he said. "Someone bought the Brownings' house." Then he looked over at me and Emily, sitting at the table eating our cereal. "Girls, maybe they'll have some friends for you to play with."

And those *friends* came down the street a moment after the moving van, in a black minivan. It had parked on the side of the road, near the mailbox with the name Tomlin engraved in cursive that I hadn't noticed until then.

A moment later I heard the whoosh of the minivan's side door opening, followed by the smacking of flip-flops against the pavement and the muffled sound of the radio coming from inside the car, forecasting the weather—sunny with highs in the eighties. That was when I saw Griffin's brother, Brandon, for the first time. He was older, with wheelies on his shoes, playing a game on his

Nintendo DS. I wanted a Nintendo DS badly and as I was watching him, wondering how much allowance money one of those would cost, Griffin Tomlin came around the side of the minivan.

He had knobby knees that were crisscrossed with scabs under a pair of cargo shorts that shook around his thighs when he walked. He was holding a game chip in his hand and reaching out to grab the Nintendo DS from Brandon.

"It's my turn!"

I saw the shoulders of a woman I assumed was their mother slumping as she sighed, gazing at her sons as Griffin stood on the tips of his toes while Brandon evaded him, holding the game higher and walking away without taking his eyes off the screen.

"Brandon!" Griffin shouted.

"Can't you two learn to share?" their mother said, exasperated.

She glanced over the hood of their minivan at the man I thought must have been her husband, who, instead of returning her gaze or scolding his children, stared at the house with his hands on his hips. He let out a whistle and scratched the side of his head, finally glancing over at his tired wife. He had black hair, just like Griffin.

"Look at that. Couldn't have done a better job fixing up the place myself," he said.

Quietly, she muttered, "You did fix it up yourself."

He laughed, throwing back his head, almost as if in agreement.

"Griffin, buzz off!"

Mr. Tomlin finally looked over at his sons as Griffin sulked over to the front steps of the porch. A moment later, he glanced over his shoulder to where I was sitting in my turtle-shaped sandbox. I grabbed the handle of my shovel and buried the tip in the sand.

"Griffin, why don't you try to make some friends, huh?" Mr. Tomlin called out to him.

Griffin looked away from his brother, eyed the turtle sandbox and the cracked shovel in my hand, then sighed. *Fine,* I saw him mutter as he walked down the driveway. His mother smiled at him and then me, waving, before shouting to him, "Be nice, Griffin! *Share!*"

He responded with a halfhearted nod of his head, almost rolling it from side to side, as if this had all been said to him before.

"Hey," he said, crouching down in front of me, plopping both scabbed knees onto the grass. He tilted his head to the side and looked at me with sparkling ocean-blue eyes as he asked, "Can I play?"

I looked at the sparkling ocean for one more moment before I replied, "Okay."

A glimpse of bright red caught the corner of my eye as someone cautiously sat down beside me and brought me back to the present. She wasn't dressed like everyone else in their formal attire— she had on a Beatles T-shirt, distressed, acid-washed jeans, and a pair of beat-up Converse. Her hair was dark red with corkscrew curls spilling over her back and shoulders as she glanced around the room, her freckled hands gripping the strap of a canvas bag decorated with pins.

I wasn't sure what it was about her, but something in me had to know, needed to know, and it compelled me to quietly blurt out, "Hey." She nodded in acknowledgment before looking away from me again. "Do I know you?"

Her tone bordered on taciturn when she replied, not meeting my eyes, "No."

I didn't know how to respond—because I knew her from somewhere, in the kind of way that bothered me. I was about to say something when I looked over the frizzled curls of her hair and saw her, standing in the entrance of the ballroom, clenching an invitation.

My mother was here. Her familiar and disconsolate green eyes glanced around the room, seeing the tables where the people she used to know sat before she found Mrs. Tomlin standing in front of the photo montage with an older couple. Mrs. Tomlin tilted her head to the left and noticed my mother standing there, the invitation in her hand. Her chest sank beneath her shawl, her face paling. My pulse quickened as my mother looked at her, almost helplessly, as if she hadn't been the one to bring herself here, before tentatively smiling. But Mrs. Tomlin just stared at her, the muscles in her neck tensing.

"Lisa," my mom said as she took a step forward, the invitation Kolby had mailed to our house beginning to crinkle in her grip as she looked at Mrs. Tomlin, her former best friend, so desperately it ached somewhere within me. I stood up but my feet were planted to the floor as my mother took another step and then another. "I'm sorry, I just—I wanted to talk to you.

"I've been trying to tell you how sorry I am, for months. To you, your family. And you have every right to ignore me, but . . . I never thought that this could *happen*. Every day, I see your house and I couldn't do it anymore. I needed you to know that I'm sorry. I'm so, so sorry, Lisa."

"*You* can't do this anymore?" Mrs. Tomlin asked, her voice collected and low. "You can't do this anymore. And what about me, or my family?" Her voice became tighter the more she spoke, before she smiled, somberly, and shook her head. "*I'm* the one who can't do this anymore. *I'm* the one who can't do this anymore because my son is dead. And I tell myself that if it happened any other way, it would've been easier. Cancer, an accident, anything. Anything that was out of my control, out of anyone's control, because then it would have been his time. I could *accept* that, but that *didn't* happen. It wasn't his time because he was murdered by your daughter. Your *daughter*, Samantha."

The room had grown suddenly silent, the chatter and screeching of knives against plates quieting. Her voice almost like a gunshot going off in a crowded room.

"How could you not notice? Because that's something I've been thinking about since he died. But then I realized you had and you did *nothing* about it! And because of that, my son, my child, is . . . is . . ." Lisa started to cry, her shoulders heaving with each breath as she looked at my mother, pleadingly, her face red and crumpling.

Mr. Tomlin stood by his wife, rubbing her shoulders as her tearful eyes glared at my mother, and I noticed his own eyes were glassy, distant, almost unreachable, looking at the wall instead of her. A second later, Kolby was standing in front of my mother. He looked over his shoulder at me, but I did nothing, said nothing, felt nothing. He turned back to her, wrapping his hand around her elbow. I saw his lips moving, his quiet voice a murmur too far away to hear, and he tried leading her away.

But she never looked at him, just at Mrs. Tomlin, tears sliding down her cheeks. "I never thought it would get this far," she said, raising her voice to be heard. "I never thought it was this bad. She's . . . I didn't . . ."

Kolby motioned for me, but I couldn't move. I couldn't go to him, I couldn't go to her. I couldn't take her by the other elbow and lead her out of the room, using the same soft voice he was using to calm her, to remind her that we knew. We knew she was sorry, we knew she'd tried. I couldn't bring myself forward, to do anything, because I knew. I knew everything. Everything that ached in my bones and curdled in my stomach and scarred my skin and hurt everything around me, lives withering in front of me because of something I'd told her.

I looked down at the empty chair beside me and sprinted out of the ballroom, away from my mother, from Kolby, from everything that reminded me of the boy they all thought he was, and after the girl with the red hair.

Because suddenly I knew.

I knew that she knew too.

I felt the brush of a cold, late winter's night breeze on my face as I walked through the parking lot, maneuvering around parked cars. The dark pavement glistened and I felt salt rocks scattered across the ground beneath my shoes. Then I found her. The girl was sitting on the bench at a bus stop, her hair illuminated by the streetlight hovering over her. Her hands were in her canvas bag, shifting items around inside, an unlit cigarette dangling from her lower lip. A second later, her hand emerged with a blue lighter. She readjusted the cigarette in her mouth, her cheeks concaving as she blocked the flame with her hand and it reflected against her face.

"You're not waiting for the bus," she remarked as the smoke drifted from her mouth.

"I do know you. You were that girl. You were that girl at his locker, a couple of years ago." I looked at her, waiting, almost desperate. "You *know*."

She lifted her hand from her lap, bringing the cigarette back to her lips, before she hesitated. And then her voice, quiet and bitter, mumbled back to me, "Yeah."

She exhaled slowly.

"I know."

Her name was Sloane Spencer, and she had graduated from Madison High School last spring, a couple of months before Griffin was murdered.

"I was cleaning a neighbor's pool for extra cash when I saw this patrol car speeding down the street with sirens going off," she told me. "I didn't really think anything of it until the next day, when my neighbor asked if I knew a guy named Griffin Tomlin." She shook her head, pausing to take another drag from her cigarette. "I said that I'd seen him around, I guess. Whatever. And then he was like, *They just found his body, he's dead, probably drowned in his pool.* A couple of days later, they were saying on the news that he was hit in the head with a rock, *then* dumped in the pool in the middle of the night. And I *knew*, I just knew it. I knew it had to be one of us. I thought it was the girl who killed him."

I shook my head. "She did it to protect me." Then, realizing she didn't recognize who I was, I added, "Emily's my sister. She knew about Griffin."

"I was waiting for her to say something, use it as, like, her defense or something, but when she didn't, I decided I wasn't

215

going to say anything either. It's not as if what happened with me would've changed anything."

"What did happen to you?"

"I met him when I was working at the concession stand for the school games, including his baseball games, and sometimes, he would come over, like before the game, when we weren't even supposed to be selling anything yet, but we always made exceptions for the team players, so it was, like, no big deal. He would ask for Skittles, always Skittles, and sometimes I complimented his pitch. And then one day, after a game, he brought me a bag of Skittles. It was a blue bag, because he said it matched my eyes."

She rolled her eyes as she said this, but her voice sounded soft and sad. I wanted to say something, but I couldn't think of anything that would actually matter.

"After that, he always brought me a blue bag of Skittles. Sometimes he would pay for his stuff with a five and tell me to keep the change. He was always asking me questions, like he actually cared about the answers or something. Like, all the buttons on my bag. They're of all the cities I want to visit, and he acted like he thought that was so cool. It's not, but the fact that he even pretended made it feel special."

I thought back to him sitting in the auditorium during the spring musical a couple of years ago, before he'd found me when it was over and wrapped his arms around me, how he'd raved about how good I was. It wasn't as if my family or friends never said anything like that, but hearing it from Griffin made it matter more somehow. Like if he thought it, it must be true.

"Then one night, after a game, he told me that one day, he was going to take me to one of the cities on my buttons. I was laughing, and like, *No way*. And then he just kissed me. Then he said he would prove it—if I waited outside for him later, he'd show me one of those *little cities*." She laughed, a slight sound through her nose, as she flicked her cigarette. "I thought he meant something cheesy, that he'd make up something cute, but instead he brought me to a party. He was like, *There are so many people here, so many lineages, dozens of nations.* Then he gave me a wine cooler and it tasted . . . fine? A few minutes later, he said he wasn't feeling good and wanted to leave, wanted to go upstairs to get his coat. Okay, fine. We held hands going upstairs, and went into this one room. And as soon as he closed the door, I was like, *Wait, you didn't bring a coat.*"

I took in a breath, my fingers clenching around the edge of the bench seat, his voice echoing in my head. *Come on, I want to show you something.*

"I think I scratched him on his neck before he pushed me down onto the bed. And it was like I was *melting* into him, like I could barely move or anything. Last thing I remember is him trying to undo the buttons on my miniskirt. When I woke up, he was gone and my clothes were tossed over my body. I was bleeding. And when I got dressed, I realized my underwear was missing."

"He took your underwear too?" She nodded.

"Summer break was the next week," she continued. "I didn't see him at all that summer. I think he was scared. Because the next fall, he was going out of his way to avoid me, and I thought . . . I don't know. It just didn't make sense, you know? So I concocted this *idea* in my head that it didn't really happen. Maybe the wine cooler had already been tampered with and I'd just passed out and he freaked out and left. Maybe then someone else came in? It seemed like the *only* thing that made sense, which is crazy because it doesn't—didn't.

217

"I asked him about it, at school. I never saw him anywhere else. And he just . . . shut me down. That was it. He never admitted it because he knew I barely remembered. You tell a cop you were at a party, drank, and then blacked out, he assumes you got drunk and passed out. Especially if you went braless and in a miniskirt."

I noticed in the glow of the streetlight that she was starting to cry.

"My mom saw the scars he'd left . . . on my ribs. She thought I was *cutting* myself. She reads books on teen suicide all the time, watches me like a hawk, all to fix a problem I don't even have."

"He cut your ribs?"

She smiled sadly, and then looked at me for the first time since she'd started speaking. "I came here tonight thinking that I would *finally* tell the truth about Griffin Tomlin to these people. You know, like, *Happy freaking birthday to your dead son, the rapist!* Right." She dropped her cigarette onto the ground without even looking as it fell, grinding it into the pavement with her shoe. Distantly, I heard the roar of a bus barreling down the road.

"You know what's funny," she told me, her voice not phrasing it as a question, as she reached out, taking a tendril of my hair and gently twisting it, focusing on it instead of me. "My hair was the same color as yours when it happened. I dyed it red during the summer. I thought it would help, but now everyone just thinks I'm a Scottish princess-wannabe with suicidal tendencies."

I watched, a lump forming in my throat, as the fingers that held my strawberry blond hair, the same color hers was when he'd brought her packages of blue Skittles, released the lock. Tears gathered at the bottom of my vision, transforming everything into watery colors that bled into each other, as she stood up. She disappeared into the bus without looking back. I sat there, watching as the doors closed behind her before the bus started to drive away and left me there, alone, with a cavity in my chest and scars singeing against my skin.

I looked over my shoulder through the gold-speckled plexiglass walls and the rain starting to pelt against the hotel parking lot. I knew that Kolby was waiting for me, that somewhere my mother probably needed me, that I should go back. Back into the ballroom transformed into an elegant shrine to him, with his favorite music flowing from the speakers and pictures of him looped on a screen and an assortment of his favorite foods on a buffet table. It was dedicated to him and the kind of person they thought he was. The kind of person he pretended to be until he died. Griffin Tomlin was immortalized for what he wasn't, for the lie he'd told them every day until he was gone, and the truth had gone with him. And it left me here, with a cavity in my chest and scars that burned against my skin, because there was nothing left for me to do. I would have to swallow down the truth he'd left with me. Hold the hand of his best friend, watch my sister's trial, and suffocate in it all, because the storm was never him. The storm was never his eyes, searching for me, reaching out to me, grabbing me.

It was him, leaving me. Leaving me with the truth, the scars, the aftershock. And with nothing else.

And then suddenly the breath I was holding disappeared into the rainy night air, and I couldn't breathe it back in. I was gasping in breaths of thick air that never reached my lungs, and my eyes blurred the street in front of me. My sides ached as I tried to breathe in, inhale, take in, but there was nothing there to breathe in because everything was gone. Everything had ended the moment he was murdered. Everything stopped after she was arrested. There was nothing else. Nothing to grasp on to, and I was left, at a bus stop, alone. I was suffocating in what he'd left behind and now I was without her.

Anywhere but here.

But she wasn't here.

I tried again to breathe in, inhale, take in, but all I heard were the strangled sounds of my voice.

She was never going to be here.

It was what she'd sacrificed for me to be safe.

But that feeling—safety—was still a stranger to me.

"Hey, I sent your mom home—Clara?" I felt warm fingers brushing the side of my arm and a blurry figure appeared in front of me as I sat there, taking in the huge rain spots on his blazer and his damp hair when he crouched down in front of me. His eyes kept glancing away to look over my body, as if he were searching for something, a visible wound, a bleeding scar, a pain he could see with his eyes.

"Clara? Hey, hey, hey, baby, what's wrong?" I knew he was trying to sound calm, but desperation submerged his tone with each word he spoke. "Clara, are you okay? What's—I don't know what to do, Clara—I don't . . . please, just talk to me, Clara. *Talk to me.*"

I felt the warmth of him brushing off my tear-streaked cheeks as he held me, held my face. My eyes found him as he leaned closer to me, perched on the toes of his shoes, alarmed earth-brown eyes searching mine, almost pleadingly.

And then I finally took in a breath, a gasp that scratched against my throat, and it all slowed. The rain against the plexiglass, my pulse whirring in my ears, my breathing, his voice. Everything seemed quiet and still, and it was just us, staring at each other with fear ignited in our eyes. His hands on my face, and my scars between us.

"Griffin," I breathed, taking him in as he crouched so close to me, almost convinced I felt it against my face every time he blinked. The whirring reappeared in my ears. "Griffin . . ."

Kolby interrupted me as he pressed a kiss against my temple and whispered that he knew, he knew. The heartbeat thundering through my veins abruptly stopped for that single moment that I believed that he knew, until he said he knew Griffin was dead. He was so sorry he was dead.

My eyes fluttered closed. He thought I was grieving for him, grieving for what I could never have with him. I started to shake my head away from him when I heard what came after his apologies, and it was so silent, it might not have even been there. *I know I'm not him. But I love you, though. I love you.*

Something in me collapsed as I pressed against him, his lips against my hair, and I felt a single teardrop sliding down my face before I shook my head. "I don't want you to be," I whispered, feeling him still against me. "Please don't ever be him."

I felt his chest tensing against my shoulder, hesitating before he leaned back, a crease between his eyebrows as he looked at me, bewilderment flooding his gaze.

"What do you . . ." His lips barely parted to form the words, and I forced myself to hold his gaze until something changed in his eyes. Then he took in a breath, his shoulders rising beneath his suit. After a minute, he asked me in a quiet voice, "What are you saying?"

I wasn't sure what else there was to say, or if there was anything else I *could* say. If there were any more words I could form about Griffin Tomlin and what he had done, who he had been to me, without completely shattering in front him, breaking at the seams of the scars Griffin had left me, because I knew I was about to lose him. Once he knew, he would be gone.

But there was no going back now.

"Griffin, he . . ." A trembling breath slipped past my lips as I finally whispered the words that had been between us since the moment he'd kissed me in his driveway. "He raped me."

And then it all slowed again.

I listened to the trickling of the rain from the edge of the bus stop roof as I waited for him to say something. He was still crouched in front of me, his lips just barely parted, and looking back at me, thunderstruck. Then he closed his eyes and released a slow, steady exhale that started to shake at the end before swiftly standing up and turning away from me. I caught his reflection in the gold-speckled plexiglass as he brought his hands to his face, over his nose and mouth, staring at a defaced ad against smoking. He stood there silently for what seemed like minutes before he turned back to me. His eyes were blazing and glistening, the gold flecks in the brown now ignited sparks.

"Griffin," he said, his voice low and thick. It sounded almost as if he were forcing the words out, expelling them like a bad taste. He cleared his throat before he continued, the muscles in his neck tensing. "Griffin raped you."

He shook his head, almost in disbelief, maybe in actual disbelief, and fear sparked around my chest. I realized with a painful jolt that I needed him to believe in me, over Griffin, over the boy who'd never deserved someone like Kolby Rutledge to believe in him. "That's—I would've . . . I would've known . . . I don't . . ." He let out a humorless laugh and looked up, blinking. "I don't get it."

"It was after the Super Bowl party," I told him as his gaze lingered on the roof for a moment, his Adam's apple bobbing as he swallowed. Then something in him shifted. His shoulders went rigid and his breathing suddenly became quiet before he looked up, something gleaming in his eyes I couldn't recognize.

"Last year I was in love with him, or at least I thought I was. And it seemed like he was finally noticing me. He asked me to go to that party. You were there. I remember you, sitting in the back seat. Playing *Ten Second Trivia*." I attempted a smile with my trembling lips, but his eyes were glassy and unfocused. "He took me upstairs and I thought . . . I don't know what I thought. But that's where it happened."

He held both of his hands, pressed together, in front of his nose and kept his gaze hidden from me. Distantly, I heard a siren blaring, and a tear slipped from my eyes as I closed them. We both stayed that way for a few moments, our eyes closed, our clothes dotted with rain, with a distance between us. Then he spoke, his voice quiet and catching on his words. "The Super Bowl. It happened at the *Super Bowl* party."

I opened my eyes, my gaze blurred and brimmed with tears. His hands were dangling at his sides, and there was an emptiness in his eyes. The ignited flecks were dull, drowned in something I couldn't identify, the whites of his eyes now red. I wanted to reach out, grasp one of the hands at his side and hold it in my own, but I stayed on the bench.

"Please believe me," I whispered, my voice cracking, and he flinched in response, closing his eyes again. His chest fell under his suit as he breathed heavily. "I know he was your friend," I continued as my choked voice shook past my lips, too quickly, too fast, "but I'm not lying, Kolby. Please."

I reached my hand out for his, desperate, but he stepped away from me. I felt it in my chest as the heart that had been thrashing a second ago dropped from my body, leaving me as empty as his eyes.

"Kolby," I whispered tearfully.

"I was there," he told me. I looked away from him, another tear escaping my eyes as I painfully realized he didn't believe me. Bile crept into the bottom of my throat as I thought of Kolby Rutledge believing in *him*, being on his side instead of mine.

"You don't believe me."

His jaw clenched, his tearful gaze finally turned to me. "That's not what I said." His voice was so quiet, so fragile, so broken that I bit down, hard, on my lower lip until it felt like my teeth pierced through the skin.

"I was *there*," he said again, and his voice cracked on the last word. I stood up, stepping toward him, relief coursing through me when he didn't back away. I touched my hand to the side of his face, feeling the wet strands of his hair against my fingertips, and gently angled his face toward me. I slid my thumb across the trail a tear had left on his cheek and started to say something when he unexpectedly looked past me.

He went rigid under my hand as I looked over my shoulder. Through the plexiglass, I saw Mrs. Tomlin standing on the sidewalk behind us, her hair windblown and her clothing dotted with the rain. A package of cigarettes was clenched in her hand as she stared reproachfully at us.

I took my hand from his face, keeping my eyes focused on her, before I realized, as I heard his shoes shuffling against the ground, that her glare was only directed at me. Then I realized something even worse, my scars burning against my skin as if they were fresh and still dripping blood.

She'd *heard* me.

When I looked away from her and back over my shoulder, I saw that Kolby was gone and halfway across the street with his hands still limp at his sides. I watched, a lump forming in my throat, as he headed for his father's car in the parking lot of a closed drugstore and reached for the door handle, yanking on it. His fingers slipped because he'd forgotten to unlock it. After he grabbed his keys, he looked back over to where I stood. It almost seemed like he was hesitating, a breath rising in his shoulders. But then he looked away from me, unlocking the car, and slid into the driver's seat. And then he was gone, like I knew he would be.

When I turned around, I realized, with dread like ice water in my veins, that she wasn't.

The heels of her black pumps sank into the hotel's front lawn as she strode toward the bus stop, the sound of the ground squishing beneath her muddying shoes soon replaced with the clicking of her heels against the pavement as she rounded the corner. Her eyes were wide as she stared at me, stepping into the cramped space. For a moment, she just stood there, incredulous, and I realized that his ocean-blue eyes were hers, and that they looked just as dark as his had been that night.

"What is the *matter* with you?" she whispered harshly, and her voice shook with anger and resentment. I tried to ignore the sting I felt within my chest as I heard her tone. "My son is dead and you're . . . *you're* out here claiming that he . . . my son would *never* do something like that. He was a *good* person."

I could only stand there, uncertain of what to say or do, my lips parted as if I was readying to defend myself, to say that he wasn't, but every breath I took in felt like it was all I was capable of. Inhaling, exhaling, inhaling.

"You are *just* like her. I *hoped* that you weren't, Clara. I really did. But you are just like your sister. Always out to hurt him. Can you just leave him in peace? Hasn't your family taken enough from him?"

"What?" I shook my head. "No. I never wanted to hurt him. I loved him, Mrs. Tomlin. I really did. But then he—I'm not lying." Then I told her what I had been holding in since September. "It's why Emily killed him."

She scoffed in response, shaking her head so forcefully it caused locks of her hair to fall from her bun and land against her shoulders. There was a bitterness in her gaze that looked so unusual on her it was almost startling. "So are you saying my son has been *raping you* since he was eight years old then? That's why she killed his puppy, right? To get back at him?"

"That wasn't her," I said quietly. "That was Griffin. My friend, I don't know, she thinks she's Nancy Drew or something, but she figured it out. He killed your puppy. It's, like, a part of a triad. Hurting animals, starting fires, bed-wetting—"

"That was Emily," she interrupted, and there was something in her voice that made me hesitate. "You were younger. She used to come over and ask to play with the dog all the time. And I let her. One day, he came back limping and she said she'd accidentally closed a door on his paw, and I believed her. So the next time she came over to play with him, I let her. A couple of months later, she asked to take him out for a walk and when she got back, she said that he'd run away from her. Griffin was devastated. Cried for days. Eventually, someone at the police station called us and said they'd found his collar covered in blood, and a paw in the woods. My husband thought it must have happened *after*, but I think I knew. I think I always knew."

"Mrs. Tomlin—"

"Stop spreading accusations about my son. Find another way

to get attention or a defense for your sister or whatever it is you want. Let Griffin rest in peace."

And then, as the pounding of rain quieted against the bus stop, she turned away from me, lifting one of her hands to brush back a stray strand of hair.

I remembered what Bex had told me, about Emily hurting Wilson Westbrooke the same way Griffin Tomlin had hurt me. The lies she'd told about his friends hurting her, or even him hurting her. Each truth rammed into my ribs, knocking me off-center. I remembered that she'd stabbed Griffin Tomlin with a knife the police never found, the clothes she kept in plastic bags in her closet, the funeral and her eyes looking empty as she listened to the tearful eulogies his family delivered.

Then I remembered Elizabeth Monner, buried beneath the roots of my father's dead vegetables and clumps of frozen dirt. Griffin would've had to sneak away into our backyard to bury her without being seen or heard. I remembered how Griffin had said he would bury me in my father's vegetable garden in the text messages he'd sent, and how Emily was the only one who'd read them. I thought about when I'd overheard detectives theorizing that the reason the killer had given up on dismembering her was because he wasn't strong enough. But Griffin was a pitcher, he was strong enough.

I took a step backward, the beats of my heart shattering my rib bones as I slowly sat back down on the bench. She'd disappeared the day after he'd broken into my bedroom, when I was asleep in the abandoned barn, drunk and alone because she'd left to get more beer. The pocketknife I'd brought with me from the night before was gone when she left. Elizabeth Monner was stabbed with a knife they never found.

Aniston said not to tell the police about Griffin. Because she knew. She knew it wasn't him.

Suddenly everything seemed too real, too clear, too strong. I leaned forward, sure I was going to vomit onto the concrete. The rushing sound of my pulse thrashing in my ears echoed against my skull, overwhelming me, as I realized the truth. The truth that felt too big in front of me to not be shattered underneath it.

Emily killed Elizabeth Monner.

chapter twenty-three

before

After the night he'd ambushed me in my bedroom, it was like Griffin disappeared. The text messages every five to ten minutes either professing love or disgust stopped, and so did the unmarked letters and packages. I saw him in the hallways sometimes at school after summer break ended, slamming locker doors or slapping the shoulders of guys I barely recognized, pretending as if I wasn't there, but something felt strange about it. I wondered if now he was the one who was afraid. Maybe he thought he'd gone too far and was a phone call away from being arrested and charged with assault.

He passed me in the halls with his eyes directed at whatever was straight ahead of him, completely ignoring me. If he was outside when I stepped out through my front door, mowing his lawn, the material of his shirt darkened with sweat, he kept his eyes down on the clipped blades of grass. Guilt or fear motivated him, or maybe he was actually through with me. He had felt my life in his hands, my body beneath his, and maybe that was enough, for now, but I was still afraid for later.

I'd thought later might come at the block Labor Day barbecue, when I noticed him swimming in one of our neighbors' pools with Kolby and a couple of the neighbors' kids. He'd looked over to me and my family as we arrived, taking us in for a moment before calling out a weak, "Polo."

Sometimes I wondered how no one else saw it—the boy he really was underneath—but then I watched him play pool games with the neighborhood kids. No one expects boys like him to play Marco Polo at block parties, swimming slowly in the pool to let the kids still in floaties catch him. That would be too sweet, too kind. Boys like him had to always be fraught with malice.

About an hour later, he was gulping down his soda, condensation clinging to the cup, and he cast one quick look over the rim from across one of our neighbor's backyards. He was shirtless, the curls of his hair still wet, his swimsuit clinging to his thighs as he stood there, barefoot. But then he looked away from me, finding something else to my right and something changed in his eyes. It was something I couldn't quite understand or identify, but then he looked away from that too.

"I'm heading back to the pool," he announced, slapping a mosquito from his forearm. I looked over after he walked away, a tense arch in his shoulders, and saw it was only Emily, slouched in a lawn chair, her flip-flop dangling from her toe as she observed him, lips pursed.

I thought it must have been disgust that made her lips press into a thin line like that, her eyes never abandoning him as he left. So he walked off, and that was the last time I saw Griffin Tomlin.

The next morning, he was dead, found floating in his pool.

chapter *twenty*-four

I was too afraid to drive her car to school the next day, the early morning chill crawling up my spine as I stared at its red, gleaming paint in the driveway. There was too much of her there. I couldn't flip the turn signals or adjust mirrors and act like maybe Emily hadn't kept Elizabeth Monner in there somewhere. Maybe in the trunk or the back seat. Maybe even when we'd driven home later that afternoon, while I relaxed against the passenger seat and hummed along to the radio.

"Hey, Mom?" I called out. "Can you give me a ride to school?"

"Sure, I can drop you off on the way to work," she said as she swallowed her sip of coffee. "Is something wrong with the car?"

The car was what she had been calling it since Emily had been arrested and I started driving it. Not hers anymore, but still not completely mine. I thought about lying to her, that it wasn't starting or a tire was flat or something, but suddenly it felt exhausting keeping everything to myself.

"No," I said. "I just don't want to drive it today. Or maybe anymore, I don't know."

My mother placed her coffee mug in the sink with a slight clunk. "Okay, but sweetheart, you should know that we can't afford to get you another car right now. My practice hasn't exactly been thriving the past few months."

"I know. I could just start taking the bus or something."

She shook her head. "No, I don't think that's a good idea. There's just so much going on, I don't want other kids to start bullying you about it." She paused, rinsing out her mug under the faucet. "I can drive you to school, and maybe when Scoops! opens up again in the summer, we can work something out between that and what we make selling the other car."

"I don't know if I'm going back to Scoops! this summer." I shrugged. "The owner probably doesn't even want me to work there. Everyone would probably think I'm poisoning the ice cream or something."

"Mrs. Connor loves you!" she scoffed. "And besides, you need a job, Clara. You have to earn money for college somehow, and if you tell me . . ." she said, pointing a finger at me, a teasing smile on her face, "that you're not sure you're going to college next year, you can forget about that plan." She set her coffee mug on the drying rack and dried her hands with a dish towel.

I nodded. "I know." I hesitated for a moment before asking, "Mom, why were you there last night?"

She paused, like that was something she wasn't expecting me to ask. I wasn't really expecting to ask her either. Then she let out a soft sigh. "I just wanted their family to know how sorry I was for everything that happened. I found the invitation Kolby sent you, and it seemed like a good opportunity."

"You know you're neighbors, right? You could've just walked across the street without making a scene at a party."

"I've tried. And I'm sorry about making a scene last night." She smiled sadly at me before reaching out and tucking a strand of hair behind my ear. "I should've just accepted that what I needed to say wasn't what they needed to hear. Anyway, we'd better leave now if you don't want to be late."

I kept glancing around the hallway for Kolby, wondering if maybe he'd waited for me this morning, standing by the front door and listening for the familiar sound of the Mini Cooper's engine approaching his driveway. Or maybe he'd never even considered riding with me, the girl who'd accused his best friend of raping her before her sister murdered him. But I never saw him, not in any of the hallways or at the water fountains or even in the cafeteria during lunch. I looked around, searching for his familiar frame standing in line or sitting at one of the tables. When all I saw were the usual staring faces, I turned away and went into the girls' restroom to hide.

When I came out of the stall a few minutes later, just before the bell for our next period rang, I noticed a girl with short brown hair and thick eyeliner standing at the sink. When she saw me standing behind her in the mirror, she hesitated, staring at me. I turned on the tap, running the ice-cold water over my palms like I'd just used the restroom like a normal girl. I was pumping the soap when she finally spoke, uncertainty lacing her voice.

"So did Griffin Tomlin really *rape* you?"

~

I left the restroom with my hands dripping wet, soap suds between my fingers as I stepped out into the hallway. I felt the droplets slipping off my fingertips as I tried to focus on something. A locker door slamming, a voice shouting, the static crackling through the speakers of the PA system. But there was nothing, only the words the girl had said at the sink reverberating through my mind.

Someone said they heard Mrs. Tomlin telling her husband about it. She sounded, like, really mad. But did he really rape you, though? You could tell me. If he did. It just . . . it's Griffin, you know?

I walked slowly to my locker, noticing random heads turning to look as I maneuvered between people, backpacks bumping against my shoulders. A couple of awkward-looking girls stood near the water fountain, uncertainty on their faces, and a lanky boy smacked his friend's chest to make him look up from his phone as I neared my locker. I hadn't realized it before. I'd thought they were looking at me like they normally did, the way they had since October.

Then I lifted my gaze and found him. Kolby stood alone near the turn of the hallway, with his hand clenching the strap of his backpack. There was something in his expression, in his jawline and eyes, that sank deep into my chest, but he kept the distance between us before he turned away. Someone tapped him on the shoulder as he passed, gesturing to me, but he shrugged his shoulder out from under their hand before he disappeared.

"Hey, Clara, wait up!" I heard Aniston's voice, a blur of pink appearing from behind me. "I take it from the rumors buzzing around school that Griffin's weird dead birthday party thing didn't go so well. That's okay. I mean, it's not okay *okay*, but it will

234

be. People just care right now because it's fresh. Like, you know, eating avocados and doing internet challenges."

I shot her a look as I opened my locker.

She made a face. "I get that people knowing is bad but it's not *terrible*, Clara. They'll, you know, get over it and it'll—"

"You knew."

"Knew about what? I found out what happened last night at the party through the rumor mill. Which is fine. I mean, you could've texted me. If you wanted. But, I don't know, maybe you thought it was too late or something, and in that case, thanks for the consideration—"

"No, you knew about Emily," I interrupted, watching as she tensed. "You knew that she killed Elizabeth Monner. You knew the entire time and you *never* told me. I mean, what was even the point of asking me to help you if you were just going to keep things from me?"

"I wasn't sure you'd believe me," she stammered. "I wasn't *hiding* it from you. I just wanted proof before I accused your sister of murdering another person!"

"You had no problem telling me you thought Griffin was becoming a serial killer without proof." My anger flared as I looked down at Aniston, her stature still so tiny even in three-inch heels. I was suddenly furious that she'd lied, that everyone seemed to be someone else, their mask slipping away and revealing someone I did not know. "You think you know people. That because you write for a *high school newspaper* and read Sherlock Holmes, you know everything. You know better than everyone else but, Aniston, you don't. I mean, you are so *conceited* that you thought you could figure this case out better than actual detectives!"

Something passed over her face, a fleeting emotion that

touched her eyes and the corners of her vibrant pink lips before it faded away, but a flicker of annoyance still showed in her expression. "If by *conceited* you mean confident, then yeah, I am. You might not know the emotion because you've spent your entire life doubting yourself."

The words stung and made my skin prickle when I heard them. "You know what—"

"Look, it didn't make sense how someone, even a guy like Griffin Tomlin, could sneak into someone else's backyard with a body and just bury it. It also didn't make sense that he didn't torment you about it. And . . . Emily is a killer! Just because it's insanely obvious to everyone doesn't mean it's not true. At first I thought maybe she'd killed Elizabeth Monner to try and get Griffin arrested, but that didn't make sense because then why hide the body in your backyard and not do anything with it? And I spoke to Bex. I tried to speak to Wilson, but he was having none of it. Anyway, what she said matched with what Emily did to Griffin. She . . . used one of the beer bottles to sodomize him. Just like Bex said Wilson told her she used to do to him."

I closed my locker door. "Since when did we start believing anything Wilson says? He's an abusive loser who probably taught Emily everything she knows."

"Did you ever actually see him being abusive? With Emily or Bex? I don't know what kind of impression Emily gave you of him, but I think it's pretty obvious now she's untrustworthy!"

"That doesn't mean Wilson Westbrooke isn't too." I turned around and headed to my next class. "I have to go."

A few hours later, standing in the parking lot, clenching and unclenching my fists at my sides, I stared at the tan van with the dirtied windows rolled down, muffled rap music coming from the stereo. Because my mother's veterinary clinic didn't close until five, I had a couple of hours before she was coming to pick me up. And when I'd walked outside and noticed his van, as he waited for Bex to finish practice—which I'd skipped—I hesitated.

His dark blond hair touched his shoulders and his thin gray T-shirt was too big on his slender frame. His thumb was counting the beats of the music as he looked out to the street, watching the fleeting cars go past.

What was he like before he met Emily? Maybe he was different then. I tried to remember if he'd looked different. Maybe with shorter, fuller hair, with arms that filled out his sleeves instead of disappearing into them. Basketball shorts that didn't slip down his hips when he walked.

That was when I realized he'd done the same thing I had. He wore sizes too big, never anything that shaped or flattered. But he was Wilson Westbrooke. He was a boy. Even though he was so lanky, he had to be stronger than she was. It almost didn't seem to make sense that he couldn't stop her, shove her away from him. But then I remembered when Griffin threatened me to be still that night, whispering he would kill me if I tried to scream again, and I didn't. I was quiet and still and never fought back either. And that was when I understood who Wilson Westbrooke really was, not just who my sister told me he was or who my parents thought he was, but what was really there beneath.

He was just this lonely boy who thought he'd found someone who was so brilliant and mesmerizing that maybe it meant there was something kind of like that about him too. And when he was wrong, he knew no one would ever believe it, so he kept it all to himself.

Griffin Tomlin was not Wilson Westbrooke. I was Wilson Westbrooke.

As I approached the van in the back of the parking lot, its scent wafted out toward me: lingering cigarette smoke that clung to the cracked, yellowing leather of his front seats, and a perfume I recognized as Bex's. The car stereo was still blaring a rap song I hadn't heard before. Wilson was drinking from a bottle of soda when he glanced over and saw me. He seemed to take me in with an intensity I wasn't sure I'd ever thought Wilson Westbrooke capable of, and somehow it was suddenly obvious. He knew. Everyone knew now, and I stopped myself from wondering how the news had reached him. Maybe he'd known before, seeing something in me he saw in himself, or maybe Bex told him.

"Wilson." I was shouting to be heard over the pulsating beat that I felt under my shoes through the pavement, and Wilson held up a finger, his mouth still full of soda, and turned the radio off. The abrupt silence was almost as jarring. "Wilson," I repeated, quieter now. "I want to ask you something, and whatever you tell me, I'll believe it. Did my sister—did she do the things Bex said she did?"

Wilson turned to me, and before he said anything, it was clear. Clear from the nonchalant expression that didn't reach his eyes, a familiar reluctance lingering there, afraid of the truth.

"How am I supposed to know what she told you about her?" he asked, his voice gruff with feigned indifference.

"You want to know what I think?"

"No."

"I think you were a decent guy before you met her. I think you probably fell in love with her a lot faster than she did with you, if she ever did. And now I think you say things you know will hurt other people because you're afraid that if you don't, you'll be right back where you started, getting hurt yourself. But I also think you hate that. I think that you hate what she turned you into and you blame her more for that than anything else."

I let out a breath, realizing as I said those words that they were true, and watched as he slid his thumbnail down the label of his soda bottle, tearing it, and clenched his jaw. But I also noticed he wasn't saying anything. He wasn't trying to hurt me. He wasn't trying to get under my skin. He was just sitting there, tearing the label off a bottle.

"Emily—she took a lot of things. But you, who you are, it doesn't have to be one of them," I said. "You don't have to add yourself to a list of things she stole. You . . . are here! You have a chance to *push back* and take what's yours."

He turned, gnawing on his lips and his fingers clenched white around the neck of the bottle, but there was something in his eyes that softened as he took me in, standing there beside his passenger door. "That was a really long speech. And dramatic," he remarked.

"Long and dramatic are what make it effective." I tapped on the door of the van. "Do you think you could drive me somewhere?" He tilted his head to the side, raising his eyebrows at me. "Please?"

He leaned across the console and popped open the door. I climbed inside, the leather firm against my shoulders and the hinges screeching as I yanked the door shut. Wilson glanced at me as he started the engine—his eyes were a different shade of blue than Griffin's, brighter, almost glittering. I leaned back against the cracked leather, feeling the curled corners of duct tape graze my neck.

"Where are we going?" he asked, pulling out of the parking lot.

"The greatest place no one will ever find," I said.

He hesitated. "Sure, but which way do I turn?"

chapter twenty-five

The barn loomed eerily in the distance as Wilson steered the van onto the dirt clearing, potholes causing the tires to dip under us and my elbow to bang loudly against the door. The apple orchard behind it was barren and brown, snow on the branches, and crumpled, dead leaves weighed down by snow littered the ground. With a dull white sky behind it, it didn't look like the place I remembered it being: safe and warm.

"A barn," Wilson observed flatly. "That was close to what I was hoping for. If you took off the letter *N*."

"I think Emily killed someone else. Other than Griffin. Her name was Elizabeth Monner. You remember the body they found in my backyard a couple weeks ago? That was her. And I think Emily did it. I just have to prove it, and maybe there's something in there. I don't know."

"Wait, you actually want her to get *more* time?"

I turned toward the apple orchard a couple of hundred feet away from the warped and graying barn, thinking that beyond lifting a couple of old blankets and peering into the stalls for some hint—something that would somehow shift everything into place, locking it all into a picture I could understand again—I hadn't thought about what I would do if I actually found something.

"Come on," I said to him, instead of answering his question, yanking on the door handle. "Let's go."

The cold air drifted through the spreading gaps between the boards in the walls, brushing against my neck and my bare hands as I stepped into the barn, Wilson a couple of paces behind me. I felt a small pang of disappointment as I looked around. It looked just like it did before. Bottle caps from the afternoon we'd spent here still scattered across the cracked concrete, straw crunching beneath our shoes, the blanket we'd spread out crumpled but still on the floor. Even though I'd already known I probably wouldn't find anything here, the sight created a hollowness in my chest when my instinct was basically confirmed.

"She brought me here the day Elizabeth Monner disappeared," I told him, taking another step, noticing a crumpled fast food wrapper in the corner. "I fell asleep after she gave me a beer and said she was going to go get some more. I woke up a couple of hours later and she said she'd been waiting, like, the whole time."

"She probably lied. She was probably gone the whole time and told you that. I bet she even drugged you." He laughed bitterly and kicked one of the bottle caps. "She knew how to do it."

I glanced at his hands, balled in the pocket of his hoodie, the strands of hair that hid his eyes from me. "She said you hit her," I said. "She had a black eye once and said you hit her because she thought you were cheating on her. Did she give herself a black eye just to convince me you were hitting her?"

"No, not really," he sighed. "I did hit her, but not because she thought I was cheating on her. She tried something and I had just had enough, I guess. So I flipped out. Pushed her off and ended up smacking her in the eye and she ran out crying. *Her*. She was so *twisted* that she actually made me feel bad about what happened. And then a couple of days later she comes back, tells me that she forgives me, and I'm so relieved I don't even remember why I smacked her in the first place. I knew what she was doing but doing something about it just felt wrong. And then she started telling me my friends are trying to gang rape her when I'm not around, that she thinks my father, my *father*, wants to touch me and I need to stay away from him. We broke up not long after that, but she didn't really leave me alone until she went to jail, and even now I still get letters from her."

"She sends you letters? From jail?"

"Locks of her hair too. Says to put them in a jar or something so I can still smell her until she gets out." Wilson took a step away from me and into one of the stalls, the one farthest away in the back corner of the barn. He kicked at the random clumps of hay scattered across the dusty, splintered concrete.

I wasn't really sure of how I was supposed to respond to this, if I was supposed to tell him about the letters Griffin used to send me or apologize that Emily Porterfield was my sister.

"Aniston told me that teenage killers are sloppy," I said to him instead. "They're so convinced they won't get caught that they make mistakes. But what if Emily wasn't like that? What if she really was good at this stuff? Or what if I'm wrong and Griffin really did kill Elizabeth Monner? I don't know. I don't try to figure these things out! Aniston just does it and tells me in really long sentences."

"Well, it would help if you actually looked around instead of just standing there," he retorted, lifting a handful of multicolored blankets from the ground. He shot me an almost amused look, as if to say *see*, as a water-damaged cardboard box was unearthed. "Emily was sloppy. Manipulative, but sloppy. The only thing that kept her from getting caught sooner was that she was a pretty blond cheerleader."

Wilson used the side of his shoe to edge the cardboard box from the corner, the bottom scraping against the concrete, and something rattled inside. Sliding his sleeves over his hands, he reached down and pried it open, ripping the duct tape from the edges and peering in. He looked at me, an uneasiness in his eyes, before he kicked the box toward me. It slid a few inches before it was stopped by a crack in the concrete.

"Is it human stuff?" I asked.

"Sort of."

He grabbed the flaps of the stained cardboard so the sunlight could illuminate its contents. Inside was the pocketknife she'd taken from me last summer, mostly wiped clean but with dried blood still clinging to parts of the steel, two phones, and a roll of duct tape. But that wasn't what my gaze focused on as I stared into the box, my heart sinking somewhere deep and unfathomable. There was a grocery bag filled with women's underwear. And through the plastic, I could see the familiar white fabric crumpled inside—my underwear, the pair Griffin had shoved into his pocket the night he'd raped me.

Air lodged somewhere within my throat as I stumbled out of the barn.

"Clare?" Wilson said, gingerly sorting through the box's contents, his brow furrowing. He was confused, something contorting the corners of his lips as he noticed the bag of multicolored women's underwear. I gestured vaguely in the direction of the box, tears blurring in my eyes as he glanced between me and it.

"That's—" I said. "My underwear. The pair I was wearing when—"

He placed the box down on the ground, his sleeve retracting from his palm when he lifted his hand to gesture that he got it. And that almost made me choke on a bitter laugh, because I was suddenly tossed into a world where Wilson Westbrooke understood me. Where Emily was just like the person she'd claimed to be protecting me from. Where monsters were humans and humans were monsters.

"She was in on it," I rasped. "She helped him. She knew what he was doing, what he did, and I—that night, the night he was in my room, I was the only one home! Maybe she told him my parents were gone. And my window was *open*! I never leave my window open. I just thought he was, I don't know, an amateur locksmith or something, but she *opened* it for him!"

"Clare."

"Stop calling me Clare!"

He flinched, glancing away from me. I wondered then, with a sickening feeling spreading out from my chest, if I reminded him of her, like how Brandon Tomlin always reminded me of his brother. The same eyes watching, even if they weren't actually there.

"Sorry," I said quietly. "Can you just—"

I nudged the cardboard box with my boots until it reached one of the front tires of Wilson's van. My hands were shoved into my pockets. I was afraid that if I touched it, my fingerprints would cling to it and the evidence would condemn me as much as it did her. But I couldn't leave it there. And it wasn't until I stood at the bumper of his van, my eyes focusing on the fruitless apple orchard in front of me, that I realized where I needed to go.

"Can you take me somewhere else?" I asked Wilson. "Like the police station."

"You want to take this to the—?"

"Yes," I said, noticing that even though he had taken his keys from his pocket, he'd made no move to unlock the van. "We don't have to tell them about you and her. We just need to take this in. This knife could be the one she used to kill Elizabeth Monner."

When Wilson still didn't look convinced, that glint from earlier in the school parking lot back in his eyes, I took a step closer to him. "She's one of us. But unlike us, she never got away. Her nightmare did. And we have to do something about that."

"We're not talking about some random pervert, Clara. It's *Emily*, your sister. She could be in prison for the rest of her life because of some of the stuff in there."

I nodded, reaching down and grabbing the box through the sleeves of my coat. "I know."

The engine was running when I opened the passenger door at the police station. Wilson's fingers were almost dancing along the steering wheel as he gazed at the building in front of him through the windshield. An anxiousness swirled into the indigo of his eyes as he took it in, the red-brown bricks and white pillars apparently as intimidating to him as they were to me. I slowly slid out of the van, something occurring to me as I did.

"Why did Bex believe you?" I looked down at the cardboard box I had grabbed from the dashboard, shrugging, my glasses sliding down my nose a little. "She didn't believe me when I told her about Griffin. And if she could believe you, then I don't get why she couldn't believe me."

Wilson leaned into his seat. I almost thought he had no answer. No idea why Bex would choose to believe him but not me. "Bex is one of those people who needs proof of everything. But she comes around. It just takes her a minute."

There was something in his voice, a softness, something so unusual to hear coming from him. But then I remembered all the other things I'd learned about Wilson that day, and it felt slightly less surprising.

"But for the record, I think she does believe you. I think what was so unbelievable to her wasn't that it was Griffin Tomlin or whatever. It was that she'd had no idea." He frowned. "People think you're supposed to notice those things. They expect it to be obvious. And when it isn't, they're ashamed. And you think they're ashamed of you, when actually they're ashamed of themselves for never seeing it in the first place. That's why Bex, and your boyfriend, need a minute."

"I don't think he needs just a minute," I whispered, my voice thick. "What if he blames me for Griffin dying? Or he does believe me but he's so—so disgusted by that he can't even . . ."

"He probably is disgusted," he replied, and even though I knew this was true, I shot him a look. "He should be. But he's not disgusted with you, or anything you did. You're probably the last person he's disgusted with right now, Clara. People don't always react in the best ways when they're caught off guard, but if they care about you, they'll find a way to make things right. And Kolby cares about you. A lot."

"If you believe all that, then come with me inside the police station. Tell them what happened between you two."

He shook his head. "That's . . . different. I know it sounds like an excuse, but it isn't. People are going to believe a pretty young girl way sooner than some borderline alcoholic punk with a record. That's just how it goes."

I let out a sigh, turning to hop down from the van. "I get what you mean," I said to him, about to close the door, "and thanks for calling me pretty, I think—but no one believes me either."

He made a face, one that looked sort of apologetic. "I didn't—"

I nodded. "I know. But for a borderline alcoholic punk, you've got a couple of people who already believe you. That's a start, right?"

"You're stalling."

"I know. But still. It's just something to think about."

The inside of the police station was always brighter than I expected it to be whenever I walked inside. When Emily had still been just a suspect in Griffin Tomlin's murder and the police brought all of us there for interrogations, I remembered thinking that everything would be darker, with minimal windows and unsmiling faces everywhere I turned. Instead the walls were a cream color, gleaming white tiles stretched out over the floor, and now, months later, cheap St. Patrick's Day decorations decked the lobby. There were even a couple of black leather couches near the windows in the waiting room, and they had a television mounted in the corner.

The receptionist looked up from her computer, her artificial nails clacking at the keyboard, and smiled when she spotted me coming through the doors. "Can I help you?"

"I'm here to see Detective Marsh? If he's available. It's about my sister. Emily Porterfield."

As I spoke, the receptionist turned back to her computer, her hand reaching for the mouse. When she heard my sister's name, she paused. "All right, why don't you have a seat and he'll be with you as soon as he can."

I headed to the couches near the corner of the room, the muffled sound of voices shouting at each other from the television becoming louder as I neared it. I curled my fingers a little tighter around the edge of the box and looked out the window to the parking lot. My eyes searched for the van I already knew would be gone.

As I stared out at the patrol cars parked outside, I heard footsteps coming from behind me, soles squeaking on the tiles. I turned around and saw Detective Marsh standing there, wearing a suit with a Bugs Bunny tie. He looked taller now than I remembered him being, his graying hair shaved close to his head, and his face was creased with wrinkles.

"Hey there, Miss Porterfield. I heard you wanted to talk to me about something."

I nodded. "Yes, sir."

He gestured for me to follow him. "You want something to drink?" he asked as he led me down the hall. "Snack maybe?"

"No, thanks."

Detective Marsh led me into one of the interrogation rooms. The walls were a bland shade of white, and my feet shuffled against gray carpet. There was a bare table beside the wall farthest from the door, and there were three chairs positioned around it—two on one side and only one on the other. I already knew which one was meant for me.

Detective Marsh looked at the box as I set it down on the table. "We've been looking for you today, Clara," he told me. "We've heard a few rumors around town about you. Do you know what those rumors are?"

"Yes, sir."

"Do you mind if I ask you a couple questions about it?" I shook my head, even though that wasn't totally truthful. I did mind. But it wasn't like it mattered now anyway. "Before we start, you want us to call your mom? Let her know where you are or ask her to come down here?"

I shook my head again. "She doesn't know about any of the things that happened."

"It might be helpful to tell her what's been going on. And for her to hear it from you."

"Can you just call her and tell her I'm here? So she doesn't worry about me. She's supposed to pick me up from drama practice soon."

He nodded. I gave him the number to her vet clinic and waited until he returned a few minutes later. "All right," he said as he closed the door behind him. "I talked to your mom and she said she was going to come down here, *but* we'll just talk in here, okay? Just you and me. And if you want her to come in at any time, we can go grab her. Sound good?"

"Yes," I said.

"All right. So had you and Griffin Tomlin ever been in a romantic relationship?"

"Sort of. At first, I mean," I said, kind of embarrassed to be talking about this with an older man who was listening more intently than I was used to people doing. "I had a crush on him for a really long time. I thought I was in love with him, but now, I don't really know. But I thought he never, you know, never really saw me. But then one night, after the school musical, he texted me and asked me to meet him in my backyard, and he kissed me. But nothing really happened after that. Then a couple weeks later, he gave me his number because he'd got a new phone, and we started *really* texting. And in February, he finally asked me out. Like, really asked me out, and I said yes. He took me to this party and gave me a beer before we went upstairs to someone's bedroom."

"What happened then?"

"He raped me," I said, my voice thicker than I wanted it to sound in front of him, but he didn't seem to notice. Just nodding and listening. "He, um, cut me too? With his pocketknife on my ribs, in between the bones, and I still have the scars if that . . . proves anything. But he took my underwear, and the reason I'm here is because I found it. In this box."

"And where did you find the box?" he asked, standing up to inspect it.

"In this old abandoned barn my sister used to bring me to last summer after she'd found out about what he'd done. But now I think . . ." I hesitated, digging my fingernails into my jeans, and wondered if I was really about to do this. If I was really about to suggest to a detective that my sister had killed a total stranger. "I think she helped Griffin do stuff to me. And I also think she might have killed Elizabeth Monner. The girl you found in our backyard."

"I see. What makes you think that?"

"It just kind of makes sense? Like, she buried her in our backyard, and I don't know where she was when Elizabeth went missing." I shrugged, suddenly realizing just how weak this all sounded. "Do you think that they might have been working together? Hurting girls or something."

"It's a possibility we're looking into," he said finally, with some reluctance, and then his features softened considerably, the crinkles of his skin around his eyes and mouth easing away. "We're investigating Griffin Tomlin and taking all things into consideration right now."

"I think I have something that could help with that," I told him. "I still have the pocketknife he used when he raped me."

chapter twenty-six

It had been a few hours since I'd arrived at the police station and finally I was through with all of Detective Marsh's questions. I'd scheduled an appointment to meet with a forensic nurse after school in a couple of days about the scars between my ribs. A forensics expert took the cardboard box I'd brought in with me to be tested, and Detective Marsh sent someone to the house for the pocketknife I told him I'd taped under the driver's seat in Emily's car. Before, when it was still in my bedroom and Emily was arrested, I'd been afraid the police would search my room and find it, but the search warrant had been limited to only her bedroom and car, and the family areas of the house. When Elizabeth Monner's body was unearthed in our backyard, they didn't include the car in the search warrant, since it had already been combed through after Griffin's murder.

It was nearing nine o'clock at night when I came out into the station's lobby and found my mother sitting on one of the couches, distractedly watching a rerun of a comedy show from the nineties, still dressed in her scrubs with cartoon kittens and paw prints over its teal fabric. When she heard my boots squeaking against the tiles, she clenched the purse strap tighter over her shoulder and stood up.

"Clara—"

"Can we just talk about this at home?" I glanced around the police station, at the receptionist still on her computer a few feet away, pretending like she couldn't hear us. "Please?"

She hesitated, fingers tightening around her purse, but nodded. "Okay."

It was quiet during the twenty minute car ride, except for the humming of the engine that droned in my ears and the radio station that immediately turned on when Mom started the car and neither one of us went to turn off. She glanced over at me occasionally, when she flipped on her turn signal or switched lanes, but other than to ask me if I was warm enough in the first few minutes, she said nothing else.

It wasn't until we got home and she hesitated behind me after we walked through the front door, dropping her keys in the dish with a series of jingling clanks that felt deafening in the otherwise quiet house, that I realized she *knew*. Not just that I'd found a cardboard box filled with evidence incriminating her other daughter, but about *him*. Maybe she'd heard it at work earlier that day, a teenager telling a parent that their vet's daughter had accused a murdered boy of raping her at a party she'd snuck out to attend or something. But she, along with the rest of Shiloh it seemed, knew about what had happened with Griffin Tomlin.

I remembered Wilson telling me that people don't always react in the right ways when they're caught off guard.

I couldn't handle that anymore.

"I'm tired," I told her, feeling as if I had interrupted her even though she hadn't said anything. "I'm going to go up to my room."

"Clara." Her voice was firmer than I'd expected it to be. It was a tone I hadn't heard her use since before Emily was arrested, and it was enough for me to pause on the first step of the staircase. "We have to talk about this. Look at me, please." I slowly turned to face her, still standing on the step, and something wavered in her expression as she looked at me. I could hear it when she swallowed. "Are the rumors in town true about Griffin Tomlin?"

I felt parts of him on me, touching my sides or the muscles in my neck, fingernails scratching at the lower half of my stomach as he tried to undo my jeans. The ripping sound of the zipper being yanked away from the button almost similar to a gunshot firing in my ears. Before, it had been something I'd had completely to myself, but now it was out there, for anyone to imagine or disregard.

"Clara?"

"Would you believe me if they were?" I murmured.

The muscles in her chin dimpled as it trembled, and she took in a shaky breath. "Oh, honey," she whispered, her voice choked, and I felt parts of me slipping, falling, crashing to the ground before my fingers could grasp them again, regain control, and steady myself. "Yes. Yes, I would—and I do, I do believe you. I'm so sorry, sweetheart. I should've seen it."

I shook my head. "Mom, it's not your fault. *I* should've seen it and maybe none of this would be happening right now. Everything would be fine and we wouldn't be—"

"But I'm your mother. I'm supposed to protect you from these things, and I couldn't even tell you had a crush on the neighbor boy. If I wasn't so focused on how perfect I wanted things to be, then maybe I would have seen them for what they really were."

"But it wasn't like I wanted you to. Half the time, I don't even know why I keep stuff a secret, I just do," I told her, my breath hiccuping between the words.

"Still, I'm your mother and I should've known, even if you didn't want me to. I'm sorry." She let out a shuddering exhale, wiping her fingers under her eyes. "I should call your father. He needs to know about this too." She glanced at me, her face softening as she took in my reluctant expression, and she gave me a watery smile. "Tomorrow. I will call him *tomorrow*. Tonight, let's just go to bed."

I shrugged, desperate not to be alone again, and my mom felt like the only person I still had left. "Or we could watch a movie?" When she blinked, surprised at this, I added, "Or something."

She shook her head. "No, let's watch a movie. I'll go pop some popcorn and you pick something out, okay?" She leaned over and wrapped her arms around me, tightly. Her perfume reminded me of when I was younger, when we hugged more. "I love you, sweetie, no matter what."

"I love you too, Mom."

Everyone's gazes shifted toward me as I walked down the school hallway to my locker. A part of me tried to convince myself that it was because I was back at school the day after everyone had found out about what happened with me and Griffin, but I knew it was also because I looked different. And not just because suddenly I was the girl who'd accused a dead boy of raping her, but because the loose-fitting sweaters and leggings I usually wore were replaced with distressed skinny jeans and a sleeveless top with a neckline that revealed a hint of cleavage. My boots were switched out for small heels I'd found in the back of my closet, along with the other clothing I hadn't worn since last February.

I was even wearing makeup, and had sprayed perfume on my wrists.

I hadn't taken anything from Emily's closet when I was getting dressed that morning, like I would've before, even after she was arrested. Now I refused to touch anything that belonged to her, wanting to separate myself from it, her. Slice away the parts of her like a medical procedure, until she was completely detached.

And I wanted to abandon Griffin, the ocean-blue eyes I still felt lingering on my exposed skin as if he were still here. I wanted to pry his fingers from me and leave them like the bones they were becoming in his grave.

He didn't get to choose what I wore anymore.

"Oh man," someone chuckled from behind me, his back turned. "You dress like that and you call it rape?"

I glanced over my shoulder at the speaker, recognizing him as Xander James, one of the lacrosse players. He was spinning the combination of his locker, almost as if, despite his comment, he was completely oblivious to me.

I felt a twinge of self-consciousness, my exposed skin tingling and suddenly cold, and I thought about maybe changing into my gym shirt before I remembered ocean blue. Ocean blue observing me, controlling me, following me. Ocean-blue waters had surrounded me, nearly drowned me, and then left me scrambling for breath. A mumbled comment wasn't going to leave me breathless and afraid again.

"You think you can just joke about something like that?" I

whirled around at the sound of the voice coming from behind me.

Kolby.

Xander stared at him as if he wasn't sure he was serious. "Just relax, man."

"I heard what you said. *She*," Kolby told him, pointing to me, "heard what you said."

He shrugged, still looking incredulous. "Okay, fine, whatever. I made a joke, so what? When you're dressed like that, you're asking for it. You can't complain when a guy acted on it."

"Are you hearing yourself right now?" Regardless of whether Xander was listening, everyone else could certainly hear Kolby, his voice echoing against the lockers as he yelled.

"Kolby, it's fine," I muttered as the other students in the hallway started to stare.

He shook his head, shooting me a look. "No, it's not fine! Morons like him can't just say whatever they want—"

"Oh, so now I'm a moron?" Xander asked. "Geez, man. I thought he was supposed to be your friend. Why are you taking this slut's word?"

"What did you call her?"

I caught a glimpse of pink rounding the corner down the hall, and I turned to her, confused and almost scared.

Talk to him, calm him down, Aniston mouthed to me.

I looked back at Kolby, anger contorting and coloring his skin. I felt my own sense of anger. He'd left me, stranded at a bus stop with Mrs. Tomlin, and now I needed to talk him down.

"Kolby, seriously. It doesn't matter. Let's just go."

He ignored me. "What did you call her?"

When he didn't listen, I reached into my backpack and grabbed one of my textbooks, smacking it against the back of his head.

Out of the corner of my eye, I saw Aniston jump as Kolby paused, in the middle of a sentence I hadn't understood. He brought his hand to the back of his head as he looked at me, bewildered.

And then, over his shoulder, the history teacher headed toward us.

We had been left sitting in the chairs outside the principal's office, the receptionist turning to glance over at us every few seconds while our parents talked inside. Xander was on the last chair, closest to the principal's door, occasionally casting a look over at Kolby that he either missed or ignored from where he sat in the middle. I hadn't seen or spoken to him since he'd left me at the bus stop two days ago, but I almost wondered if he was trying to be a wall of flesh and bone between me and Xander or if he'd just randomly sat there.

Sometimes I thought I could feel him glancing at me, but I never looked over at him to see if he was.

Xander's mother emerged first, apparently frustrated and exasperated as she threw open the principal's door and sharply told her son, "Get up right now." As they were leaving, I leaned back to look at the principal's door, hoping to see my mother come out next.

When it was obvious that our parents were still going to be in there for another few minutes, I couldn't help flicking my gaze over to Kolby for a split second. "What were you trying to do?" I finally asked.

He let out a sigh, tilting his head back, a reluctance already tensing his shoulders.

"Did you really think that getting into a fight at school was a good idea?"

"It wasn't really a fight. I never touched him. And anyway, he said something stupid," he muttered.

"I'd take that over someone *doing* something stupid any day."

I turned away from him, crossing my arms over my chest and slouching in the chair—even though it felt juvenile, I wanted to look as irate as I felt, a rebelliousness stirring that needed to be visible to him, to anyone.

His jaw was clenched, the muscles twitching beneath the skin, but after a moment, he slowly leaned closer to me, his voice soft, and there was something lingering underneath it, a shift I couldn't quite recognize. "He was my friend. I don't even remember meeting him, he was just always my friend. And I thought I knew him better than anyone."

I waited in the silence, let Kolby continue. "I was there, at that party. I was downstairs, on my phone, and I see this guy taking a girl upstairs. And I just go back on my phone."

"You saw—?"

"I thought it was Brandon," he told me, his voice small and broken, the whites of his eyes beginning to tinge red before he looked away from me, coughed, and then swallowed. "He'd said he might show up later. I thought it had to be him because it couldn't be Griffin. I knew something was off, and I just went and played a stupid game on my phone while . . ."

"You told me about that."

He nodded, forcing a small, choked laugh. "You'd think I would've noticed, right? I would've been able to recognize him or you. The only reason I went was because Griffin said you'd be there, then it becomes so *stupidly* obvious that you guys were on a date. And I remembered all those little things that were so clearly wrong, but *no*. I noticed *nothing*. My best friend raped my girlfriend and I—" he scoffed, shaking his head as his voice deepened, "I couldn't even tell."

I wasn't completely sure of what to say to him, or what to even think, but before I could come up with a response, the principal's door opened and our parents came out to tell us that we had detention for the next two weeks.

"Getting into fights at school? Really, Clara?" my mother was saying to me as we trudged through the slush-covered parking lot, pausing between words as she fished through her purse for her keys, making a muffled jingling sound.

I shrugged. "I didn't get into a fight, Mom. It just kind of happened around me, and I—"

"Hit Kolby Rutledge on the head with a textbook," she retorted, glancing up for a moment to glare at me. I shrugged again as she sighed, turning back to her purse. "What was that about anyway? I thought you two were going out."

"I don't think we are anymore."

She stopped walking, her hand still deep in her purse but the rummaging temporarily paused. "What? Did he break up with you because of what people have been saying?"

"No. I mean, we haven't actually *broken up* or anything—like, no one's said it—but when I told him about Griffin and everything, he didn't take it that well." She was still looking at me, sadness softening her focused gaze, and I waved a hand through the air, trying to brush it off. "You were right anyway. Dating the best friend of the guy my sister killed was a bad idea."

My mom hesitated, retracting her hand from her purse—fingers now clutched around her keys—and looked as if she were about to say something when she suddenly glanced over my shoulder. "Is that Bex?" she asked, and I turned around.

There, sitting on the last concrete step in front of the school, was Bex on her phone.

Then, before I knew what was happening, my mom was waving her hand in the air, calling out, "Hi, Bex!"

"Mom!" I hissed as Bex looked up, glancing around the parking lot before she saw my mom and me standing near the handicapped parking spaces, her brow creasing.

Mom was smiling, still waving. "I haven't seen her in forever! How come you girls don't hang out anymore?"

"Same reason Kolby and I don't date anymore."

My mom blinked, turning to me and dropping her hand. "Wait, you—"

"Hi, Mrs. Porterfield." Before I even realized Bex had got up from where she was sitting a moment ago, she was standing in front of us, an awkward smile going back and forth between my mom and me. "It's nice to see you again."

"It's really nice to see you again too, Bex," she said, and I almost rolled my eyes. "Clara told me you have the lead in the musical this year. That must be really exciting!"

"I probably only got it because Clara didn't want it," she said, laughing.

"You didn't want it? I thought you auditioned."

"Not exactly," I answered reluctantly. I wasn't sure I wanted to tell her I'd missed the audition deadline and only accepted a background role because I'd thought Bex was being abused by Wilson Westbrooke, which I was wrong about. I also really couldn't tell her that in front of Bex.

She looked at me for a few seconds before she turned back to Bex, her smile reappearing. "Did you need a ride home? You were just sitting on that step over there, and it's a little cold outside." I shot my mom a withering look.

Bex shook her head. "No, it's okay. My boyfriend's going to drive me home. Thanks, though."

"You have a boyfriend?" My mother grinned teasingly at her. "That's exciting! Do we know him? Is he from the musical too?"

I caught a glimpse of panic in Bex's eyes as she blinked, her mouth opening as if she were about to respond, but then she said nothing for the next couple of seconds before I blurted out, "Mom, can I meet you at the car? I want to talk to Bex about something."

"Sure," she said, a little too cheerily. "It was nice seeing you again, Bex. Can't wait to see the musical in a couple of weeks!"

After my mother walked a safe distance away from us, Bex said to me, "Thanks?"

"I didn't really do it for you," I told her. "My mom still thinks Wilson is sketchy and I don't know how she'd react to finding out you two are together. But there was something I wanted to ask you."

"Hmm?"

The stale scent of cigarette smoke drifted from her clothes as I crossed my arms and glanced over her shoulder to the empty parking space I knew his old and broken-down van would be idling in soon. "Do you think you could talk to Wilson about going to the police and telling them about what happened between him and Emily?"

"He wouldn't do it," she explained. "He thinks people will think he's just making it up or, if they don't, that they'll start pitying him."

"But he can still do something about it. He can press charges against her for what she did."

"He doesn't care about that. It's not like she's out free or anything. She's already in jail."

"For now, because the judge denied her bail, but she hasn't actually been convicted or anything," I told her. "She deserves time for all the things she did to everyone, including Wilson. Don't you want him to get justice for what she did to him?"

"I want what he wants, and that's to just move on. I don't get why *you* can't get that."

I stared at her, incredulous. "I *do* get it, Bex. That's why I'm saying this. He has this chance I'm never going to have. The last time I saw Griffin was at a Labor Day block party and then, the next morning, he was dead. And that was *it*. He basically got away with it and there's nothing I can do about it, ever. But Wilson can. He can prove to her that he doesn't belong to her, and I need you to show him that."

She glanced down at the scuffed toes of her combat boots and let out a breath. I wondered if her reluctance wasn't because she disagreed with me but because she really knew he wouldn't do it. She knew him better. She probably knew his middle name, his birthday, the name of his favorite song, and whatever else he might not have told me about Emily, about them, together. But I knew him in a way that she didn't—we shared that tightening ache in our chests and scarred wounds that throbbed as if they were still exposed.

"Bex," I said after a moment of tense silence, remembering my mom was still waiting for me. "Talk to him about it, please."

"I still don't think that he'll do it." She crossed her arms, glancing over my shoulder as I heard the familiar medley of a sputtering car engine and muffled rap music coming distantly from behind me. "But I'll ask, okay?"

I was almost tempted to smile at her before I realized that would mean I was smiling at *her*. "Okay," I responded as she nodded, walking around me and starting to wend her way between the cars parked around us. "Cool."

"You realize you're talking to no one, right?" I jumped at the voice from over my shoulder, whirling around and noticing Aniston standing on the sidewalk. "I mean, it's fine. Like, I talk to myself all the time too, but I get that's not really what was happening here. *But* you *could* talk to me instead? Or, you know, no one."

I glanced away. "I don't feel like talking." I almost wanted to add *to you*, but I thought better of it. "My mom's waiting for me."

"Wait, Clara. Are we really not going to talk or fight about this at all? You're just going to keep coming up with excuses to walk away?"

"My mom really is waiting for me. That's her car over there."

"I get that when I wasn't completely honest with you about Emily, I broke your trust, but the thing is, Clara? You haven't been completely honest either, with a *lot* of people. And I'm not trying to deflect here or bring up an *ad hominem*—"

I frowned. "What?"

"Whenever you weren't honest with me, I *got* it. And I was hoping you would too. I wasn't holding anything back to hurt you. Emily's your sister and I knew that I couldn't just accuse her of murdering Elizabeth Monner with no real evidence without seriously imploding our friendship, so I held back. I mean, you're *literally* my only friend and I wanted to protect that, and you. I'm sorry if I didn't really do that right."

There was a small, glimmering part of me that wanted to just let that be the end of it, tell her that it was okay and ask if she had any new theories or had bought any pink accessories recently or something, but I couldn't quite give into it. There was still something tethered to me, holding me back.

"My mom's been waiting for me a long time. I really have to go."

I headed for my mother's car before I could hear a response from Aniston. When I climbed into the passenger seat a moment later, my mom was leaning over the steering wheel staring at Aniston as she stood on the sidewalk. "That's Aniston, isn't it?"

"Yeah."

"Her mom was so nice when we stayed with her. You should invite them over for dinner some time, to thank them." When I didn't say anything, she shot me a look. "You girls are still friends, right?"

I reached for my seat belt, stalling for a second. "Not really anymore."

My mother let out a sigh, pausing before she turned her key in the ignition. "Clara, honey," she told me, pulling out of the parking space. "You're starting to run out of friends here."

chapter twenty-seven

I went for a walk after dinner to try to clear my head, and when I got back home, I noticed my father's car was parked in the driveway, muddied and dusty, with slush embedded in the treads of the tires. It was almost like I could see how unkempt my father had become since he'd left. My father loved his car. He used to spend every Saturday afternoon washing it in the driveway, waving to dog walkers and gardeners. He even had a strict no-food policy after an incident at a drive-in theater regarding the loud boom of an on-screen explosion and a napkin covered in ketchup landing on the car door. But now there were crumpled bags of fast food and deli sandwich containers lying on the seats, their labels torn.

I was just about at the front door when I heard the familiar rumble of an old brown van. Wilson stepped out a few seconds after pulling alongside the curb. His hands were shoved into the pockets of his jeans as he walked across the front lawn, and I could see the prickles of goosebumps protruding on his arms, since he wasn't wearing a coat. He nodded in my direction as he approached me.

"You talked to Bex," he said.

I nodded, a bit reluctantly, feeling the slight twinge of panic that I had overstepped my bounds, and he responded with silence, looking away from me and tensing his shoulders with the intake of a breath. "I did."

"Clara—I don't want to do this." His voice was soft, nothing more than a whisper left to drift through the wind and find me. He looked like a small boy, filled with fear and confusion, and so unlike the person I'd thought he was before. So I reached out to him, my hand gently wrapping around his wrist—his muscles flinching beneath my palm but his arm remaining there, not pulling away—and I felt his pulse throbbing against my fingertips.

"Then you don't have to," I said. His blond hair blew in front of his face, his eyes lingering somewhere unfocused and unreachable to me, but he slowly slid his hand out of his pocket and interlocked his fingers with mine, his skin cold. I squeezed them, angling my face to meet his distracted gaze. When he found me, he offered a small but unstable smile. "But I want you to know you can. You *can* do it, Wilson."

His hand remained in mine, clasping it tightly, as if he was hoping it would anchor him to this place, prevent him from drifting away to somewhere unknown and frightening. Wilson looked as if he were about to say something when I heard the front door being thrown open, the doorknob banging against something loudly, and then footsteps rushing down the front steps with an urgency that alarmed me. Wilson's eyes widened as his hand unlatched from mine, and he stepped away from me.

"*Wilson!*"

I whirled around as I heard his name being spat, a deep and enraged growl from behind me. My father was charging from the front porch, his face red with resentment, as he sped past me and toward Wilson.

My mother followed behind my dad, shouting, "Eric! Eric! Eric, stop!"

Before I could realize what was happening, my father's fist slammed into Wilson's mouth with a crunch. He was shouting so hurriedly and so harshly at him that it didn't even sound like words. Wilson stumbled backward while simultaneously bending forward, bringing a hand to his lips, blood painting his fingernails.

"*Eric!*" my mother gasped, covering her own mouth with her hands.

My father was reaching for Wilson as he backed away from him, his steps unstable and wobbling. Then his hands struck against Wilson's shoulders, slamming against his collarbone and knocking him down to the ground, his back colliding with the concrete of our driveway.

"Dad!" I shrieked, rushing between them and crouching down by Wilson. "Stop! He wasn't doing anything!"

"Get away from him!" my father shouted, his hand gripping my shoulder, nearly dragging me back and onto the ground, but then I felt him abruptly let go.

"Are you okay?" I asked Wilson, gingerly touching a hand to his chin, his blood warm underneath my fingertips. His eyes had just met mine, bewilderment and shock staring back at me, when I heard my father shouting again. But this time, not at Wilson.

"Let me *go!*" he yelled. "Clara, get away from him! Get off me!"

I looked over my shoulder, my jaw falling slack as I took it in. My father, with someone's arms wrapped around his chest, restraining him, holding him back.

Brandon Tomlin's arms.

"Sir, you need to calm down," Brandon said over my father's irate voice as he demanded to be let go, struggled underneath the weight of his arms, the hands braced against his chest. Brandon pulled him backward and away from us.

A few minutes later, after Brandon Tomlin had forced my father to sit down on one of the front porch steps, he had somewhat calmed down, but not before commanding Brandon, "Get that filth off my property." A part of me wanted my mother, standing a few feet away from him, to remind him that this wasn't his property anymore.

Brandon came across the driveway toward us—wearing a football jersey and sweatpants, his socks dirtied from the slush as if he'd rushed out here—and said to Wilson, "I got some ice for that mouth over at my place, if you want."

Wilson's lips were reddened and swollen, and I could see blood was staining the crevices between his teeth. It was as if he was searching for something as he looked at me and I realized after a beat that he was asking if I was okay with it. And that was how we ended up in the Tomlins' garage, with me wordlessly following them after Brandon had extended his hand and lifted Wilson from the ground. I noticed him giving me a distrustful look before turning around and leading us to the house that was so familiar and yet unfamiliar at the same time.

We sat on lawn chairs while Brandon went inside for some ice, my shoulders stiff against the seat. I was almost waiting to see Griffin come through the door Brandon had passed through before I thought of something worse and more probable: one of his parents walking out and finding me sitting on their lawn furniture, as if we were still just neighbors who hadn't accused each other's families of doing awful things.

Something nudged me, a gentle touch against my boot. I glanced down, seeing that Wilson had extended his leg out from under his own chair and bumped the edge of his worn and untied shoe against mine.

"You okay?" he asked. I nodded, and then Brandon emerged from inside, a package of frozen corn kernels wrapped in a paper towel in his hand.

"Sorry," he said, handing it to Wilson. "We didn't have any actual ice after all."

Wilson brought it to his mouth nonetheless. "It's all right, man," he said, his voice muffled around the frozen corn. "Thanks."

For a moment, Brandon just stood there after nodding in response, leaning against the hood of a riding lawn mower with his arms crossed over his chest, and I realized as I looked at him that I really had no reason to be wary of him. He might have been Griffin Tomlin's brother, but I was Emily Porterfield's sister, and I wanted nothing to do with her or what she'd done.

And I knew one of the things she'd done was irrevocably hurt Brandon Tomlin and the rest of his family, and that they didn't deserve it, even if they didn't—or maybe couldn't—believe me.

"Brandon," I said after a moment, feeling that I owed him this much. "I'm sorry my sister killed Griffin."

He let out a breath. "I'm sorry about what he did to you."

"Wait, you—" I hesitated, not totally convinced that I'd heard him right, my heart beginning to hammer in my chest as I looked at him. "You believe me?"

"I didn't want to," he admitted quietly, and I heard the corn kernels shifting in the bag as Wilson adjusted it against his chin. "But yeah, I do. Sometimes he just said these things that didn't sound right. Kind of like he was bragging. I didn't really know what to make of it before my mom told me about what you'd said at the party the other night."

"She doesn't believe me, though, right?"

"No," he told me. "She thinks it's something Emily's defense lawyer came up with and that you're spreading it around to make it seem more believable or something. Is that why she did it? Like, to get revenge on him or something?"

"I thought that was why she did it," I said, feeling a little embarrassed as my voice trembled on the words. I cleared my throat, looking down to the concrete. "But now I think she actually was attracted to him because of what he did . . . maybe she killed him because he didn't like her back or she was jealous. I don't know."

"She thinks Emily killed that girl they found in her backyard a couple of weeks ago," Wilson mentioned.

"I know she did," I replied, looking over my shoulder at him. "I just—I don't really know why she would've. She was a total stranger."

Brandon grunted, shaking his head. "I wouldn't go trying to make sense of the stuff your psycho sibling does," he informed me, his voice becoming more somber as he spoke. "None of it's ever going to make any sense. It's just what's left, I guess."

"I don't think that's enough for me."

"Well," he responded, bracing his palms on either side of the riding lawn mower and pushing himself off the hood, "you have more than what I got." Then he shot us a tight smile that didn't quite reach his eyes and turned away, slipping inside the house a second later and leaving us there in his garage with a bag of melting corn.

I was about to get up from the lawn chair when Wilson brought the corn away from his mouth, still swollen and tinged red, and held it in the air, raising his eyebrows. "Am I supposed to just keep this now?"

chapter twenty-eight

It had been almost a week of spending detention together on opposite sides of the room before I found Kolby Rutledge lingering outside of the study hall afterward, leaning against the lockers as I gathered my homework and brushed the eraser shavings off the desk. I hesitated for a moment as I hitched the strap of my backpack farther up my shoulder, then started walking toward the exit when I heard his voice from behind me.

"Hey."

I turned around, halfway. "Hey."

"Can we talk for a second?"

I pointed my thumb behind me, over my shoulder. "My mom's waiting for me. We have to go meet the detectives at the police station about some new evidence."

He pushed himself off the lockers, his shoes squeaking against the floor as he approached me. "Can I walk with you, then?"

"I guess."

We ambled through the school hallway together, wordlessly

for a few moments, before he glanced at me out of the corner of his eye, tilting his head just slightly in my direction. "I'm sorry about leaving you at the hotel last week," he said, his voice soft but resolute. "And for getting us stuck in detention for another week. But mostly about the first thing. I shouldn't have left you with his mom and not given you a ride home. Especially when I practically made you go," he added, shaking his head with a dry laugh.

"You didn't make me go," I said, turning to look at him. "It was important to you, so I wanted to go." He shot me a look, and I shrugged sheepishly. "Okay, maybe not *wanted* but I wanted to do it for you. And I'm sorry I ruined it."

"You didn't ruin it," Kolby said. "It was ruined before we even got there. It was stupid, having this birthday party for a dead guy who doesn't even deserve it."

Back before anyone knew about what happened, I'd thought that I would've savored hearing someone—especially him—speaking about Griffin Tomlin like that, like the facade had finally shattered, the curtain dropped, and revealed to the crowd the boy that I had seen for months. But now I almost flinched hearing Kolby talking this way about his best friend.

When we reached the school's front doors, I turned to face him. "Thank you for apologizing," I told him. "I really do have to go now."

"Wait," he said quickly, but there was still a lingering hesitance in his voice. "Do you want to maybe meet up somewhere later? Not detention, I mean?"

"No." I shook my head, taking in his expression as he nodded, as if he'd anticipated this but was still hurt by it anyway. "I'm not still mad at you or anything. It's just—I mean, I know you're sorry, but I still don't want to just go back to how things were before. It hurt and I'm not over that."

I wasn't totally sure of how I expected him to respond, but I hadn't thought that he would just nod again, glancing down at the salt stains that rippled across our shoes, and murmur, "Okay."

He reached for the front door, opening it and stepping outside. It took me a minute before I realized he was holding it open for me. As it closed behind us, he told me again, "I'm . . . I'm really sorry about everything, Clara."

"I know you are."

It just wasn't enough.

> *hey, can u talk??*
> *hello*
> *clara?*
> *seriously, u gonna start ignorin me now?*
> *come on u i kno u c me*
> *ur thinkin about me*
> *u were starin @ me all nite just like u used to cuz u want me*
> *u need me*
> *kolby can't give it to u like i can*
> *answer me, slut*
> *SLUT*
> *SLUT*
> *SLUTSLUTSLUTSLUTSLUT!!!!!!!*

I stared down at the printed sheet of text messages Griffin had sent me, spanning from the middle of February to almost the end of August last year. Across the table from me, Detective Marsh interlocked his fingers and waited as I looked over the pages, nine in total.

When I glanced up at him, my brow creasing, he told me, "Those were the messages we found on one of the phones in the box you brought in last week, sent to your phone. Do you recognize the number?"

I did. I remembered the feeling of a ballpoint pen etching part of it into my palm more than a year ago. "About a year and a half ago, Griffin came to this ice cream parlor I worked at and told me he had to get a new phone, so he wanted to give me his new number. That's the number."

Detective Marsh nodded, taking the papers when I held them back out to him. "I think what happened here is that Griffin didn't really need a new phone and bought a burner phone to send these messages to you. The phone we found when Griffin was murdered was one he'd had for a couple of years."

"So Emily took it when she killed him? I don't get it. Why would she do that?"

"The other phone belonged to her. She started sending him text messages sometime in July and continued until his death in September. She probably hid them in the barn after we brought her in as a suspect for Griffin's murder. But there were a few messages mentioning an incident that occurred around your birthday?"

I nodded. "The day after my birthday, my bedroom window was unlocked, and Griffin climbed inside. He attacked me, but my parents came home and he ran out. I think maybe Emily opened it for him. I never unlocked my window, ever."

"Okay," Detective Marsh said. "Did you ever consider calling the police when he broke in and attacked you?" When I shook my head slowly, feeling sort of ashamed and embarrassed to admit this to a detective, he nodded gently. "How come?"

"Everyone loved Griffin. My parents did, the school did, I even thought I did. I thought if I did something like call the police, then maybe nothing would happen. I mean, I've watched those news stories about politicians and old comedians. Everyone just thinks the girls are lying for attention. And then Griffin would know I'd called the police and maybe he'd get back at me for it."

"Clara, did you know I have a daughter about your age? Maybe a little younger," he said, and I shook my head, not totally sure where he was going with this. "Whenever I'm working a case with a young girl involved, I think to myself, *If this were my daughter, what would I want the detectives to do? How seriously would I want them to treat this case?* And I know I'm not the only officer here who thinks that way. Now I can't speak for other departments or people, or whatever. But we don't ignore cases because, what, it's Griffin Tomlin? Everybody likes him?" He shook his head, making a dismissive face and waving his hand through the air. "That means nothing. That's just a name."

I nodded, although I wasn't entirely convinced. "Why do you think she killed Elizabeth Monner? It's, like, I can't even understand. It makes literally no sense."

Detective Marsh considered this for a moment before leaning back in his chair. "There were other text messages between Emily and Griffin. It seemed as if your sister thought killing Ms. Monner would strengthen their bond, so to speak."

"Their bond?"

"They shared a common interest. Sexual torture and manipulation. It was like a grand romantic gesture to Griffin in Emily's mind. But things didn't go quite according to her plan. Griffin was only focused on you and he was scared of actually killing."

I thought back to what Aniston had told me before. "So he wasn't on his way to becoming a serial killer?"

Detective Marsh guffawed at this. "I mean, it's hard to say one way or another what a dead eighteen-year-old kid would've done decades later. And whether he had some set of morals deep down or just didn't want to get his hands dirty, it doesn't really matter." He leaned forward, his voice lowering to a whisper. "I don't like the guy."

I smiled. "Are you always allowed to talk about homicide victims like that?"

He feigned innocence. "Like what? I didn't say nothing." Then he winked, like he'd used the double negative on purpose.

When I stood up to leave a few minutes later, I remembered something that made me hesitate. I was still really upset with her, but I felt I owed her this. "Detective Marsh?" I asked tentatively from his doorframe, watching as he looked up from his computer. "Do you think maybe you could look into Santino Hernandez's murder? It happened around four years ago. It's never been solved."

"Do you think it has something to do with Griffin and Emily?"

I shook my head. "No. I just—I know his daughter. And it would mean a lot to her if she could find out what happened to him."

"I'll see what I can do."

I smiled. "Thank you."

~

The sputtering sound of an engine echoed through the air as a van parked on the shoulder of the road outside my house. The sunlight was dimming and turned the snow on the lawn a glittering peach hue. A few minutes later, I walked outside to see Wilson leaning against the bumper, his hands shoved into the pocket of his hoodie, and I hesitated just as he looked up.

The long strands of greasy blond hair that had hovered close to his shoulders were gone, cut shorter and exposing the back of his neck. It made him look different. Not like the Wilson Westbrooke I'd known before, the one my sister let me know, but maybe more like the Wilson Westbrooke I had got to know over the past couple of weeks.

When he saw me, he smiled faintly and then looked down, somewhat uncomfortably. "Your dad's not home, right?"

"I don't really think this is his home anymore, but no. He isn't here."

He laughed, nodding, before blurting out, "Wanna come with?" His voice tried to exude confidence, but a sense of sheepishness lingered beneath it.

"Where?" I asked, my arms wrapped around my chest.

"The police station," was all he said before he turned around, the color of his ashen cheeks beginning to tinge a soft pink, and headed back for the driver's side of his van.

I stood there, dumbfounded for a moment until he reached for the keys that dangled from the ignition and gave them a twist, the engine coughing and rumbling beside me. When I realized that was all he was planning on telling me, I climbed into the passenger seat.

As the glow from the dashboard became the only source of

light in the vehicle, I turned in my seat to look at him. "Is Bex going to be there?"

"She knows some stuff," he responded finally, his foot slowly easing on the gas as we approached a yellow light. "But not everything, and I don't really want her to either. I don't want her to . . . think about that stuff."

I glanced away from him, feeling as if the seat belt strapped against my chest was starting to tighten around me, constricting me to the duct-taped leather of the seat. I thought of Kolby, because I knew what Wilson wasn't saying was that knowing everything, all of it, would change everything for them. She would start seeing the Wilson Westbrooke that had existed a year ago, not the one who stood in front of her now. She would look where Emily had hurt him and that would be all she could see.

He would become a souvenir of someone's darkest moment instead of a boy with blue eyes and, now, short blond hair and a beat-up van.

"Can I ask you something?" I said tentatively, focusing on the taillights of the car in front of us. He nodded, easily and nonchalantly. "Why did you ask me to come?"

"Bex doesn't really get it," he admitted, almost embarrassed. "She tries, I mean. She tries really hard. But she doesn't. She can't." And then, for the first time since he'd pulled up in front of my house, he turned to look at me, *really* look at me. He held my gaze, his eyes flicking to the road every few seconds, before shrugging, as if it were easy, obvious, and clear. "You do."

He pulled into the parking lot of the police station, retracting the key from the ignition but not making a move to get out of the car or even unbuckle his seat belt.

"Come on," I told him, unbuckling it for him and popping open the passenger-side door. "They're not going to ignore what you tell them. They're going to listen and take you seriously."

"That's what they did for you. You're this," he said, stammering as if he couldn't quite get the words out, his hands vaguely gesturing in the air, "pretty blond girl. You've got this trustworthy, innocent face. Have you seen my face?"

I nodded. "Yeah, it's pretty too. You're also blond, so you're two for three." He laughed, looking down at his hands on his lap. "Regardless of your face, I know at least one detective who'll listen to you. But he can't if you don't get out of the car."

He nodded, a little too quickly. "Okay," he breathed, glancing at me for a fraction of a second before he reached for the door handle.

chapter twenty-nine

When I came home and walked in through the garage, I noticed that a couple of six-packs of my father's beer had been pushed against the wall, along with the type of high fiber cereal he used to eat that looked more like pellets than actual sustenance. Beside them both was a garbage bag filled halfway with other assortments of food, like the granola bars Emily ate or the hot mustard she liked on her hot dogs.

I walked into the kitchen, seeing cupboard doors left open, before I noticed my mother's wedding ring behind the sink, near a bottle of dish soap, unattended. It wasn't as if my mother never took off her wedding ring to wash the dishes, but it somehow seemed different there, alone, with no dishes in the drying rack. Like it was there for good now.

It wasn't until I heard footsteps upstairs, creaking against the floor, that I understood what my mother was doing. I went up and ventured closer to the doorframe of my sister's bedroom, to the door that had been closed ever since she was arrested. It was now open, and my mother was standing inside. Emily's dresser drawers had been pulled open and emptied, the surface that used to be cluttered with perfumes and tangled jewelry now cleaned and bare.

Garbage bags were scattered throughout the room, objects inside protruding against the plastic, and her bed had been stripped of its sheets, the duvet and pillows discarded on the floor. My mother was running a hand through her hair when she saw me, a garbage bag clenched in her hand. She offered a tired smile, as if she had replaced gardening with this new hobby of cleaning out her homicidal daughter's bedroom.

"I figured it was time to maybe throw this stuff away," she explained, even though I hadn't asked her anything. "I'd donate them, but it just feels wrong giving the less fortunate a killer's clothes. I don't know."

"You're getting rid of their stuff?" I took a tentative step beyond the threshold and into her room, the familiar scent of her perfume masked by the chemicals my mother was using to clean the windows. I had a feeling that if I went into my dad's office, the remnants of him and what he'd left behind would be stuffed into bags just like hers, or they would be soon. "Even Dad's?"

"I don't think we can really work things out anymore, sweetheart," she said. "Your father loves you girls so much. And with your sister—I think he can overlook some things that I'm not sure I can."

"Do you still love her?" I murmured, wondering what the right answer was supposed to be.

It was easier not to love her after I'd realized what she'd done to Elizabeth Monner. But now as I stood in her room, starting to remember the moments that had nothing to do with Elizabeth

Monner or Griffin Tomlin or Wilson Westbrooke—like the nights we'd spent in her bed watching movies on her laptop, or doing our makeup together in here before school—I felt torn. Torn between whether to believe that version of her had ever really existed or that she had been like Griffin, a mirage that turned to mist when you got too close. I wasn't sure what I was supposed to do with her now that everything within me felt dulled.

"I'll always love her," my mother said. "I love her more than I'll ever be able to tell her, but there's still so much I don't understand. She's done *horrible* things, and I'm not sure I could handle seeing her again until I've forgiven her for that." She walked to the closet and began pulling sweaters from the hangers. "If you want any of this, you should grab it now before it gets tossed. I doubt she'll be coming back to get it. You still don't want the car, right? I already put an ad in the paper."

"No." I grasped one of the perfume bottles sitting in a cardboard box, bringing it to my nose and breathing in the scent of berries and whipped sugar. I thought of the things Emily'd done, not just to Wilson or to Griffin or to Elizabeth, but to me. "Do you think you can forgive her?"

She folded one of the sweaters. "I'm never going to be okay with any of the things she's done," she said. "But I think that someday I'll forgive her for them. I love you girls too much to never forgive either of you."

I put down the bottle, the smell suddenly sickly sweet. "It's not like she deserves it."

"I don't think forgiveness is about what someone else deserves. I think it can be about what you're willing to let go of." She took another sweater off the hanger, glancing over her shoulder at me. "That's something I think we need to talk about, sweetheart."

285

"Mom—"

"Your sister isn't Griffin." She smoothed her hand over the knit material of the sweater she held over her arms before she set it gently in one of the garbage bags. "She committed awful crimes, but she isn't the boy who raped you. And I know it must be so frustrating that he died before you could prove what he did, but convicting Emily isn't the same as convicting him. And it won't feel the same either."

I looked away, uncomfortable and unconvinced. She'd left my bedroom window open for him, her violent version of a romantic gesture, like flowers or a box of chocolates.

"It's okay not to feel the same way about Emily. You don't have to group her with Griffin Tomlin. She's your sister. You two had such happy memories together. That doesn't have to change."

"Mom, she killed people. Raped them. I can't just focus on everything else."

She hesitated thoughtfully before she sat down on the edge of the bed. "Right now, I think you're focused more on what she did than everything else. But you don't have to ignore it, just remember there was more to her, even if it was just to you."

Then she smiled, reaching her hand out to me and rubbing my knuckles with her fingers. "You're so much like your father. You focus so much on one thing, you forget everything else. Like Kolby. You focused on him not taking the news so well. Or Bex—you remember her, right? Best friend a few years back." She smiled as I rolled my eyes, nodding. "Did you and Bex get into a fight about Griffin?"

"It wasn't really a fight, but she didn't really react that great either when she found out."

"Has she talked to you since then? Tried to apologize?"

"I mean, yeah, but—"

She widened her eyes. "Then let her! And what about that other girl? Aniston? You used to be friends with her too. What happened there?"

"She lied to me. She knew Emily killed the girl they found in our backyard, but she didn't tell me, and we were supposed to be"—I glanced at her, almost embarrassed to be saying this out loud—"solving it together."

"Did she tell you why she kept it from you?"

"She wanted proof first because she didn't think I would believe her without it."

My mother shot me a knowing look. "I wonder who here can relate to someone keeping a huge secret because they were afraid no one would believe them . . ."

I groaned. "Mom, that's not the same."

"It doesn't have to be the same. It just means you should understand." She tugged on my hand and brought me down beside her onto the bed, wrapping an arm around my shoulder and bringing me into her chest. "I know Emily and Griffin were two really important people in your life who let you down. But that doesn't mean that you have to shut everyone else out when they make a mistake. Felonies, maybe, but not every mistake."

I sighed into her shirt. "You didn't even like Kolby. Why would you want me back with him?"

"I never said I didn't like him. I've known him since you were all kids. I know he's a sweet boy. I was just worried about what people would say when they found out, or that maybe unresolved feelings about what Emily had done would end up making you hurt even more than you already were. But you were also normal with him." She leaned back and smiled at me. "You were going out on dates and talking late at night on the phone, and I thought, *This is what I want for you.*"

"A boyfriend?" I asked drily.

She gave my shoulder a light smack. "No. For you to act like a normal seventeen-year-old. And I think Kolby gave a little bit of that back to you. And Aniston too. That's why I think you should forgive them. I don't want you to turn into a hermit." Then she feigned an innocent look. "In fact, you might even find the time to forgive Bex this summer."

I frowned. "What?"

"I called Mrs. Connor and when Scoops! opens up again next month, your job will be there waiting for you."

"No," I moaned. "Why would you do that?"

"I want you to have a normal life, Clara. I also want you to earn your own paycheck so you can help with the insurance and gas for the car we'll get for you sometime this summer. And again, I don't want you to become a hermit."

I slumped against her shoulder. "No one's ever going to see me as anything more than Emily Porterfield's little sister. Except when she was just a popular cheerleader, it didn't have such bad connotations."

"That's only how they'll see you if you never make anything more of yourself. Which you can't if you stay inside this house all the time by yourself." Then she patted my knee and stood up from the mattress, turning back to the closet. "Now come on. We have a lot of work to do here."

I found Aniston the next afternoon at school, slipping dollar bills into a vending machine in the cafeteria, and I smoothed my hands over the chenille pink material of the sweater I had kept from Emily's closet the night before, still sort of scented like berries before I'd washed it and put on my own perfume. It was the only pink shirt I had.

When I approached her as she pressed D3 for an orange, she glanced over at me through the loose strands of hair she'd kept out of her French braid, her gaze drifting down to the pink sweater before turning back to the vending machine. "This is the only pink top I could find in my whole house," I told her. "And it's kind of warm outside today, so I'm sweating a lot right now."

"Thanks for the update," she replied, her tone clipped as the machine released her orange.

"You're welcome. But the reason I'm wearing it is because I know pink is super important to you, and I wanted to do something that was important to you to let you know I'm sorry for not trusting that you had good reasons to keep Elizabeth Monner's killer a secret from me. And you were right when you said I was being a hypocrite about it. So I'm sorry for that too."

She was still looking away from me, her pink nails picking at the skin of the orange.

"You're pretty much my only friend too, so if the reason we're not friends right now has anything to do with me being a total idiot, will you please forgive me and let that *not* keep us from being friends?"

"Only if I can borrow your sweater sometime," she teased softly, running her hand over the sleeve. "Pink looks good on you. Also you just totally ranted, which means I'm rubbing off on you in more ways than one."

"Heaven help me." She laughed, and I hesitated for a moment

before I told her, "I'm ready to do the interview. The one you asked about, like, two months ago. I'll do it."

"You don't have to do that. We're good. And besides, people were right about me being this nosy journalist wannabe. I shouldn't have gone so deep into it. I mean, I got blocked by a lot of different phone numbers." She sighed, sticking her thumb in the top of the orange. "My mom's right. I'm obsessive."

"Maybe, but that doesn't mean you should go back to writing soft-hitting exposés about disappearing urinal cakes in the boys' bathroom or something. It just means you have to try a new approach. And if you hadn't got so deep into it, then I would've never told anyone about what happened with Griffin and me, and we wouldn't have become friends."

"Yeah."

"So let's do the interview. The *exclusive* interview that no news station or other reporter is *ever* going to get. Putting you, Aniston Hale, on the map of journalism."

A few days later, I looked down at the stacks of thin *Madison Register* papers on the table in the hallway, my picture on the front page. Aniston had told me she would use one, but I'd originally figured she'd meant my school picture. Instead it was a picture of Aniston's—one I hadn't even realized she had taken.

It was black and white. I was in the cafeteria, my elbows perched on the edge of the table, and I was staring somewhere to the right, my gaze unfocused, with my short hair tucked behind my ears. My glasses were off, folded and beside one of my elbows. I was just looking out, my expression almost blank, as the sunlight filtered in through the windows behind me and cast a brightness over one half of my face.

I wasn't really sure why she'd chosen that photo when she showed it to me last week—or why she'd taken it in the first place—but she told me it was supposed to be symbolic or something. Me, without my glasses and revealing my eyes—green the only color on the whole page—was supposed to be a representation of me finally uncovering the truth. I wasn't completely sure I got it, but she seemed to be really into it.

As I stepped away from the table and headed toward my locker, I felt the hesitant and slightly unnerved glances of the other students when I passed them, the pages of the article bookmarked with their thumbs. They knew everything now, from the moment I'd caught a glimpse of Griffin Tomlin in the audience to the last moment I'd seen him, evading my tentative gaze the night before he was murdered by my sister.

The trial for Griffin's murder is at the end of the year, I had been quoted. *I've heard that since Emily has been officially charged with Elizabeth Monner's murder, the trials will be combined, since the prosecutors believe that Griffin was murdered because he knew Emily killed Elizabeth. There were texts on their phones, talking about it. Emily thought killing her would be impressive to Griffin, but he seemed freaked out by it. Eventually, he blocked her on their burner phones, but the night he died, she texted him using their real numbers and he agreed to meet her outside. They think he rejected her again and she killed him because of it.*

I was spinning the combination on my locker when I noticed Kolby standing near the corner of the hallway, one hand clutching the strap of his backpack and the other just barely in one of his jeans' pockets.

Kolby had read the article. I knew he had, even though I couldn't spot any obvious reason to think so. I wondered if knowing the details of everything—what had happened once he'd taken his eyes off Griffin and me as we wandered up the stairs, the letters and texts, him waiting in my bedroom—had changed something for him. Altered the way he looked at me right now, his breaths slow and even. Despondency filled his eyes and contorted his features, and I didn't know if that was because of what I'd told him before or because of what he'd read in my interview.

I wondered if he was thinking of saying something right now, maybe apologizing again, or if he would repeat what I had pushed to the back of my mind until this moment as I looked at him from across the school hallway. How minutes before I'd told him the truth about Griffin, when he'd found me outside of the hotel at the bus stop, he'd told me he loved me.

I know I'm not him. But I love you, though. I love you.

I caught his eyes darting away from mine and down to the ground after a minute had passed. He tightened his fingers around the strap of his backpack and turned around, slipping out of sight within a few steps. I looked down at the lock I still held in my hand, scratching my fingernail against the engraved numbers as I came to a conclusion.

Kolby Rutledge was truly on his own.

~

The scent of fresh soft pretzels and melted butter topping found me as I approached the food court, glimpsing the bright purple stripes of the counter for the pretzel shop In Knots, sandwiched between a closed fast food restaurant and a pizza counter. I hesitated when I saw Kolby behind the counter, standing to the left of the cash register, in a bright purple T-shirt that matched the stripes and the chalkboard menus on the wall behind him. A black baseball hat obstructed half of his face from me as he wiped down the counter beside a display case of pretzels.

My boots squeaked against the tiles as I neared the counter, a twenty dollar bill pinched between my fingertips. I stopped and waited. He didn't notice me at first, tossing the paper towel he was cleaning with to the other side of the register and moving the spray cleaner under the counter before he looked up. His lips parted as if he were already preparing to ask me what kind of pretzel I wanted before his expression shifted as he took me in. Instead of bored and prepared, a vulnerability crept into his eyes and uncertainty closed his lips.

I held up the twenty dollar bill in my hand. "I have a twenty. Is that enough for one of your pretzels?"

Kolby blinked without responding, as if he wasn't sure what to say to this. Then he let out a breath through his nose and gestured to the display case beside him, an assortment of soft pretzels lined up together on wax paper. "Yeah," he told me, reaching for a box of plastic gloves. "I think so. Any one in particular?"

"Whatever you recommend," I told him.

I watched as he pointed to a soft pretzel with peanut butter, chocolate sauce, and sprinkles of salt drizzled over the golden crust, and I nodded. "I'm actually not just here for your expensive pretzels," I admitted as he picked it up. "I wanted to tell you that I'm sorry. I wasn't understanding and I never really heard you out. I know it was hard for you too, and I should've given you time. So I'm sorry."

He looked away from me as he dropped the soft pretzel into a bright purple bag. The muscles in his jaw were tensed as he set it down on the counter. "You were right, though," he whispered. "I shouldn't have just left." He cleared his throat, turning to the register and jabbing his finger at the buttons on the machine. When the total came to $6.48, I extended the twenty to him, but he ignored me as he pulled out his wallet and slid his card through the credit scanner. "I'm really sor—" He hesitated, his voice thick and tight, before he swallowed. "I'm really sorry I didn't do anything that night. I should've known something wasn't right and I should've—I should've done something instead of playing a game on my phone."

"It wasn't just you, though. No one thought—*I* didn't think he could do something like that. You believed in your best friend, and there's *nothing* wrong with that."

He shook his head. "He's a piece of—"

"I know." And then I smiled at him. "But he was also your best friend, for years. And I know not everything you remember about him is going to be bad and that's okay. It's okay to not be sure how you feel about him. You knew a completely different Griffin, and it's okay to miss that person. You don't have to hate all versions of him." He looked away from me, unsure, and I shrugged one of my shoulders. "And if, you know, you're looking for a new best friend, then I think I'm available?"

He let out a small laugh and shook his head once before meeting my gaze. "Yeah," he responded, and a familiar look filled his eyes, one I'd seen when he first asked me out to the movies and I told him I couldn't go. "Okay."

I reached out for the pretzel on the counter, feeling the plastic of the bag crinkling beneath my fingers. "You told me you should've known about what happened with Griffin. But that's not really the way I see it. I see it as you letting me find you, coming to you on my own. You were the only one who wasn't searching for something. And that means something, Kolby. It means a lot, actually."

He lifted his head, a slight smile forming on his lips that reached the corners of his eyes, the flecks of gold twinkling beneath the russet. "That's the nicest way anyone has ever told me I'm dumb before."

chapter thirty

I had to borrow one of Emily's black dresses for his funeral. Most of what I owned now were oversized sweatshirts and leggings. But what I wore didn't really matter anymore since he was gone. He would be in a funeral home or in a hearse or in a church or in a cemetery, and that was it. Those were all the places he would ever go now until he was buried. And I never could admit it to anyone, but I was so relieved there was going to be a permanent barrier of six feet of ground between me and him.

The local news channels spent every moment on air devoted to the coverage of the mystery that had started to plague the small, mostly rural community of Shiloh, New York. They repeated the facts that had been released to the public several days ago—that the police had found evidence of blunt force trauma to his head but chlorinated water in his lungs, so he'd most likely drowned after being dumped in the pool, and they'd also speculated he knew his attacker. After the fifth time one of the anchors regurgitated the information, my mother grabbed the remote and turned the television off.

She shook her head, sniffled loudly, and then looked through the gaps between our curtains to the Tomlin household, which looked almost desolate, foil-wrapped packages overflowing from the trash cans. She tried calling Mrs. Tomlin every day, but each time she was forced to leave a voicemail asking her to please call her back anytime, even in the middle of the night if she needed. But Mrs. Tomlin never called her back, day or night.

I wore a pair of black leggings under the dress to his funeral, even though it was hot that day. Hot enough that humidity clung under my arms and made my thighs stick to the pews—but there was still a part of me that felt I needed to be covered, even though his eyes would never see whatever I exposed again.

It didn't feel completely real, that he was simply gone. It didn't feel as if I had actually seen that curly black hair or his ocean-blue eyes for the last time. I would never have to glimpse him from across the backyard at another block party, lounging on a lawn chair, trying to balance a full paper plate of mayonnaise-based salads and a hamburger on his lap, or feel that clench in my stomach whenever I heard his laughter or his voice, because it was gone. Everything about him was gone now and all that was left was about to be buried and abandoned in the ground.

The air in the sanctuary of the church was stifling, almost as thick and apparent as the unspoken truth of his death that everyone skirted around. They talked about how he was such a good kid, always offering to mow lawns or shovel driveways in the winter, or what a great pitcher he was and how far he would've gone, maybe even to the *big leagues*. I overheard half a dozen stories about him, about his kindness, about his goodness, about his sweetness. I couldn't help but look down at my hands, pale and clammy in my lap, thinking that if he was really that kind, that good, that sweet, then he wouldn't be in a casket wearing the tux he'd worn to prom.

Whoever had murdered him would be obvious, unmistakable from the corners of the church where they stood in the back, observing the grief they had caused, a different type of sweat collecting on their temples. It would be clear. You would look in their direction accidentally, trying to find the restrooms or one of the Tomlins, and just know once your gaze fell on them. So obvious you would be left wondering how no one else was seeing it yet.

I thought that they would look so ashamed, so guilt-ridden, that you couldn't help but feel an uneasy tingling in your bones that wouldn't go away until they left your sight. In fact, I didn't really even believe that whoever killed him would be at his funeral, I thought they would be so remorseful.

I leaned over Emily's shoulder to read the hymnal lyrics from her program and I stood beside her as we waited our turn to exit the pew when the service was over. I watched as she embraced Mrs. Tomlin, wrapping her arms around her and whispering condolences in her ear. I listened as she tried to joke around with Brandon, giving him a light punch on the arm that nearly toppled him because he was so unsteady on his feet, but he only nodded at the things she said, sweat glimmering on his neck.

She had tried to talk to Kolby Rutledge but he'd left the funeral so quickly after the service ended, face reddened and blotched, that she never got the chance to say more than his name.

~

I was in my room, my fingers grazing against my blinds as I stood in front of the window. I was trying to decide whether to finally open them and let the glow of the mid-September setting sun infiltrate my bedroom. I told myself I didn't needed to be afraid of him anymore. He wasn't in his bedroom, fingers peeling back his own blinds so he could look across the street and into my room, watching as I undressed or did my homework. Now I could do whatever I wanted and he wouldn't be there, lingering somewhere beyond the pavement of the street separating us.

But a part of me still hesitated as I tugged on the string, the cord wrapped around my fingers. I thought of Brandon Tomlin, spending his evenings in his basement playing video games or leaving for his job at the local movie theater. He could look into my window, I thought. So I left my blinds alone and went back to my bed and my history textbook, thinking of two facts at the same time.

The first being that Sir Edmund Hillary was born in 1919 in Auckland, New Zealand. The second being that Griffin Tomlin was truly gone.

I heard footsteps outside of my bedroom door, the doorknob starting to twist. I thought it might have been my father since Mom had gone to bed already, having loaded the dishes into the dishwasher, then kissing me on the forehead and telling me, *I'm so grateful for you, sweetheart.* Her words had caused my stomach to twist as she walked away. Her eyes had been reddish the entire day, and she'd still sometimes randomly reached for a tissue even after we'd got home from the funeral, as if a part of her was still there, watching Mrs. Tomlin hug every attendee and swallow back the emotions threatening to overtake her.

When I realized it was Emily as she poked her head through the crack of the opening door, I blinked in slight surprise.

She'd vanished into her bedroom soon after we'd got back from the church that afternoon, saying she needed to take a nap. My mother brushed back her hair with an understanding sigh before Emily removed her heels and went upstairs, disappearing into her room, and remained there until now, apparently. She was still wearing the dress she'd worn to the funeral.

"Hey," she whispered.

My rib bones went rigid because I was sure she was going to ask me how I felt about his death, if I was okay, if it stung to see all those people weeping for a boy I wasn't sure even deserved their grief. Did he deserve to be mourned because of who he was to everyone else? Did he deserve it because he was murdered?

Emily tilted her head to the side, smiling softly at me as her temple touched the doorframe, and murmured the words that started it all, that started the shattering of the illusion of her. "Can I show you something?"

There was a yellow cotton tank top, a pair of high-waisted shorts, and a bra with underwear in the large freezer bag she held out to me gingerly, like it was a small animal or something. She looked at me expectantly as I took in the bag with folded clothing. I shot her a look.

"Why I am I looking at this? You know I've got a history test coming up next week, right?"

She looked at me weird. "You really don't see it?"

"See what?" I looked down dramatically at the freezer bag of clothing and flipped it over in my hands twice. "It's a bag of clothes. I mean, it's weird but—" I felt whatever else I was planning on saying crumbling and disintegrating in my throat when I looked down at the bag again, this time seeing red splatter marks on the thick strap of the tank top. They were on the collar too. The stains were so small, barely even noticeable on the fabric.

I couldn't even make sense of what this meant, but my spine still stiffened and the air in my lungs became a hardened mass, my heart feeling as if it were a timer in my chest, ticking away, threatening to stop, because I think a part of me did know. I think a part of me knew it was his blood, ruby splatters like paint dotting and decorating the fabric, as if it were her own version of artwork.

I felt acid in my mouth as everything started to crack and splinter, shattering at the corners, until it all crumbled in front of me and landed at my feet. It was as if she were someone else, someone other than my sister, Emily, the girl I'd spent summer evenings licking strawberry ice cream cones with or riding beside in her Mini Cooper listening to the country music songs that were always blasting from the speakers.

"Emily," I rasped, my mouth dry as sweat collected on my forehead, panicked and afraid and confused. "What did you do, Emily?" I felt as if I were about to retch onto her carpet, the room beginning to spin at the corners.

She took the bag from me and shrugged. "I killed Griffin Tomlin. It was the only way to get him to leave you alone."

My chest started to ache as my heart beat unevenly, as if the muscles were working against each other and twisting in opposite directions. My mouth filled with saliva, my stomach threatening to heave. "I never wanted you to . . . to kill him. Emily, oh my—" I covered my face with my hands and I tried to breathe in, out, breathe in, out, to stop myself from hurling at the thought that she'd actually murdered someone.

But nothing could stop the churning feeling in my stomach that caused my hands to grow clammy and my head to go dizzy. She'd killed him because of what I'd told her.

"Yeah, you did," she told me, speaking as if it were obvious, and if I hadn't been so terrified or revolted, I would've got annoyed with her for it. "That day at the barn? You said you just wanted him to go away? You know, get run over by a bus or die of dehydration as a result of massive diarrhea?"

I blinked at her, really believing I was about to pass out. "You killed him because of a *joke I made*?!"

"Okay, well, no. But I couldn't keep letting him hurt you anymore. He was never going to leave you alone, so I decided I had to kill him," she told me, letting out a slight laugh as she shrugged, like it was that simple, that casual.

I didn't want this, I wanted to tell her—I never wanted Griffin Tomlin dead—but nothing would come from my lips except for breaths I couldn't remember taking. All I could imagine was his body floating in his pool, or the casket in front of the pulpit at the church that afternoon, or all the tinfoil-wrapped dishes in the trash cans at the curb of the Tomlins' house.

That was because of me.

Because of what I had told her about Griffin.

I didn't want this, I wanted to scream but, as always, my voice left me when I needed it the most.

"Everything I do," she told me then, her voice coaxing and wrong and too close, "is for you, Clara. So you can be safe now." And then she smiled again as she reached out and wrapped her arms around me, drawing me close to her. My muscles stiffened under her arms as she nuzzled her chin against my shoulder. I stood, my hands limp at my sides, unable to lift or move them.

When she pulled away, I realized what shade her eyes looked to be in that moment. Griffin Tomlin's eyes were the color of the surface of the ocean. And Emily's were the color of its depths.

It was the end of September, just that time when the bright green leaves became tinted with oranges, yellows, and reds outside the windows of the house. I was spreading crunchy peanut butter over my toast as I glanced over at Emily, sitting on the barstool beside me, eating her cereal as she scrolled through her phone.

Every time I looked at her, I couldn't help but think of what she must have seen that night she'd murdered Griffin, if maybe he'd fought her or begged or screamed, and it made my chest ache. She'd become him in that moment, someone capable of ignoring the pleas and cries of someone else desperate to keep what belonged to them, and I wanted to retch at the thought that it was because of what I'd told her. I never wanted that. I never wanted her to become like him to protect me. I wanted to be safe. That was it. And now I was, but it felt wrong. Like everything in me was weighed down by something even heavier than the fear I'd felt before.

And all the while, it was as if none of this mattered to her. She was still the same, eating her cereal and on her phone, untouched. She'd killed someone. She'd watched the light leave his eyes. She'd left him in his backyard to drown in the pool waters as his blood tinted them red, and then she'd gone to bed, as if it had never happened at all.

The doorbell rang, and I looked over my shoulder as my father took one last sip of his coffee and got up to answer it. Emily still stared at her phone, unbothered, her thumb scrolling as I craned my neck to catch a glimpse of the front door when my dad opened it, revealing two men standing on the doormat outside.

They were both wearing blazers and ties, one wearing jeans while the other wore khakis. I thought they were from a church or something, asking if we wanted to buy a Bible or join their congregation, until I saw the glint of their badges on their belts.

"Mr. Porterfield?" one of them asked. When my father nodded, almost as if he were stunned into silence, the man continued. "I'm Detective Marsh and this is Detective Anders. We're investigating the murder of your neighbor, Griffin Tomlin."

My father's brow creased. "We already spoke to police officers a few weeks ago. None of us saw or heard anything that night."

"Well, sir, we found a couple of text messages from one of your daughters on his phone sent about an hour before he died. Is . . ." I turned to Emily as she looked up, finally no longer unbothered, untouched, something bleeding into the greens of her eyes that also resembled fear. She looked at me, speechless and astounded, and I realized it wasn't fear in her eyes. It was *shock*. She'd never thought she would be caught. "Is *Emily Porterfield* here?"

But—

My father cleared his throat. He was scared for her. "Yes, she's here."

—she was wrong.

304

chapter thirty-one

The wind brushed over my face through the strands of hair I'd recently dyed a light shade of brown as I kept my eyes closed, listening to the gentle ripples of the water wetting the beach sands and the distant calls of seagulls behind me.

I didn't look like her anymore—like Emily or the girl who'd believed in her or who'd believed in Griffin, only to be terrified by them both. I looked a little different, fresher, with bones that were a little stronger. Like someone who knew scars weren't just indications of the wounds inflicted upon us but proof we'd healed from them. Blood had stopped spilling. The bruising had disappeared. The skin had fused back together. You'd healed.

I'd healed. I'd been so consumed with what had happened that I'd clung to the pain that used to be there instead of letting it go.

I opened my eyes and took in the blue waters that glimmered in front of me as I stood ankle deep in the grains of wet sand covering my bare feet, freezing them. The bright November afternoon was warmer than usual but still cold enough for the lake's beach to be almost completely abandoned.

There was no one here who knew who I was or what had happened the day before, unlike the news vans that lined the streets outside my house, reporters clamoring for some kind of quote from me on what I thought about the verdict, hassling me as I got into the car my mom and I picked out last August—a used green hatchback—but I'd ignored them as I usually did.

I already knew who would be interviewing me about the verdict.

The jury determined the death of Elizabeth Monner had been premeditated. The prosecutors believed Emily lured her into her car on August nineteenth, two days after my birthday, with the intention of killing her. The police were never able to find where Emily had committed the murder, but there were fibers from the trunk of the car on her body and in the shallow grave, suggesting she'd been there at some point.

There were pictures from both of the crime scenes, her decomposing body in the earth and his floating facedown in a pool, and I held my breath for every moment, my ribs aching as I heard the devastated sounds of Mrs. Monner, or sometimes the Tomlins, crying somewhere in the courtroom. My mom eventually had to stand up and leave the room, wiping the back of her hand against her lips and smearing her lipstick across her skin.

My father, seated behind Emily, didn't get up from his seat or cry or even demand to know why she'd done it. He just sat there behind her with nothing but allegiance, his side clear and obvious.

He never wavered from her, not even when evidence started to mount against her, but it was as if none of that mattered to him. Emily was what mattered to him.

When he continued to blame Griffin Tomlin's death on the poor influence he believed Wilson Westbrooke had been to her, and actually blamed him for Elizabeth Monner's murder, I started to broaden the distance between us. He never told me he didn't believe me—he even said that Griffin must have tried to rape her and that's why she killed him—but I could see that my sister's last victim was my father. She had consumed him, gripping on to his trust and bringing him closer. Closer into the illusion that she was real.

One of the expert witnesses on the stand, who studied the behavior of female killers, said he believed the reason Emily had murdered Elizabeth Monner was because she'd wanted to use her death as an icebreaker to get closer to Griffin Tomlin while simultaneously indulging her sexual sadism. It was a sociopath's version of talking about a common interest, like sports or television shows, but warped and twisted. When she'd heard about what he'd done to me—which was corroborated through DNA found on the underwear he'd taken from me, left in that box in the barn, and on the pocketknife I'd kept—the expert said she recognized a piece of herself in him. It was attractive to her. They both experienced sexual gratification from manipulating and controlling others.

But he rejected her.

The prosecutor said Griffin most likely either denied the allegations I'd made against him or he was afraid of her. She'd escalated sooner than he was ready for.

"Then," the prosecutor continued, "after almost a month of rejection on his part, he finally agrees to meet with her, only to reject her *again*, and she just *snaps*. She had been leaving him gifts, like the body of Elizabeth Monner, and even offered him her own sister. Which would kill two birds with one stone, so to speak. Ms. Porterfield was jealous of the attention Griffin Tomlin paid her younger sister, and by offering her to him through an opened bedroom window, she's building trust with him and getting rid of her."

I tried not to flinch as I heard this, even though it wasn't as if I hadn't already suspected, but it felt different hearing someone say it so passionately to a selection of people who had never met me before. My mother was still somewhere outside, since she couldn't bring herself to hear about the open window again after the first time I'd told her, back when they were preparing for the trial. My father never really believed it, claiming the prosecution was twisting things or that the texts weren't actually from Emily but someone using her phone, but it changed something for Mom. She wrote Emily letters sometimes, some she sent and others she didn't, but she never went to see her. She never told me, but I thought the only way Mom knew how to love Emily now was from a distance.

"And Griffin Tomlin goes and rejects her, time and time again," the district attorney continued, gesturing to Emily. "He's not interested. And maybe he threatens to tell the police about the girl she killed to impress him, and she decides to kill him. Out of both rage and self-preservation."

His parents were in the courtroom, near the back. They'd both worn black clothing, as if they were still at his funeral. They'd moved recently, when the trial had neared and evidence started to trickle into the media that became harder and harder for the locals to deny. After someone smashed in their mailbox and defaced their garage door, they'd gathered their belongings into a moving truck and left before even selling the house.

I wasn't completely sure where they'd moved—Aniston suspected somewhere in Pennsylvania—but they still came for the trial. I kept glancing over in their direction, wondering if they were ever looking at me. I wanted them to know that I was sorry they'd got tangled into this, that I never wanted for them to feel so hurt or for their son to be murdered. But instead of saying those things—which I felt would've been left unheard in their ears anyway—I turned around in my seat and looked to Emily, taking her in for the first time since February.

Her hair was longer now, and maybe a little duller—not as blond, not as strawberry—and her skin wasn't quite as tan as I remembered it being a few months earlier. She wasn't wearing the beige jumpsuit again, but instead a navy pantsuit with a flowing light-pink top underneath the blazer. Aniston was upset about that, grumbling that she owned the same blouse as a killer now.

Sometimes I looked over at Wilson Westbrooke sitting a couple of seats down from me, wondering what he was thinking when he looked at her. She'd only caught his eye once, when she was entering the courtroom, and I'd waited for something to register within her. Guilt, dread, satisfaction, anything. But her expression was blank and her gaze was as dull as her hair. She'd finally abandoned him, dusted him from her hands and treaded on.

Wilson had started volunteering for an organization in Buffalo that helped male sexual assault victims and told me a couple of weeks ago he was thinking of getting his GED. After my mom went to apologize for how she'd treated him while he and Emily were dating, they bonded over animals, and now he was considering going to college to become a veterinary technician. He'd even got a job at her clinic, wrangling the leashes of big dogs and holding agitated cats during their shots.

And sitting beside Wilson was Bex, holding on to his hand. We were finally getting back to where we'd been nearly two years ago, helped by small moments here and there at Scoops! over the summer and on the opening night of *Shrek the Musical*, when she'd reached for my hand as we'd all bowed down at the edge of the stage and I'd let her grasp on to it. But I'd kept my eyes on the audience and grinned at Kolby and Aniston, already waiting for me to find them in the front row, two sets of brown eyes twinkling under the stage lights.

The prosecutor and defense attorneys made their closing arguments—with Emily now claiming she'd killed Griffin in self-defense when he'd attempted to rape her, and saying that she wasn't involved in Elizabeth Monner's murder at all—and then the jury left for deliberation. I watched as my father reached over the space between them, squeezing her shoulder.

I stood up, grabbing my purse and walking out of the courtroom.

I might have been able to accept that I had good memories with my sister—and I did—but I didn't think I could stomach being in the same room with her again knowing she'd offered to let Griffin murder me and then taken my rape as her defense.

Kolby was standing in the hallway outside of the courtroom when I stepped through the door, near the water fountains bolted to the wood-paneled wall, humming gently. His hands were crammed into the pockets of his jacket—an actual jacket now, not just a puffer vest—and he pushed himself off the wall when he noticed me, shooting me a soft smile.

"Hey," he said as I neared him. He still smelled a little like pretzels, since he'd come here straight from work after his shift ended a little more than an hour ago. "What's happening?"

"The jury just left," I told him, nodding over my shoulder to the emptying courtroom, the sound of muffled chatter slowly starting to spill out into the hallway and drown out everything else. "And in celebration of the end of all this, do you want to split some peanut M&Ms with me?"

He laughed and I felt myself smiling at the sound. I rummaged inside my purse while walking around him and leaned against the wood paneling, sliding down to the floor as I found the candy behind my wallet. His knee brushed against mine as he slid down to sit beside me. I tore open the package, dumped a few M&Ms into his palm, and then reached inside for my own.

"Do you think she'll be convicted?" he asked.

"Probably."

"Are you okay with that?"

I thought for a moment, chewing, before I nodded again. "Yeah, I am. I mean, I wish none of it had ever happened more than I want her to get off with a slap on the wrist or something."

I looked over at him, dumping a couple more M&Ms in his hand, and I couldn't help but wonder if he still thought about it. About how he'd said he loved me months ago. We still hadn't really got back together, even though there were moments every now and then that made it possible, but in the beginning I wanted to build a stronger sense of trust. And now it felt like it had been too long. I wasn't sure where his feelings were, if they were with me or someone else or anyone, because now we had been *just friends* longer than we had been together. It seemed like the statute of limitations on us had expired already, too late to go back now.

"Lisa Tomlin was out here before you came out. She still thinks he's innocent," he told me. "She wanted to know why I didn't want to do a victim impact statement."

Elizabeth Monner's mother and aunt had been asked to make victim impact statements if she was sentenced, and so had Griffin's parents, and Kolby. I assumed he was unsure of how he felt about Griffin. But there was something in his voice now that suggested maybe his unsure feelings weren't so unsure anymore.

"What did you tell her?"

"I told her he wasn't innocent," he explained. "She wanted me to talk about how he was murdered and then had his character taken from him, but I told her I believed you."

He nudged his shoulder against mine, and I smiled at the touch. "You deserved better," I said. "You deserved better than a rapist for a best friend."

"I like the one I have now."

I leaned over and rested my head on his shoulder, about to tell him that I liked him too, when I felt the vibration of his voice against my cheek.

"Actually . . ." He laughed, kind of shyly. "I really like her—you."

He looked at me, his expression so nervous and hesitant and endearing that I had resist the urge to smile at him. I slowly placed the bag of candies down near my thigh. "I know you said before you were still hurt about what happened and I'm—"

Instead of letting him apologize for the thirtieth time that year, I leaned over and kissed him. He made a stunned noise in his throat, but he paused for only a second before moving his lips against my own and kissing me back. He tasted of mint and chocolate, and when we pulled apart, he smiled. "I've been waiting eight months to do that."

I grinned, wanting to tell him what I realized I had known for so long it didn't even have a beginning anymore. Somewhere, the feeling had become a constant, like stars lit against a dark sky. "I love you," I whispered, just as he said to me in a breathy voice, "I like your hair brown."

Kolby brought his lips back to mine softly, the taste of chocolate and mint sweet in my mouth, and I didn't have to wait to hear him reiterate the words back to me. His feelings hadn't wavered, hadn't disappeared like the froth over the sea or shifted into something else. Just like mine, they remained constant, just waiting for me to notice.

Out of the corner of my eye, a burst of pink. "Okay, Clara, I'm totally trying to give you time to process here, but I am so excited about this new article, I might explode."

I looked over Kolby's shoulder at Aniston, who had recently taken up crime blogging—since the school hadn't reacted so well to my interview and its *mature* subject matter—in addition to the school paper. Kolby was biting down on his lips, trying not to laugh as he turned away from her. "Hi, Aniston."

"Hi." Then she paused, glancing between us on the floor, furrowing her brow. "Am I interrupting something?"

I nodded, a slight smile on my lips. "A little."

She gasped, grinning as she clasped her hands over her chest. "I'm interrupting *something!*"

The jury found my sister guilty of one count of first-degree murder for Elizabeth Monner and then one count of second-degree murder for Griffin. The judge sentenced her to twenty-five years for Elizabeth Monner's murder and fifteen for Griffin's. The sentences were to be concurrent, meaning she would be eligible for parole when she was forty-three. It was something the prosecutors had prepared us for—judges were usually more lenient toward women.

When the verdict was spoken, it was as if the courtroom awakened, brimming with so many responses articulated in one place. A few members of Elizabeth Monner's family started clapping. Her mother was crying, her body jolting at the words, her eyes squeezed tight, releasing tears out of the corners. In their places at the back of the courtroom, the Tomlins were less vocal—maybe because this meant that to some degree, the jury had also found their own son guilty—but their countenances showed relief and were streaked with their own tears.

My father's shoulders drooped when he heard the verdict, as if his chest were crumbling inward. Then he leaned over to speak to Emily. I wasn't sure what he was whispering to her, but I was sure she could barely hear him. My mother held on to my hand, her eyes glistening beneath the courtroom lights, but she didn't say anything. She kept holding on until Emily was led out of the courtroom.

Our feelings for her were always going to be complicated. There would never be an easy emotion for us to have about Emily. She would always be someone else. Someone else in our memories and someone else in front of us, our recollections and thoughts just as split and torn as her. But that wasn't wrong. It wasn't wrong to remember strawberry ice cream dripping down our wrists or afternoons shouting the lyrics to Carrie Underwood songs in her car.

That version of her might never have been real to her, but it was to us, even if it wasn't there anymore.

And now at the lakeshore, I stood in the sand that submerged my feet, the wind off the waves rustling through my hair. A graying sky loomed over the water, tingeing the color, as the cold waves swept over my ankles. It was exhilarating to stand there, a part of me breaking open and spilling out into the water, leaving me.

I'd wanted to find an ocean abundant with familiar blue water, but I'd settled for Lake Ontario. Aniston had offered to come with me after spending the night, and Kolby had already texted me that morning, but I'd wanted to come alone. It was where I'd started and I didn't mind going back to it every now and then.

I stood in the color I'd once felt had overtaken me, submerged me in its depths, and pulled me under the current I hadn't realized was there, as I tried to breathe but took in nothing but mouthfuls of water. Darkness and water had surrounded me, stuck in the center of a storm hidden beneath the glimmering, beautiful surface of bright and sparkling blue.

Every storm has to calm.

I stood in the color I'd thought had overtaken me, but now I was above it. Finally breaking through the glimmering surface and taking in that breath of air as the ocean blue finally fell away.

acknowledgments

There are so many people that I have to thank for their part in making this book a possibility, and not just that, but something I could actually hold in my hand and flip the pages of and everything. *What Happened That Night* is a real book now, you guys!

First, I have to be thankful to the Lord for giving me the idea for this book and then giving me the inspiration and motivation to take it from that spark into a story and then into this. I know I put up a bit of a fight on that one. I want to thank my parents for being really embarrassing and telling everyone they meet that I'm an author: *Look, here's our daughter's book, we're so proud.* I may look like I want to kill you in those moments, but it's okay. I promise I love you too.

I also have to thank Monica Pacheco, my talent manager, for honestly being the best. There was so much that you did for me and for this book, answering all of my questions and sending me the latest updates and spending so much time with me on the phone. I know you really fought for this book too, and I want to thank you so much for that. I also want to give the biggest thanks to my name twin Deanna McFadden! You really did *so* much. Without the help you gave me during the editing process of this book, it would not have happened. Your notes and encouragement turned a first or second draft of a *seriously* long story online into a *book*, polished and everything. Thanks to Sarah Howden too, for copy editing and leaving so many cute notes while doing so. And thank you to Ashleigh Gardner, who heads Wattpad Books, for considering *What Happened That Night* for this amazing adventure! Caitlin O'Hanlon and Leah Ruehlicke have also played a huge part in my journey on Wattpad as well. And I-Yana Tucker, who I emailed only a few times, was probably the most excited anyone has ever been to meet me before, so I had to mention her as well! Lastly on the Wattpad side, thank you to Allen Lau for creating this website for writers so we not only have the opportunity to post our work but to be recognized for it in a life-changing kind of way.

You probably realized I wasn't done yet; after all, you read the book. You know how long winded I am. I want to thank the amazing friends I've made online—there are literally so many of you that I couldn't name them all (I tried), but special thanks to Katie, Trish, Sev, Noelle, and River, who have been with me for literally almost ten years—and also to the friends I've made IRL. Laurel, Haylee, Marissa, Jadon, and Ally, our lifelong friendship has truly shown me how important it is to have a group of girlfriends (and Jadon). It's why there are so many female characters in this book. But I have probably the biggest thank you of all reserved for Laurel. Over ten years ago, you gave me this book you had written yourself, stapled together, and asked me to read it, and I was determined to write a book to give back to you. Well, I wrote it, but I never actually gave it to you because I was embarrassed. Still, I kept writing after that, and now look where we are. I never would've started writing if it weren't for you and our friendship, and I honestly don't know where I would be without it. So thank you for changing my life with not only your unwavering support, but by giving me a purpose.

To my manager, Mark, thank you for all the time off so I could work on this and for always rooting for me to be more than a cashier. You are the best boss, and one of these years, I'm going to actually remember Boss Appreciation Day.

And to the readers who have supported me on Wattpad for years, not just since I started posting chapters of *What Happened That Night* every Thursday, but before. As I'm writing this now, there are 1.1 million of you out there, and I can't even comprehend that number! Surely half of you just left the browser open, right? Clicked by accident? Even if one of those were the case, that's still so many people, and I'm blown away by it. *Thank you.* You've all supported me in so many different ways, including saying years ago how this should be a published book. Look! You're holding it right now! I honestly thought you were all just being nice but without your love for this book, it wouldn't exist. You loved it even when I didn't and nothing was working and hey, there's a trash can right over there, but the comments you left were the most encouraging things I've ever read. You read this book as an episode of prime-time television you wanted to binge-watch, and it was glorious to see.

Thanks to everyone, and cheers! We made it! We deserve some candy.

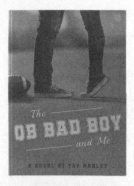

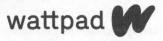

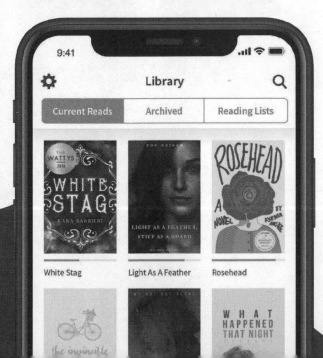